Dedicated to Clemence Cauwenbergh,

Thank you for always giving me the freedom to pursue my creative ambitions.

The Atheist

By Alpha Maurice Cidade Cauwenbergh

Preface

The inspiration to write this novel snuck up on me quietly, it was a mild autumn's bus journey home from work when the idea started filling me with thought churning joy. The feeling it gave was like picking up the rhythm and sounds of your favourite song playing in the distance of an otherwise bland and sedentary moment. It seemed random at the time but in retrospect I realise that there were many little seeds planted in my head throughout the last 6 years, seeds that were slowly watered during conversations with family and friends, until one day it blossomed into the life altering decision to write the book you now hold in your hands. I have poured every once of my strength, heart and soul into creating this story, using all the skill I could muster in architecting each sentence of every page. Completing it has been a satisfaction like no other, and all I can hope for now is that you enjoy reading it as much as I did writing it.

I also want to take this moment to acknowledge the amazing people and friends that have helped me in the different stages of my debut novel; To Kalina Mugiwara and Deda Starhemberg you were both there from the very beginning - your advice, support and positive energy were invaluable in helping me to stay engaged in this creative project. I offer you my endless gratitude.

To my mum, my brother Henri-Bruno, Eddie K., Joanne F., Mat S., Pheobe B., Gabby, Matteo, Ali R., Gabi M., Antoine R., Kit, Eugenia, Chloe Brown and Grace Liljemark no matter how large or small your contribution was - all of your help and constructive criticisms were key in the formation of this book. Thank you from the bottom of my heart. Finally, a very special thanks to Leigh Blinman, Sharmay Mitchell and Nick Thompson. The first pair for taking the time to proofread all 82,000 words! And Nick for creating the amazing front cover! You all deserve a year's supply of milk and cookies!

Now without any further ado I give you…

The Atheist

Prologue

In a time before the beginning there existed a whole being. For reasons unknown it separated into two singular parts, these two parts although from the same original whole grew to have different driving purposes and effects on the space and time around them. These effects were not always complementary and from this a great tension arose. Again for reasons unknown they then created other beings from their own selves who although only a diluted power would share their driving purposes and have a similar affect on the spaces and time around them. Following this came a period of ever growing friction between the two entities, now irrevocably opposing one another. The mechanism for which appeared to be due to a process of causality born from conflicting ideologies...

This was a period that was coming to a universe-changing climax.

Then just as inevitably as the gasp for air that causes a man to drown, one side struck first. This started the great battle between the beings from above the heavens, and just like that drowning man - they had lost. They found themselves drowning in a sea of consequences reaching far beyond their space and time and into ours. One such consequence was that those on the losing side were dealt swift and severe punishments, first of which was there sealing in a place of nothingness believed to be located in between time and space, for a length of time as comprehendible to a mortal man as the solar system is to a garden ant. The second was that once they completed their period of exile, if they choose to follow the path of the victorious being they would enter a rehabilitation program designed to test the strength of their new convictions and allegiances. If this offer was refused then return they would to their prison. In this rehabilitation program for the beings from above the heavens, they would be separated from their immortal essence and sent to a different space and time...our space and time. There they would live human lives...although not chained to the earth by death they were to endeavour to live their lives to the standards set by the victorious one. All in the hope that it would one day see fit to return them to their once transcendent state of existence above the heavens.

Chapter 1

****

I think therefore I am...I think therefore I am...but I am not, and have never been. I have been thinking for years but still have yet to see evidence for my existence; I guess that is another human saying of theirs that I don't agree with. They are always in my thoughts and in my heart...a sentiment I cannot actually fully realise as I am without substance but one I understand the meaning of. Loneliness I also understand...loneliness I also feel...but *actually* feel. Unlike the plethora of other subtle human emotions that are intangible in my lack of existence this one has resonated in everything I am not, ever since the moment I thought my first thought. Is it really my only true connection to these humans I watch continuously, tentatively and with piercing scrutiny as my timelessness elapses via their every moment, interactions and acts of great valour or evil? Or just a default occurrence of consciousness...I think therefore I am?

If I am anything and not nothing, then I am an observer. This is what I have decided to call myself; I feel I can allow myself the self-indulgence of a first name. It's very apt. My observations have always been limited to a specific line of sight, and this singular landscape I have been looking out into consists of a particular city, street, House and family. Why? I do not know... but I observe, after all it's not like I have a choice. Today the family is having a very peaceful morning for their standards...it's that time of ones breakfast and The Atheist is walking down the stairs...

****

"Bonjour fils!" François says with hopeful energy to Julian.

"Bonjour..." He quietly replies with an opposite energy.

A breakfast of omelette made with sardines and onions is served and a plate waits for Julian. Before sitting, he wonders for a moment... "why couldn't I smell this from upstairs?" This...his favourite breakfast, then as he scans the room his question is answered by two open kitchen windows. Just then he notices his father still patiently waiting for him to take his seat at the table with the demeanour of a well-trained dog awaiting its treat.

He obliges, François breaths a sigh of relief. So far so good he thinks to himself.

"So...how is the bike doing?" François asks.

"What that old ass chopper? It still has a heart beat I guess...what is it with ethnic families and passing on their unwanted rubbish to their kids? Maybe I should sell it…? But who would buy it...? With its silly sofa for a seat... do I look like Austin Powers?!"

"Hey! Have some respect son! You should be thankful and not be insulting a well meaning gift someone gave you because you failed your driving test... again..."

"A driving license would have been a better gift" he says with a smirk.

François decides to hold his tongue and just say nothing more. He feels it's better to allow silence to serenade the rest of their morning meal. Once Julian has finished his meal he looks at the time and knows he had better leave to get to school on time. He is in his last year of sixth form at Cardinal Francis Memorial School in London and with every other aspect of his education going quickly down the toilet he feels the least he could do is be on time. With his father silently watching his every move he leaves the table, places his plates in the sink and heads to the front door where his transportation to school awaited him. He resented that bike in every way, for being his father's, for being old fashioned, for just being there at all.

Before embarking on his morning ride to college he stops and stares as he has always done at the various pieces of his mum he had left. From the African pictures of animals she had once bought as a gift for his dad and proudly displayed on the walls of a house she made feel like a home, to the South American religious artefacts scattered around the place in an order he always felt was pretty random and unlike her. Then his moment of reflection would always culminate in looking at the only picture of his mother, it hung on the wall of the corridor that lead out of the living room and to the front door. He would look with nonchalant eyes as if trying to prove to her that the hole she left in his heart when she left suddenly and without goodbye had been filled and cemented over by his own strength and resolve. This was of course a lie and he would always leave just before he broke down and revealed his true emptiness and inconsolable despair. Now out of his front door he climbs aboard his Chopper, pauses to take in air and appreciate the beautiful and warm day that it is in May...he then starts pedalling away from his home and towards the familiar roads, sights and sounds that will guide him to his destination. Julian always enjoys this part of his morning, especially on a day such as this one. The sound of birds chirping in trees always makes him smile a gentle smile, even though they are hidden to his eyes by the density of flourishing trees and the speed of his movement through the semi-empty roads of early morning London. As well as that and in spite his own distain for his father's bike he always enjoys the looks given to him by middle-aged men acknowledging the retro coolness of the chopper and by association his own coolness. This temporary high almost makes him forget the various aspects of his life that usually leave him low and socially dysfunctional. But as he approaches his destination his reality starts creeping back towards him, and as he turns the last corner of his journey the building where he's studied since the age of twelve appears before him and not even the beauty of this day can illuminate the darkness this building fills his heart with...

After chaining up his bike in the school car park, he takes a moment to menacingly stare back at the other students who from library windows are, as far as he is concerned, obviously making fun of him and his old fashioned bike. Then once he's had enough of that little song and dance Julian heads into the reception area with a slouched posture and demeanour that is in total contrast to the other students and teachers floating about the place all seemingly eager to get to where they need to be and assumedly learn and teach a great many things. But before he can make it to his own form class room to register his attendance, he is stopped by his former P.E teacher and Football coach, who is dressed in his usual Adidas trainers, shorts and t-shirt. A casual look that seems mismatched with the assertive body language he displays as he prepares what to say.

"Ah good morning Julian" he says in a mild scouse accent.

"Good morning Lloyd"

"Would it kill you to say Mr Lloyd or just sir like everyone else?! It's a simple gesture of respect."

"What have you done for me to respect you?" Not wanting to open that can of worms, Mr Lloyd sighs and moves to conversation in another direction.

"What do you think about playing for my 1st 11 this weekend?"

"Not much"

"Listen Julian we have 2 more matches left this season and one is a cup final against our rival comprehensive school! I haven't spoken to the players yet about you playing but I'm sure they will have no problem with it, and God knows we could use a striker with your athletic physique and natural goal scoring instinct!"

"Are you enjoying your office?" Julian says with a subtle anger hidden behind an indifferent facial expression.

"Are you seriously still going to mention that after all these years?"

"Are you seriously still trying to get me to play for your team after all these years?"

"Julian when are you going to grow up and stop wasting the talents that God gave you?!"

"Please let's not involve that fabricated and useless character."

These words angered Mr Lloyd, much more then any of Julian's previous rude responses. And with shortening patience he says

"What is wrong with you boy?! You have spent 6 years in a Roman Catholic school! Raised by Roman Catholic Parents and yet you still manage to end up so confused about your faith that you can spout that Atheist nonsense so freely! Yes we all appreciate what happened to you was difficult..." Before Mr Lloyd could continue his rant Julian aggressively interrupts

"Shut your mouth! What do you appreciate??? You didn't appreciate the concept of common decency did you!? You didn't appreciate the idea of someone's pain! I will say what ever I want about that joke of a character you all worship! He's done nothing for me at all! Ever!" Although Mr Lloyd is not surprised by Julian's words as he has heard them many times before he still can't get over how this boy can overlook the many things he believes God has blessed him with; intelligence, good looks and sporting prowess and instead focuses on other less positive details of his life most of which are of his own making, well all except...that one...that loss...Either way this kind of behaviour and language is never tolerated in this school and thus he would have to respond accordingly.

"Julian! Enough! This conversation is over I'll see you on Saturday for your detention, and I will be speaking to your father and the headmaster about your continuing unacceptable behaviour."

And with that Mr Lloyd left to return to his teaching duties. Julian still a bit flustered and emotional used the long walk up several flights of stairs to his class to calm down. Once outside the classroom door he peers inside briefly, now relaxed and prepared for another day of pretending to listen he opens the door and steps in.

Now, while Julian is at college doing his usual impersonation of a student, his father is working hard as he always does Monday to Friday. François stood alone in a large warehouse filled with boxes of designer clothing items from handbags to shirts to stylish and impractical belts. He stood there doing what he always did at 1.15pm, having black coffee in a cup too small for his masculine manual labouring hands while staring at the pile of forms that was going to make up his afternoon work. He didn't mind the monotony of his work day too much though as this warehouse was his own space where unlike at home here he was the unquestionable authority. As well as that, he could listen to the radio playing his favourite songs without the judgmental moans and groans of his son, maybe even throw in a few dance moves if he saw fit, yes this space was truly a pleasant one for François a place to forget his troubles and strife.

Half way through his cup of coffee, François' attention is drawn to the warehouse front door. A man stands there

"Hello old man!" the man says.

"Haha hello" François responds with a warm inviting smile.

"You realise James that I'm only 1 year older than you don't you?"

James walks in from the door way and towards where François stood.

"Yeah but a lot can happen in a year mate you know like hair loss, twenty kilos and impotency."

"None of which I'm afflicted with."

"Oh there's still time mate."

"Hahaha yes prophet James there definitely is." Although François was enjoying the banter he was starting to wonder why James from the adjacent warehouse had come in to see him, normally at this time he would be hard at work in a nearby cafe putting teeth to meat.

"So to what do I owe the pleasure of a visit from our resident prophet? Am I really more appealing than cow meat?"

"Ha not in a thousand Sundays old man, that bloody place is closed for some reason! Tell ya what I flipped my lid! I go there every day and it's never closed! But this time it was and not even a note on the bloody door to explain why! Got me well annoyed."

"I can see."

"But after I'd finished giving birth to a few kittens I decided to come here and see if you knew another good little place I could stuff my face?"

"I'm very sorry but I don't actually know any, I am a man of packed lunches and very dark coffee."

"Shit! What bloody good are you, eh?" Then with a momentary pause and a huff, James now seemed acceptant of his meatless lunch. So he decides to take his mind off it by changing the subject.

"So how's the boy?" he asks in a deflated tone.

"Hmmm, well the same stubborn and difficult idiot he always is, you know I just don't understand why he behaves the way he does? I try so hard to provide him with a good life but he never seems to appreciate anything I do for him like this morning for example, he was complaining and insulting my Chopper that I gave him so he could get around as I can't afford to pay for more driving lessons for him at the moment! While he's at school no doubt not actually making an effort I'm actually working so he has something to eat when he gets home."

"Yeah mate, tell me about it, my daughters take everything me and the Mrs. do for them for granted. I think it's just how today's kids are. I blame MTV."

"Haha." François can't help but laugh despite his memory recall induced frustration, which was one of the aspects of James's personality that he liked best he could always make him laugh and smile no matter his mood. Just then his mobile phone rings with a default ring tone unpleasant to the ear that perfectly gave away his lack of technological savvy. He recognises the number...

"Hello" he says answering the phone acceptant of bad news

"Hello hi Mr Mufunga? The voice on the other side says making sure to pronounce the name properly, François recognises this voice very well.

"Good afternoon Mr Lloyd what has he done now?"

"Well, Mr Mufunga I was speaking to Julian this morning about possibly playing for the school football team and he responded by telling me to shut up! Now I don't need to tell you that this is totally unacceptable and way below the standards of behaviour we expect from all our pupils here at Cardinal Francis."

With a sigh François interrupts

"I know but you should really stop trying to get him to play for you, you know how he feels about you and what happened, he'll never play for you so why waste your time?"

"Yes well irrespective of that he still needs to learn to behave in a proper manner befitting of this school. So I've given him a Saturday detention." Another one, François thinks to himself.

"Okay I understand I'll have a word with him when he gets home from school, thank you for letting me know."

"Yes please make sure that you do, he is an intelligent boy Mr Mufunga and we need to make sure that he doesn't waste it." With decreasing patience François answers

"Okay okay I know, now I need to get back to work Mr Lloyd if there's nothing else?"

"No there's nothing else"

"Okay then goodbye"

"Goodbye" the conversation ends and François is left with a familiar feeling of anger and disappointment. He then notices that James is gone, thinks to himself that he must have left to go find himself some lunch. Now, in no mood to enjoy his own lunch, he finishes off his coffee and gets back to work.

Back at school, Julian has decided to skip out on his afternoon French class, which he often does. He rationalises that being fluent in French makes going to the classes quite pointless. Though deep down he knows his limitations very well and that going could actually benefit even him. But nethertheless there he was, not in his French class but standing in front of the entrance to the school's chapel. Why he was there he did not know, he seemingly just ended up there by chance during his stroll through the empty corridors of the school. Corridors that always remained cool despite the warmth of the outside weather. He always appreciated that and the marble floors architectural design of the interior even more for being the cause of these fridge fresh hallways. But now that he found himself in front of a chapel he never paid too much attention to and in fact had refused to enter since that day, he felt different about it somehow...indifferent to it, not resentful or angry, just a nothingness. Was this newfound stone coldness to a situation that used to burn a molten lava of emotions in him, due to an emotional maturity he'd undergone without even being aware or a beyond explainable internal emotional response to the cool temperatures his outward self was feeling? Julian certainly didn't know the answer, nor was he going to waste anymore of his skipped French lesson thinking about it. So he walks in, slowly and cautiously at first but as his memories of the layout return to him he moves around the chapel with the comfort of a priest all the while observing everything in the room with an analytical eye. "Ridiculous" he mutters to himself as he looks at a large cross mounted high on a wall that was certainly the front of the room. He wasn't sure himself why he said that, it seemed to slip out accidentally. Without even being aware of it he had positioned himself so that he was standing at the back of the room beside the votive candles as if trying to maintain a safe distance from the large cross. He stands for a while just staring at it...thinking about her, thinking about how it let him down, thinking about how the beliefs that gave birth to such places are just simply wrong. That everything that happened and happens is just the result of poor judgments and selfish human decisions, and everything this room stood for had no part in it.

That thought comforts him and he tends to find a lot of solace in logic and reason. His calming thoughts spread throughout his body into feelings of stillness, he has now stopped thinking and is just staring without focus at the cross, looking without seeing, totally calm and relaxed as if in a trance. Minutes passed by with Julian in this state...then he was slowly brought back to a more awakened state of mind by a slight warmth he could feel in and around his legs, he just dismissed it as the moments leading up to a sensation of pins and needles in his feet, probably from standing in one spot for too long in his ridged & unforgiving school shoes. But this it was not...that warmth got a bit warmer and he shook his legs in an attempt to improve his blood circulation and even joked to himself that this was the warmth of hell under his feet preparing to swallow up the Atheist blasphemer. This thought made him smile, but that was soon to be erased. In the moments that had passed since the first feeling of warmth, a chain reaction had begun that was putting his life in danger and altering the course of his future! And now it was no longer slight warmth he was feeling but genuine heat! He looked down to investigate and he saw flames! That joke wasn't sounding so funny now. "Damn I'm on fire!" He yells! "Where the hell is it coming from??!" Remembering the candles behind where he was standing he spins around, more flames! He stumbles back in shock his heart was now racing and adrenaline coursing through his veins, taking a second to analyse the flames he could see that they had waved and danced their way to the curtains that framed the only windows in the room and were rising ever higher at a frightening rate! Smoke of darkening grey was spreading across to the ceiling above his head, like water into a kitchen towel. His breathing became erratic and he tried to calm it down so as to not breathe in the smoke that was descending down and filling the room like an ominous fog of impending doom! But he was now too aware of the smell of different materials burning to calm down his respiration, it filled his nose to the point of tasting it! He found it sickening. Temporarily being able to summon some rational thought in the noise of RUN RUN RUN that filled his mind, he looked to the door he had entered, what seemed now to be a day and age ago, to see that he had closed it and the flames were now consuming the alter boy gowns that some lazy kids hand hung there!

"Shit shit where do I go?! Damn it! I can't go out like this! The irony alone is reason enough to get my ass out of here! I will find a way out I've got time I just need to relax!" But his time was running out...and his destiny was drawing ever closer...in mere minutes the atheist would meet his end burnt in front of a God he didn't believe in and in a chapel he didn't respect.

Chapter 2

****

I the observer, the existence without existing could see without looking the events of today. Like on all other days of all other years in the life of The Atheist. The Atheist was the he and the him I observed more closely than the others...the one I was more close to than others...Not in terms of space or distance as none of those human terms apply to the nothingness that I am. But in terms of attention...my consciousness was always attentive to him. During today's events I thought more so than on others, why did the he and the him that was behave in ways that made the people who he had to constantly share space and time with reject and resent him...? Did he seek the loneliness I feel? Why? It's a feeling so negative in energy that even I, one without heart physical or metaphorical could feel it without feeling. If he existed in my space would he change his mind? Yes I think he would...if I shared his space closeness is all I would seek, all I would desire and all I would be. Was he thinking these same desire-changing thoughts as the heat of that place caressed, kissed and bit his skin..? My attention was all there and there it remained with the he and the him that was.

****

Noises of a man hard at work rustled, scratched, cut, bumped and banged throughout this large cold warehouse for hours. Then eventually interrupted they were by a ringing mobile phone. Damn that annoying tone François thought to himself as he put down a box of designer bags he was checking, he pulled his phone out of his pocket to see the number of Julian's school was once again light across his phone screen. He sighs dreading answering a phone call he is sure will drain his motivation for the hours of work he still has left...

"Hello."

"Mr Mufunga."

"What has he done now?"

"Oh hi sorry to disturb you at work sir but I'm calling from St Francis Memorial school and need to inform you that there has been a terrible fire at the school and the form teachers have done their class register and your son Julian is...!" François' whole body started to go numb as his parental instincts began to imagine the worse, he barely heard the rest of what the school receptionist had to say. His mind and emotions were already becoming too saturated with worry to take in any more of what she had to say. As soon as he broke free of his state of shock he shouted

"I'm on my way!" He hung up the phone, left his work and place of tranquillity without a seconds thought! Almost tripping as he burst out of the warehouse doors and ungracefully stuffed himself into his car and sped off towards his son's school.

François arrives at the school...his car is parked hastily in the first space he saw, he is standing out side the main entrance still fearing the worst. He's had the whole journey here to think of all the worst fates a parent could imagine having befallen their child. He is so focused on the entrance to the reception area that he barely takes any notice of the fire trucks all around him.

"S'il te plait Dieu, pas mon fils" he asks God not to take his son, his distress momentarily making him forget certain truths of the world. Just before he takes his first step forward, he notices that he can't see any damage to the school building, this gives him a sensation of relief he can feel right in the pit of his stomach. Forward he walks towards one of the many possible fates his mind's eye had shown him, he enters the school and is immediately taken aback by the assault on his senses. He feels a heat not usually found in these halls, he smells the heavy thick aftermath of burning and his eyes looked upon a sight that is in complete contrast to his view from the outside. In here a huge blackened ruin without wall or ceiling was present where he remembered a chapel, staircase and teachers staff room to be...that whole side of the building had been destroyed! He thinks to himself how fierce must this fire have been?! Just before he falls back into complete panic at his son's possible fate a teacher he doesn't recognise runs up to him

"Are you Julian's father?!"

"YES! Where is he?! Is he okay? S'il te plait! He has to be! It's my fault I know it must be! I'm not good at this life vraiment je peux pas! Pourquoi?! Why?!" François was hysterically rambling away in French and English as he always did when he got very emotional, not giving the teacher a chance to tell him what she was desperate too.

"Mr! Mr! HEY!" She yells into his face, François responds and finally makes eye contact. "Have you seen your son?! He is the only student unaccounted for! And the receptionist says she saw him enter the chapel." Just then François looks around and notices all the students, teachers and firemen standing around.

"He's not here?" He asks with a calmness that shocks the teacher.

"No, that's what I've been trying to tell you! The firemen haven't found a body! So we're desperately trying to find out where your son is." François unlike the teacher was very relieved that they could not find him...in fact, in spite of the disaster before his eyes and his son's unknown whereabouts, he was somehow certain that he was not dead. Not wanting to continue talking with this teacher he did not recognise, he searched the room for a familiar face. Ah there he is! He thought to himself and brushed passed the teacher and walked hastily almost jogging towards him.

"Lloyd! What the on earth happened here?! And where is Julian?!"

"Ah François, I've been waiting to speak to you, we're not sure what exactly happened here but a fire burned half the west side of the school and the preliminary reports from the firemen is that the source of the fire was the chapel where, apparently, Julian was before the fire started."

"Then where is he?! Why can't you find him?!"

"We're not really sure but we believe that he must have escaped the fire somehow maybe through a window but at least no one was harmed in the fire." François agitated by the lack of a concrete answer responds angrily

"Through the window?? Are you serious? Écouter moi ces bêtises?! I've been in there before and the windows of the chapel are not only too narrow for Julian to fit through but are double glazed and reinforced. Even if one was open it would be too high up for him to get to!"

"I know François but it is the only possibility we can think of at the moment. When the fire department has finished its full report we will know more but for know we need to focus on finding him. But you realise that when we find him we will need to ask him questions about how it started..." François stares straight into Lloyd's eyes with an intensity that fully expresses his contempt for Lloyd's comment. Lloyd, knowing François very well, feels the very real malice in that look and ceases to speak, disengages eye contact and looks to the ground.

"I'm going home to see if he's there, if he's not I'll go out looking for him. I can rest assured that you are doing all you can to find him?"

"Yes you can, together we will find him."

"We'd better...she would never forgive me..." And with that François left the seen of carnage and fiery destruction and headed home.

As the sun begins to set, a lonely figure is wandering the streets of west London not knowing which way to turn...this lonely figure is locked in a deep contemplation of things. What the hell happened to me? Wasn't I surrounded by fire fighting for my life?! The last thing I remember is the smoke filling my lungs and starting to feel dizzy...then I put my hands on the wall, I think to stop myself falling over...but the next thing I remember I'm outside miles from my house. Did someone from school find me and save me? Of course not you idiot! Like someone would go through the hassle of saving you to then carry you miles away and leave you in the streets unconscious. Hmmm this is very strange... Look at me I'm dirty as hell I must look like some kind of lost chimney sweep! "Haha" Julian laughed out loud forgetting that his situation was not a laughing matter. Okay, well either way I am alive...what should I do now? Should I go back to school? No that stupid place is probably full of police and firemen looking for me probably trying to blame me for the fire! Yeah they would love that; it would give them the perfect reason to finally expel me for good. Should probably go home and get changed, plus I'm sure my dad is all kinds of worried about me. It's his fault anyway, all he does is stress me out with his nagging and stupid rules, I'm so tired of him in fact I'm tired of that whole house! It's just a reminder of things I want to forget! I need to move on no one understands me anyway! They can't see the pain I feel every day all they do is try to talk, talk and talk! They never listen...idiots. Maybe this is my chance for a new beginning? Yeah they probably all think I'm dead anyway, I'll find somewhere new where I'll be happy. I'm never going home. Julian, now certain of what he wants to do, starts walking in a new direction, one that will lead him away from the painful past and into a future of emotional serenity.

Hours pass and Julian's feet are sore, he realises that his school shoes were not the best for long journeys. The night has come and with it a new set of questions that need answering...Damn it! I really didn't think this through...I'm hungry I need food soon not to mention a place to sleep?! Julian keeps walking for a bit still pondering these questions and then suddenly off to his left in the distance he spots what appears to him to be an extremely large church. He thinks to himself if Jesus was around today he'd live there! He also recalls hearing from somewhere that the church would have to shelter a person without a home and provide them with food. Not sure if it was true or not, he headed there anyway, it was currently his best option.

He arrives outside the main entrance...he's temporarily frozen in his tracks as his mind recalls what happened the last time he entered a place of God. But he quickly shakes off his fear with sobering thoughts of spending the night on the streets. As he walks towards the door he is overwhelmed by the scale of the church, it has several buildings around and connected to the main building all in typical Roman Catholic design. What were they for? He thought, and as he got within yards of the door he looked up at the huge spire that seemed to reach heaven itself. Although very much daunted by this church's scale, he presses on and places one hand tentatively on the door's handle. It opens difficultly, he struggles with the weight of the door for a second...then he gives it an extra push to reveal a room bathed in candle light with a woman on the other side standing by the alter. She's noticed his ungraceful entrance and looks his way...Julian's vision adjusts to the light and distance of where she stood. He pauses, his eyes widen, his heart seems to stop beating in his chest, a sound is stuck in his throat...he strains and forces his vocal chords to tighten as he prepares to speak..."MUM!!!"

Chapter 3

****

As ever I was watching him with intent. His journey had taken him away from all the love that he didn't know he knew - one that I, without the flesh of man could feel and into the arms of an unknown embrace. Why was his faithlessness leading him towards hope? His apathy towards truth...? Strangeness had woven itself into his life but with all the familiarity of the covers that envelope his rest during the dark of night. Did he notice the snowball of events that were leading him to the very thing he has always rejected? He doesn't...Without seeing I saw the love of men that was showered on The Atheist daily & by his father always... a love I didn't fully understand, though I have always been observing from my first moments of nothingness. He had pain...a deep pain that he carried side by side with his love...somehow with all my presence-less presence he, the father, still knew things I did not. I could see it in between the lines of the speeches he spoke. Now at the helm he was of a ship he found accidentally and boarded willingly, a great ship that I feel will conquer a great many things in him. But Atheist be wary of the false one I already see... Don't let isolated flames become oceans of fire... Stay on the ship, it will carry you over.

****

Earlier that day a 6ft 4 blonde haired man sat in a park at noon...bathed in the rays of the sun he was, enjoying it immensely he was too. The warmth he felt on his skin pleased him...a smile hung on his face as he watched the many people who covered the fields of the park like wild life in the Serengeti. Passers-by who saw him always smiled at him, his attire seemed to invite warm affection from them. This pleased him too...and for reasons these casual onlookers would never know. In that man's mind there were thoughts that played back stage roles to his smile, a smile from a handsome man was the perfect play to seduce all who saw it. They would clap, they would scream, roses red with love would be thrown at his feet with stems of all the hope a soul could hold. And while carrying that smile, he would step on them all. As he sat watching...his attention turned to a mother, father and a son just old enough to walk. He thought to himself Look at these three...that's so very nice...I like how they are so consumed by their argument that they are unaware of their son's impending fall. 5, 4, 3 the man counts down to the little one's fate...2, the parents scream at each other about some unimportant disagreement from earlier that morning. The mother's hitting the father on the arm as she yells...1, the infant steps off the pavement...haha nice the on looking man thinks. The father gesticulates ironically to the mother...0, the child's early and limited control of his centre of gravity fails him, in a split second his momentum builds, forward he falls and crack! His head slams into the concrete ground! The seated man intensely watches the toddlers face as he desperately tries to witness the very moment when the little child becomes expressive of pain and anguish...there! He sees it! The ignorant cries of helplessness and pain begin to scream out of the boy as it lay on its stomach with its body stiffened by pain and adrenaline..."Yes that was nice" the man says out loud this time... "Haha, so fragile" he says returning to his inner voice. Oh wait, the disgusting two still haven't noticed and now I get a bonus, I doubt it will survive this. Still carrying his smile, he takes a deep breath of the fresh spring air. It feels good in his nostrils, just as the child's unheard cries sound good in his ears. Rubbing his well manicured thumb and index fingers together he patiently waits... A helmet-less cyclist is riding quickly towards the family, with all the carefree joy of a 70s hippy. His attention is in a distant part, of the park away from the scattered clusters of lunchtime urban tan seekers and soccer mums. A group of people have noticed the crying boy, but his parents have not. Fingers still rubbing with anticipation, the seated man waits... The cyclist's attention is now drawn to the arguing couple and he's annoyed that they are spoiling his mood with their negativity, but his velocity was unrelenting. "Damn!" he says, almost falling off his bike. "Someone left a freekin' bag in the middle of the bike path!" He brakes and looks back to see who could have done such a dangerous thing...but to his horror it wasn't a bag at all. He looks down to see splashes of red that weren't there before. His shock seemed to slow down the hands of time and provide him with a slow motion experience of the panic, and startled distress that was spreading through the people unfortunate enough to be witnesses to this midday tragedy, none more so distressed, panicked or unfortunate then the mother and father, as they had now noticed their son and the full extent of the waking nightmare. "So nice," the previously seated man said as he stood up, brushed the dust from his clothes and walked off. He had walked several miles returning to the building he called home. It was a very large building with several other smaller ones attached and surrounding it.

"MUM!!" Julian screams out across the aisles, his voice being enhanced by the emptiness and excellent acoustics of the room. Realising he was forgetting the kind of decorum usually shown in a church, he held in his next screams. The woman says something back to him that is too quiet to transverse what feels to Julian like a chasm of space between them. He has begun to shake from the anxiety he is now feeling. Is that really her? Why and how is she here?! He asks himself. Although wanting to move towards this woman, he was frozen in shock, his emotions feeling like lead weights shackling him to the hard floor under his feet. Realising how distressed Julian, this boy who had wandered into a church at night was, the woman stopped what she was doing and began to walk towards him. Julian's every sense was strained and transfixed on her like a wild animal trying to decipher from a creature it has never encountered whether it's his prey or predator. As she was walking she looked majestic to him, like a floating, darkly robed, Angel, whose skin reflected candlelight in the most soft and beautiful way. He enjoyed these seconds as they felt like a musically accompanied prelude to the most beautiful and anticipated moment in his life - her return. But no, this was not to be, as she approached ever closer he could see that in actuality the beauty and familiarity he thought he saw in her face and silhouette was that of another's and not hers. "Hello mister," she says softly with a smile on her face. He is speechless and sad and fails to give any response. "What happened? You seemed very eager to speak to me a minute ago but now you just stand there with that adorable, sad puppy dog face?" But still no response from Julian. He looks her up and down and comes to terms with the fact that he was probably just feeling tired and emotional, which is why he thought he saw his mother. This woman is obviously not her, she is just a nun trying to be polite and converse with a total stranger. "If you really have nothing to say to me, mister, then I have to ask you to leave as I have to finish my duties and lock up." Julian felt that it would be very rude to stay quiet any longer, so he composed himself and began a conversation that would be a catalyst for many unexpected changes in his body, mind and soul.

"Hi, sorry I didn't mean to disturb you miss Nun"

"My name is Aeryn-Sun," she says with a giggle. Julian became stone faced at the peculiarity of her name.

"What kind of name is that?"

"Oh that's a bold tone for a lost boy to take, especially one who hasn't even had the decency to introduce himself or explain his inappropriate presence." Julian noticed that he enjoyed the sound of her voice just like he did hers and he begun to smile.

"Oh we're laughing at me now, are we?!" Julian let out a timid laugh and replied,

"No sorry, you're right, my father raised me better than that. My name is Julian and I'm in your church because...Well I guess because I've not got a home to go to and was looking for somewhere to sleep and maybe even get some food."

"Food and a bed?! You must think you're in Bethlehem, Julian" she bantered and he laughed, but mainly because he loved the sound of his name being spoken from her mouth, it had never sounded so good. He could now also pinpoint where her slight accent was from.

"Are you from Brazil, Aeryn? And yes, I am really hoping this is Bethlehem!"

"Ah, you have a keen ear mister. Yes I am from Brazil, Rio to be exact."

"How did a sassy woman like you end up a Nun in London?"

"Well us Brazilians are a very religious people and the rest is a long and personal story. I'm not sure I want to get into right now especially with someone I just met."

"I'm sorry I understand, how about you just explain to me your interesting name I doubt it's your birth name," he says with a cheeky smirk.

"Haha. Well that's not an easy one to explain either my life is sort of like a very sad soap opera. But I think I can give you the PG 12 explanation. Well my birth name was Consuela Marta. This is a name I share with my mother," she seems troubled by the mere thought of her, like just saying her name leaves a bitter taste in her mouth. "That woman wasn't like the other working class women of Rio who cared and loved for their families, she instead was violent and abusive in ways I care not recall. She was a drunk, a women swayed by the devil and his friends. This was not a women whose name I wanted to share, so when I left Rio and the nightmare of her parenthood I decided to legally change my name to the name of a woman I greatly admired, a strong courageous woman... A woman I was not, but wanted to be with all my heart."

"Wow I'm sorry to hear that. With your confidence and poise, I would never have thought that. But now I want to know more about you, honestly you already fascinate me." Julian instantly regretting saying that, worried that he had just admitted a premature infatuation with a woman he just met and a Nun on top of that! She just smiled as if she already knew and didn't say a word. "So who is this woman who inspired you so much as to take her name? I've never heard of any famous person called Aeryn Sun."

"Haha, that's because she's a fictional character from a TV show I loved watching as a kid, I was basically raised by the TV to be honest"

"Oh really? So you're a geek?"

"Maybe... But geek or not, I have got duties to attend to, and our priest will not be very happy if I delay attending to them any longer. So I'm afraid I'm going to have to ask you to go back home to your family who I'm sure are very worried about you." Julian was shocked. Why didn't she buy his story, he thought? Why was she sure that he had a home to return too?

"What makes you think that I can just go home? I told you that I need a place to spend the night," Julian pleads. But with confidence she replies,

"Because Julian, I have seen broken kids, I have seen the eyes of a youth who hasn't known love, who hasn't known the security of four walls and a roof and, mister, sorry to tell you this those just aren't you. Your eyes have hope, your posture has strength and your voice reveals a loving nature that was learned from the limitless affections of parents. So please return to them Julian, I know they are worried."

"It's not they, it's just him... I lost my mother a long time ago... You kind of remind me of her," he says coming to terms with the fact that the Nun is right and he should return home.

"Sorry to hear that, but I am not her and one is better than none." Julian was taken aback by her words. It showed a level of understanding of him and this situation that went far beyond the words they had been exchanging between them. He realised he had overstayed his welcome and it was time to leave, and when he thought about it he did feel bad for his dad and what he must have been going through, something he would never have thought about previously but it seemed that this beautiful Brazilian Nun was already beginning to have a positive affect on him. He said thank you to her for her words of advice and was about to leave through the large wooden doors he had recently entered, as what felt like a slightly different person in a completely different mind-set. Just before he opened and walked through the doors she said, "And mister, when you come back I'll tell you the rest of my soap opera." He looked over his shoulder at her, smiled at her a smile he hadn't shared with someone for months and said, "A bientôt".

Chapter 4

****

I, as the observer see a great many unseen situations of circumstance...I have observed a particular one... an atheist moving forwards along a holy path. By human definitions, if said path is holy, the circumstances are then as far from situational as light and dark...so do I, in all my consciousness, give credence to the beliefs of beings who perceive and feel in ways I cannot? I want to...and this desire weighs heavy on me. A contradictory existence is one I grow weary of even though a body and mind, to lose stamina, I have not. I use my uncontrollable existential fix on The Atheist, and all that surrounds him, to look into his universe for reflections of myself. But only questions are reflected back... I observe that he also feels the same everyday, but now my senseless perceptions tell me this Nun The Atheist has crossed paths with will reflect many truths if he looks like I can't into her eyes and soul.

Why is it that I feel fear? Is that even possible? What can I be fearful of..? But around The Atheist I feel something other than me approaching...Another presence-less presence? No, impossible. How can I use that human word? I am the impossible. In a previous moment I heard from the human world that 'evolution requires fear.' Maybe those words had more substance than I originally thought back then...and as substance is all that I seek, in fear I will believe.

****

Julian has arrived home, he notices the kitchen light is on and pauses. The glow from its lights spread ominously into the darkened corridor where he stood. He knows that to enter that room is to get involved in another argument with his father... He looks at the staircase to his left, knowing that he could seek the easy way out of this situation. But thoughts of the Nun still float in his mind and are seemingly giving him strength, so he puffs out his chest, walks a few steps forward then turns into the kitchen. There was his father sat at the table where they had shared breakfast, his face rife with emotions and eyes red from tears. He didn't utter a word to Julian; instead he just kept his eyes locked on him. Julian had never seen his father like this; it sent chills down his spine and sent his heart rate racing. It had been years since he'd been scared of his father, but in this moment he knew that fear once again. He had been stood in silent fear for a few moments but recognised that it was time to sit down. He walked slowly towards the chair; his father's eyes followed him like those from a portrait on a wall. He sits and wonders why the confidence he had before he entered the room had completely seeped out of him. The time had come... He sat patiently for his father to speak first, it felt like what he was expected to do.

"Je veux te dire la vérité fils," François says with a stern and steady voice. The truth about what? Julian thought. "I thought I lost you today son... And I just... I just. Of all the thoughts running through my mind as I headed to your school, the one that weighed heaviest on my heart was the thought of you never knowing my truth, your truth and your mother's truth." With those words Julian got butterflies in his stomach.

"What do you mean yours, mine and mother's truths?! That doesn't make any sense. We have different truths?? What, like I'm adopted and you're both actually brother and sister?! Haha," he laughed nervously. "I thought you were angry about the fire at school and going to give me one hell of a lecture about how I'm irresponsible this and immature that?! Or maybe how the fire was my fault! And I committed some kind of blasphemy on the stupid room built for a worthless God?!"

"SILENCE, Julian!" his father's voice pierced straight through him and echoed throughout the house. Julian was overwhelmed and not sure how to react to his father's strong words, powerful voice or intimidating demeanour... "All that is of no consequence right now. You are safe and the only other casualties were made of bricks and stone. So be quiet and listen to your father. I do not know whether what I'm about to do is permitted or if you'll even be able to hear the words I say. So much is unprecedented... You are a first, the only one." An awkward quiet filled the room... Julian sat submissively in his chair, staring at the coffee stains on the table. His father was very serious and he prepared himself for what he was about to tell him.

"Bon, je veux commencer au début... This is the truth, son. Originally there was a whole being who came before everything else... Similar to your notions of God. We refer to him as The Whole One." Julian found it strange that he used the word 'your', as if he didn't share the same notion, as if he wasn't a Christian too... But he remained silent and kept listening to his father's strange words. "Then at some point in time The Whole One separated himself into two lesser beings with their own individual existence, thoughts and prowess. They are referred to as The One and The Other One. No one knows why The Whole One separated himself, but many believe that it was a decision born from a loneliness incomprehensible to lesser beings. A loneliness found only in the purest of perfection." Julian just stared in awe as his father continued his unnerving story... Unnerving because Julian was already questioning his father's sanity. What the hell is going on, he thought?! "Either way, it had happened and now these two beings shared a space and time. It is said that for an aeon, things were fine and they were able to exist without problems. But then one day, well a day is the wrong word to use as in that place there are no night and day just, erm, well it's hard to explain, just a kind of constant forward and backwardness. Sorry son I'm going off track, well what I was saying is that one day there was a disagreement between the two. You see The whole Being had created this universe and this earth we live on, even most of the creatures on it. That included human beings... But at this point in the earth's time they were very different to how they are now. More like the cavemen you learn about in school but even more regressed living from one instinctual moment to another. The One wanted to give these humans a mere fraction of his own essence to help spark what he believed was their hidden potential, whereas The Other One felt this very idea was obscene and never should such lesser beings receive even the smallest amount of their divine essence. It believed they were created by The Whole One to be observed for the sake of amusement, like all other creatures of the universe. The One disagreed and from this, tensions grew and this conflict created an ever-increasing dissonance between them, to the point that the fibres of their beings became polar opposites, so much so that they were almost unrecognisable as two equal parts of a whole. Are you still with me, son? You haven't said anything."

"What am I supposed to say? Just... Just.... Just finish what you have to say." Julian was now becoming sad as he resided himself to the idea that his father had somehow become sick or mad and maybe the traumatic events that he caused were what broke him.

"I know it's a lot to take in but you need to know the truth. Okay well after a period of time, they became isolated from each other seeking a separate space to exist. Then they both started to create new beings from their own essence to share their space, who would intrinsically lean towards their own ideologies. These beings are similar to the angels and demons your church teaches about, but I don't like using the word demon, it's not very accurate to be honest." There he goes again talking like it's not also his church, Julian thought, as he watched his father's lips continue to move preaching these bizarre things. "Now these new creations are called the The Ones and The Other Ones, and individually they are A One and An Other One. Yes, I know it sounds a bit confusing but you'll get used to how it works, son. After this, it seemed that the two beings were now surrounded by an army of followers who would never disagree or question the desires of their creators. Looking at it now, it seems pretty much inevitable that the contentedness of both sides to rule separate spaces without interfering with each other would not last. The spark that lit the flame of war was the act of The One, to finally risk the wrath of his great and powerful opposite by placing a small amount of his essence into the human race. The result of that act was everything humans are today; their intelligence, free will, language, creativity, empathy, love and now flesh and blood shells to a soul." Julian's eyes starting to water, he didn't understand what was happening, and was becoming very upset at his father's continued talk of things that were quite simply crazy. He felt like he was losing him, that this sudden madness would take away from him the only family he had left. Not knowing the best way to respond to all of this, he simply asks with a whimper,

"Dad, what has any of that got to do with us?" Francois could see how upset his son was getting and it brought a lump to his throat. But he was convinced that he had to tell him the truth and that it was too late to turn back now.

"I'm getting to that, just bare with me please.... You have to know, I see now that it was very wrong of us to keep this from you," his use of the word 'us' didn't go unnoticed by Julian, but he just kept listening, choosing not to pull him up on it. "Okay where was I? Ah, oui Je me rappelle. So a great battle started in that realm and many beings from both sides lost their existence. This battle had been going on throughout the entire history of the human race ever since they first stood upright. Dark times..." Julian noticed a look on his father's face, like he was recalling a traumatic event. But before he could make any deductions, François carried on. "But in the end, there was a winner, The One was victorious. Now all Other Ones and The Other One himself were subdued and at the mercy of The One. What would happen now, eh? Well it was clear to The One that as long as his opposition and their opposing ideologies existed, there could be no peace in that realm, but the nature of his essence wouldn't allow him to destroy that which was helpless and not able to fight back. So instead he made the decision to incarcerate all the Other Ones in a prison where time didn't exist," a haunted look ran across his face... But then it changed as he remembered something, " As for the leader, no one knows what happened to The Other One... What The One decided would be an appropriate punishment for his great opposite has, since that moment, always been unknown to all. Mon fils écoute moi bien, it was in this timeless prison that we were offered a chance for redemption." Julian was shocked upright in his seat... He said 'we'. That can't be, I must have misheard him, he thought. But he hadn't and what was to come would be of greater shock. "We were told that our only chance to escape this place between time and space would be to enter a rehabilitation program where our immortal essence, which is like a soul but far more dense, multi-layered and infused into our existence, simply put a human soul, is like a 2 dimension square drawn on a piece of paper and placed inside a jacket pocket and our Immortal essence a 3 dimensional sphere that is continuously in flux as it infuses itself throughout every particle of our being making us more than our exterior appearance and defining our existential form. Haha, excuse moi, that wasn't simple at all." Julian was just still with shock, not saying a word. François, realising that this was not the moment for laughs continued his explanation. "Well anyway... our immortal essence will be stripped away from us as our exterior shell is turned to that of a human's and placed into a rehabilitation program where we'd have a life and history constructed for us. In this constructed life, we'd have to live as the very creatures we were once fighting a war to destroy and endeavour to learn to see the beauty in humanity, to prove to those watching us through our actions that we have abandoned our original ideologies, those we inherited from The Other One. This is what I've been doing ever since I got here...I've worked 9 to 5 for 30yrs, made friends, raised a son and yet they still don't believe me to be rehabilitated. What else can I do to show them that I've embraced humanity? I long to be back with her." Taking a moment to check Julian was still listening he continued. "Now this is where you and your mum come in.... Son the truth about your mum is that she is like me... She was also in the rehabilitation program. When her and me met, it was a pure coincidence. In fact we didn't even know each other's real identities as former Other Ones until she became pregnant with you. Something that I was told was impossible. You see one of the rules of our rehabilitation is that we are forbidden from revealing anything about our true selves. So when she became pregnant, it was at that point, we were visited by *them* simultaneously, and at that point we knew who each other really were, strangely it just made our love stronger." François was now smiling without even realising it as he continued talking about this time in his life that he held very close to his heart. "They came to tell us that this was the first ever conception between two former Other Ones and as we were just impersonating humans, and in fact are empty shells without actual souls, so creating a new life should be impossible. But somehow it happened. You were and are a miracle son, the one and only of your kind. They weren't sure what this meant but decided to take the risk of letting you be born. We were so incredible happy, you were happy...I learnt a type of happiness that could only come from being mortal. Years passed without problem, no bad deeds had been committed by either of us for years we were raising a child and demonstrating the love we'd always heard humans speak of but never experienced or heard. We were certain that very soon we were going to be declared fully rehabilitated. But then one day they came back and took her from us, son..." He tilted his head towards the ground as if admitting guilt for something. "You were just in your second year of secondary school doing so well, but they took her, saying she had completed her rehab. They broke up a family that, although not born from human blood, now had humanity as its life's blood. I had to watch as you cried every night asking why she left without a good answer for you. You ended up blaming me for it and taking out your anger on those around you... Eventually you just decided not to love, trust or get to close to anyone again. I'm so sorry, Julian..." Francois, now at the end of this emotional roller coaster of a heart to heart, started to cry, his tears slowly running into his mouth. Their salty flavour seemed to perfectly accompany the words he was trying to force feed Julian.

"Hold on, let me get this straight...so what you're saying is that you're a demon? Mum was a demon? And I am the soulless offspring of Demons?! And that God put you in a rehabilitation program?!"

"No, demon is the wrong word we are all like what you call angels! Is a dog that bites people a demon and the one that saves a life an angel? Or, are they both intrinsically the same and their actions just an extension of their master's will?"

"So we're angels?!"

"Yeah kind of."

"And mum has gone back to heaven?!"

"Yes... Kind of."

Julian jumps up throwing the chair he was sitting on backwards and crashing into the kitchen counter! "Are you kidding me? I've sat hear and listened to you spout rubbish hoping on the off chance that you might tell me something about mum that would bring me some kind of peace! But instead you tell me, in the most elaborate way I've ever heard, that she's gone to a better place?! What's wrong with you?! Have you lost all your marbles?! Are you trying to get yourself committed and leave me too?! You can just tell me to get lost if you don't love me anymore!!" Now Julian was crying too, and saliva spurting out his mouth with every sentence he screamed out.

"But son, it's the truth!! I should have done this a long time ago!! I'm so very sorry for everything you've had to go through!"

"Listen to yourself dad! There are so many holes in what you're saying! Like what about the pictures around the house of you when you were growing up in Congo?! The fact that you speak French! And if you and mum are the same angels or demons or whatever, that were made from that other geezer, then how come you are of a different gender and race to each other and slept together?! Isn't that some kind of incest?! Surely that would go against the rules of your parole? Or whatever you call it?! Not to mention if you felt you shouldn't tell me back then, why is it okay to tell me now?!"

"Well the answer to all of these questions is very simple, son...remember I mentioned the persons who came to visit us when your mum fell pregnant with you? Well they are called the Controllers, a section of Ones that were created with the job of basically being our sponsors but without that shoulder to cry on or the emotional support. They reside in a space just outside this dimension and just watch us. They take notes on our progress or lack of and control the implementation of our back-stories into your world and our minds. Those pictures you see, the histories of your parents, all are created by them. They usually only pass through the dimensional wall to speak to us, to tell us of any critical changes they have made to our back stories, or to tell us that we have completed our rehabilitation. Both of which are as rare as rain in the desert."

"Oh yeah, that's very convenient!"

"Didn't you ever find it strange that even though I supposedly grew up in Congo and moved here when I was in my twenties, I don't have an accent?" Julian was silent and still as he thought about what his father said...

" Whatever, you just lost it! From being here so long!"

"Now who's talking crazy?"

"Shut up!" The moment he said that he regretted it. He had never said such a thing to his father, and from the look in his father's eyes and the purposeful way he was getting up out of his chair he knew it was time he stopped talking and end this late night encounter. "Erm, well anyway I'm going to bed now. I need to rest, I'm very tired. Bonne nuit." He turned away and walked out of the room hoping that his surrender from the argument and casually thrown in bonne nuit would appease his father. François, although angry at his son's rudeness knew that this was probably the best end to this emotionally draining conversation and let him go. Julian went to sleep not knowing what to think or feel. Still in the kitchen, François sat back down not knowing what to think or feel. Both sad... Both lonely... One in the warmth of his bed, the other in the words that he said.

Chapter 5

****

The events of this evening were very strange, but they excited me... To hear about new existences that I had not seen or experienced in all my observations of their world and the empty days spent on the sand-less side of the hour glass made me feel what I believe to be the human definition of hope... But to hope, must I first despair? What can make an existence like mine despair? Loneliness, not having a significance and never thinking or performing a single act that could at least move me metaphorically forward towards an end goal. All these notions are born and the resulting feelings amplified from observing them, him and the opposite of me. Their whole lives, forward movement towards an end, good or bad, wanted or not so, the end is the final place the conclusion of the forward and the completion of purpose. This one fact, this thing I do not have, is the catalyst for all their actions beautiful or ugly, helpful or not so, that they commit in-between their start and finish. Is that fundamentally why I am nothing? Not a start, end or in-between... Nothing. These things said by The Atheist's father, his son rejects them, but I do not... They give me hope of the undiscovered, the unknown. Maybe I will find purpose? Can I defy the nothing?

****

The next morning comes with bright, clear and hopeful skies. Its cool spring air is refreshing all life outside the Mufunga house, but in that house the air was far from refreshing. The air was stagnant with the uncertainty of the emotions born of last night's great reveal. François and Julian have been awake and in their separate rooms for several hours now, not knowing what their next move should be. François stood by his window in a pensive rush to figure out the words needed to convince Julian of the sincerity in them. He had laid all his cards on the table and now could do nothing but wait. Julian lay curled up under his duvet, eyes open, staring at the stream of light breaking through the crack between the curtains and shining onto the wall and down to the floor. He was wrestling with several theories in an attempt to rationalise his father's actions. Although being in this for hours, he still was no closer to a moment of clarity. Suddenly an image appeared in his mind, 'Aeryn-Sun', he smiled... He was thinking about the beautiful nun he met yesterday. Thoughts of her soft voice and playful way of conversing brought a stillness to Julian's mind and heart he hadn't felt in hours. After a few minutes of enjoying this serenity, he decides what his next course of action will be. "I'm gonna go see Aeryn, maybe she can help me? It's her job isn't it? Yeah definitely, I'm going now." With that, he gets out from under his comfort zone, gets dressed in clothes nice enough to impress but not so nice as for it to look like it was intentional. As he makes his way down the stairs he's conscious of the fact that his father might be able to hear him, then he'd come out of his room looking to talk about what was said last night. This was the very last thing he wanted right now. He was right; François could hear every carefully placed footstep his son made on their old creaky staircase. But François would not come out of his room to confront his son, he too was still unsure about what he should say, when he should say it and why he should have to say it. So, slowly and without interruption, Julian made his escape from the disconcerting prison of tension that had become his home and headed back to the church to visit the Nun.

Julian is standing at the entrance to the church; his bike chained up to a fence, his journey here was a lot faster than he remembered it. Unlike last night, the huge doors were open and overall there was a far more inviting feeling to the whole building. There was an elderly lady sitting on one of the first few rows of benches, not wanting to disturb her, Julian stood still, deciding not to enter until he saw the Nun. Five minutes passed and while waiting he noticed that there were in fact a lot of Nuns walking in and around this rather large church complex. Frustrated, he inched towards the threshold, just as his resolve was about to fail, he saw a Priest walking on the far right side of the room. He thought to himself that he must know where Aeryn was. Just before he made a brash attempt to get his attention, the Priest walked through a door and disappeared. Julian briefly contemplates his next move and decides it would be a good idea to go inside and follow that Priest through the door, especially as the elderly lady completing her prayer was getting up ready to leave. He walks in immediately turning right, walking behind the twenty plus row of benches this church had, almost as if he was doing his best to avoid too close a proximity to the altar. After navigating his way to the far right side of the room, he finds the door the Priest had walked through minutes earlier. Standing in front of this door gave him an unnerving feeling deep in his stomach. Not sure why, he ignores it and walks through. Now he's surprised to find himself at the bottom of a single flight of stairs. It was the first time he had ever seen a church that had a second floor, not that he had visited a vast amount of churches in his life he laughed to himself. There was something though...something about where he was or more precisely where he was heading that just felt a genuine type of wrong not to be ignored. He felt cold and goose bumps covered his forearms. He contemplated turning around, but calmed himself with thoughts of, 'What could there be in a church to be afraid of?' He cautiously ascends the flight of stairs, once at the top he looks along the corridor to see a single door at the very end. The corridor is dark, its great length unnecessary and the walls a deathly bland without colour, patterns or a solitary hanging piece of religious artwork to welcome the heart and uplift the spirit. Julian just stood still looking through the darkness at the door, thinking that he should not proceed. But just then he could hear a faint sound... It wasn't recognisable at first. He strained his senses trying to make it out, "That's crying! Someone is crying?" he says, his statement turning in to a question as he realises the unlikelihood of that being true. So he walks forward, trying to verify that what he's hearing is in fact crying. The closer he gets to the door the clearer it becomes..."It's a girl crying!" he exclaims to himself being careful not to make too much noise. Now only several feet away from the door labelled 'Priest's office,' he stands unsure. He asks himself, "Man, what should I do? Someone's crying in there... But is it really my business anyway? But it's strange, why would a girl be crying in a priest's office? Oh it must be a nun, maybe she's being told off for doing her nun duties wrong?" Then he hears through the door a whimper of, "Please stop." It gives him a flutter in the pit of his stomach. He then has the thought of, "What if its Aeryn?!" Immediately his fear is gone and he's overcome by a protective instinct he has never felt before and knocks aggressively on the door several times. A man's voice yells out, "Just a moment!" Julian waits impatiently... Moments later he notices that the crying has stopped. Then the male voice says, "Please come in.' Julian opens the door without hesitation. As it swings open, the brightness of the room makes him squint. In complete contrast to the dark and gloomy corridor, this room was bathed in the sunshine of daylight that was pouring through both its large windows on adjacent walls. Once adjusted to the light, Julian uses his 20/20 ocular skills to investigate the room looking for answers to the noises he heard while outside. But to his surprise, all he found was a refined looking blonde gentleman in a Priest's collar sat behind a large desk made of a fine wood. In front of the desk, slightly off centre, stood a nun looking rather gormless. Though very relieved he was to see that it wasn't Aeryn, he was slightly concerned at her avoidance of eye contact with him. In spite her odd persona all did seem well. He looked back at the priest, who was sat there with a very confident air and a casual smile.

"How can I help you today, young man?"

"Erm I, I was just looking for someone," Julian says nervously.

"I hope it's not our friend from Nazareth, 'cause I'm afraid he's a bit hard to reach at the moment, haha," the Priest laughs loudly and proudly at his own joke. Julian and the statuesque nun stand silent, but this man seemed oblivious or totally uncaring to the tension in the room that was borne from whatever was transpiring in it earlier and Julian's interruption of it.

"No, I was just walking around your church looking for a nun."

"Well young man it would seem like you're in luck as we have one of those standing right here, she's a bit shy but once you get close to her she opens up well," he says, with a strange grin that appears to conceal something unkosher.

"Oh...ok but, I'm looking for Aeryn...Aeryn-Sun."

"Ah, lady sunshine, my angel… Well she's busy running an errand for me, but she'll be back here any minute. Would you like to wait here for her? We can get to know each other a bit in the meantime."

"Yeah ok, if you want."

"Yes, that's nice... I do want, I really want," he said once again grinning from ear to ear. It was strange to Julian how this whole time the Priest never once looked at the other nun in the room even if he was talking about her. She also seemed content with her invisibility. Everything about this man was not what he would expect of a man of the cloth. In Julian's mind, he was too good-looking, too confident and just too irreverent in his speech. He also began to notice that the longer he spent in his presence, the more uneasy he felt, agitated as if there was a magnet force of repulsion between them. Whereas, it seemed the opposite was true for the priest, his intrigue in Julian grew with every passing second. "Congolese and South American" That's a very interesting mix you are, young man. Looking at you excites my senses. You are a cocktail of intrigue and I want to drink you down like the blood of Christ and be nourished! Hahaa, yes that would be nice..." These words slightly repulsed Julian, to the point he was paranoid that it was showing on his face. To hide this, he looks towards the nun who had literally become the personification of a white elephant, and found, unsurprisingly, that she was still there motionless like a manikin. The conversation between the two men continued, but now Julian wanted to take the lead.

"So what about you? What's your name? Where are you from? Did you always want to be a priest? Because you don't seem like the priest type to me."

"Oh really? Haha I do get that quite a lot if I'm honest. I'll tell you a secret... I'm not the priest type." Julian was taken aback by his candour, and didn't know how to respond. And in that one statement the Priest had regained the conversational upper hand. "Haaahahah, no no no, I'm just kidding I am very much the type..." And with the now trademark disingenuine smile he constantly wore, he says "I love lending my skills to sooth the woes of others, lending my presence to situations of physical or emotional turmoil and leading a flock of sheep..." Nothing about that sentence sat right with Julian... Was he implying sinister things or perfectly describing the role of a priest? He couldn't be sure. His gut told him to be very wary, but the man's looks and priest collar leant itself well to the benefit of the doubt. Like the perfect disguise... "And to answer your other questions, my name is Franz Bachinger. I've lived here for as long as I can remember but my origins are

German.... Hope that quenches your thirst, at least temporarily, because I can hear lady sunshine coming up the stairs and it's about time for my lunch time walk. Goodbye young man, tell sunshine to lock the door when you're finished in here." With that he ended their conversational game of chess, stood up and casually left the room. The nun immediately followed him without being asked to, not making a sound or looking Julian's way to say good bye. The door closed, then he could hear her, it was Aeryn. The sound of her voice instantly made him happy; she must have been speaking to the priest in the corridor. Then the sounds stopped... Julian felt himself getting butterflies in anticipation, the door knob turned and she entered... She looked as beautiful as he remembered, the sunlight flowing into the room complemented her beauty perfectly like it was designed for her. And once again, her aura reminded him of his mum. She gave him a smile and their second encounter began.

"Hello Aeryn! I've been looking for you."

"Yes I heard little mister, and what for? It must be pretty important to make a man like you come to church twice in 24hrs!"

"Oh yeah well it is, kind of... I just need to talk to someone... Got a lot on my mind and just need to talk."

"I'm flattered that you regard my listening skills so highly, I guess I have no choice. After all, listening to the thoughts and feelings of one of God's children is part of my job."

"Well you were good yesterday... You kind of brought some *sunshine* into my life," Julian says, trying to conceal his amusement.

"Oh, very funny! Word of warning, do not call me by that nickname, I don't like it. *He* made it up." There was a subtle animosity in those words that was picked up by Julian.

He could tell that it was a story for a later time. There was a brief pause, then, "So spit it out mister, what is troubling you?"

"Well I can't. I'm not sure if telling the exact details is the best thing to do, but at the same time I feel the burden of this information in my mind and body."

"Hmm, have you ever tried praying?"

"Don't think I know how to."

"It's easy, you just need to find a sense of quiet from the outside, peace on the inside...then just talk to him... He's always listening."

"I think I'd rather attempt to pour my guts out to a sister, than to a father, if you know what I mean, especially if it's about him." These words intrigued Aeryn, but she held back the urge to enquire into their meaning."

"Why don't you just let me talk then? And whenever you feel like saying anything then you can, no pressure."

"Okay sounds good."

"Did you know that I love football?" Aeryn says, totally changing the subject.

"Haha no."

"Why is that funny?! I used to play football in Brazil when I was a kid and I was pretty good too, better than a lot of the boys! That's one of the few blessings I could feel in my life back then. It kept me out of the house and distracted when my mum was in one of her moods."

"It's good you found something to put some distance between you and her."

"True, but growing up in the favelas wasn't an easy thing for any of the kids there, let alone for one from a single parent home of an abusive alcoholic mum who did things I can't speak of in a house of God." Julian was stunned, he found it hard to fathom that such a confident woman who appeared to have such a strong faith could have come from such a horrible youth... It made his problems with his home life seem very juvenile and insignificant. He was now even more amazed by her than before, without realising he was forming a strong attachment to this woman, this nun.

"I'm sorry to hear that you had it so hard, how did you survive?"

"Well I was saved by two things... One, the strong mental fortitude I was blessed with from birth, may have got it from my dad... I don't know, he left before I was born. And two, a wonderful man I meet after I went through one of my worst moments...I was 19 and it was so bad... In fact that was when I changed my name in a futile attempt to escape the psychological hold my mother had on me."

"Aeryn-Sun... I must admit I love that name."

"So do I, the real Aeryn-Sun was so strong, so brave and she never took any stick from anyone! She carved out her own path in life, never yielding to the evil forces of the world. I just wanted to be her...I guess I thought that having her name would somehow help that process along." Julian didn't interrupt...he could feel that it was a big deal; she was opening up to him. It made him very happy, he kept his lips still and listened to her. "That wonderful man I mentioned earlier was a priest from a nearby church. He would often talk to the children playing outside and any persons he came across. One day he spoke to me...he changed my life. He taught me about the true meaning of religion and what prayer and faith could do to help others and me. It was thanks to him that I am here today, in every sense of the word."

"Amazing…" Julian immediately felt hot in the face, he was embarrassed by the strength of the word he chose! He tried to act natural so as to not draw attention to it. It's in moments like these that he was very thankful for his brown complexion; it made him impervious to the visible signs of blushing.

"It is amazing I guess, to come out of that environment a better person," she said with a smile. "But it's all thanks to that priest and our father upstairs." After a moment of thoughtful silence Julian moves the conversation forward.

"Talking of priests where did yours go? He said he was going for his usual midday walk but, as he strikes me as far from a usual priest, I'm curious"

"Oh Father Bachinger is in the park, like he was yesterday and the day before that. He just sits there for like an hour smiling at passers by and observing all the people enjoying themselves there. I find it very strange if I'm honest," she says, with her face turning a detective kind of serious.

"I think he *is* strange." Realising what his words might have sounded like he starts back tracking. "Oh sorry I didn't mean to be rude about a priest. It's just that, erm, the impression I got, you know, was like kinda strange. I mean I heard crying well maybe it wasn't, I was quite far away... Sorry just ignore me I'm talking rubbish."

"Are you though?" Julian locked eyes with Aeryn with a tense expression covering his face. And Aeryn realising exactly what Julian was really implying about farther Bachinger considers doing something that could very well be going against the religion she loves and be the catalyst for a chain of events that could lead to multiple disastrous conclusions. Although maybe differently to the way Julian feels it, she too also feels a connection between them. So she decides to proceed. "Can I tell you something Julian, something that has been weighing heavy on my soul for some time now..?"

"Yes, it would be good if at least one of us did."

"This is not a joke...I've heard crying several times coming out of Farther Bachinger's office too...and each time it's a Nun's voice. Then when I see them after they come out, they look like they've seen a ghost, they become very quiet, socially awkward and are quite frankly never the same again..."

"I think you should be careful with where you're going with this, Aeryn?" She already knew it was too late to stop now. She had made up her mind and, like her namesake, was going to proceed carving out her own path.

"Julian I think he's doing something to the nuns he shouldn't be," now whispering to avoid anyone outside the room hearing. "I think Father Bachinger, our priest, is sexually abusing our nuns. And I need your help to stop him."

Chapter 6

****

All that I know isn't everything, all I know is something... This one is wrong…a subterranean earth he is to the light of a golden sun. The Atheist should tread this new life path carefully, I see him developing, he is progressing and his interactions with new persons are aiding in his assimilation...but that one man feels like incorrectness...distance from him must be kept. I worry for The Atheist's fate and those who are woven into his life through blood or water. This is another something that I have used my arrogant proclamation of an existence with thought to consider. It doesn't make sense...but sense is not something that should concern a senseless me, yet it is all that concerns me. I have been troubled recently by my lack of forward, but this peculiar unfolding story is a forward I can use as my cosmic compass to a universal north.

****

While Julian and Aeryn were reaching the game changing climax to their conversation, Father Bachinger was enjoying his daily midday escape to the nearby park... During these moments he's always deeply engaged in an internal dialogue about the various things he perceives in his environment or the people he meets. "Hmm that sunshine is nice... A good day for everything, except leaving milk out that wouldn't be nice...unless you enjoyed that particularly awful taste. Does rotting flesh smell the same, I wonder? I've always left too early, note to self--linger around for longer. I wonder what curious things I'll see in the park today? Doubt it will be as eventful as yesterday. Yesterday... I like that word; it feels like destiny on my tongue. I don't know my own yesterday or yester year, but remembering that--keeps my future perfect. Its fine and dandy haha yes all kinds of dandy like the many, many I see every day at this time. Nice, nice, nice and nice but also pleasant...like that god fearer in the penguin costume. I wonder what holds more truths? The costumes we all wear to portray our chosen destinies or life roles? Or the bare naked flesh of birth? They can both be soft to the touch? The skin is no less a costume than the clothes we wear...yes I know one protects from psychological elements and the other physiological, but both protect, and both are better removed...yes...so good... so nice. Watching these people smile at me due to my costume is ticklish on a man's funny bone. Hahaha, if only they knew what I did to get here, those smiles would soon go and better expressions would be worn across their fragile faces."

Back in the Priest's office, Julian and Aeryn were still locked in their conversation. "I just find it hard to digest that this could be true," Julian says, while rubbing his forehead. "I mean yeah, I agree that he's as creepy as box full of spiders, but that?! Maaaaan, I just don't know... But then again that nun's face and demeanour was just so strange..."

"And you said you heard crying, how do you explain that?" Julian was in a puzzled silence for a moment before Aeryn interrupted his contemplation and carried on, "We investigate that's how! I've heard and seen too many strange things since he's been in our parish for me not to act. I couldn't face God if I ignored this... I just remember when I was going through my dark things with my mother, how many times I felt helpless and alone.... I thought if only there was someone, anyone to save me? Death sometimes seemed like the answer. But if it's happening here that wouldn't be an option for these women."

"But hold on, why are you so certain its sexual abuse and not another kind of badness he's doing? And why hasn't he tried anything with you? He seemed quite fond of you to me."

"Firstly, someone who's experienced the hell created by those godless acts and has felt and thought the feelings borne from them will instantly recognise them in someone else... It's like looking in a mirror of the past for me sometimes...some days I cry thinking about it, about what these women are going through. Made worse by the fact it's happening in the house of their Father... I fear they will start losing their religion if they haven't already. Lucky for me, when I was going through my dark past I had none to lose in the first place." Julian found her passion and empathy deeply moving. He could feel himself gravitating towards her... Confusion, his normal internal conflicts and psychological maladjustment's seemed to not exist around her. She was a vacuum to dark energy and to light a saturation of substance, he felt he had to help her no matter what or where it lead him. He had even forgotten about the original reason he came to see her. His father's incredible revelation seemed like background static at the moment. He could hide from it for now, but the time would come when he'd have to tune himself into it again. "And why he hasn't tried anything with me... Honestly I don't know, but I can assure you I would not let myself go through something like that ever again, EVER." With her voice resonating with determination she stares intensely into his eyes. Julian fully appreciates her seriousness. Though goosebump-inducing, her words were of no consequence to him as he had already decided to aid her with her problem.

Some time passed and the priest was back at the church walking back to his office and the newly formed tag team of justice have finished exchanging ideas for strategies on achieving their mission. As they are about to leave, Father Bachinger opens the door, almost knocking them down.

"Oh excuse me! Very sorry I didn't realise you two would still be here, let alone walking out at the exact moment

I'm walking in," the priest says, sounding very sincere for the first time in the ears and eyes of Julian and Aeryn.

"Don't worry about it, it's cool," Julian says while trying to navigate his way around him and through the door. Aeryn on the other hand is standing patiently waiting for a more polite opportunity before walking out the door. Just then, Father Bachinger felt Julian's hand brush onto his, and then in that instant everything froze! In his mind he could see columns of solid dark opaqueness, thousands of them as far as the eye could see. These columns of solid darkness are of unrecognisable textures, reaching higher than this moment would allow him to see and deep into a red mass that filled him with a feeling he couldn't understand or describe. As he attempted to investigate his surroundings he felt his body go through severe cooling and heating up at almost random intervals. His skin looked ashy, to the point that with every slight breeze this dreamscape provided parts would flake off like he were an old painting fighting to maintain its state of being. Though throughout all of this bewilderment and saturation of new familiar feelings, one thing was certain in his mind none of them was fear... That was the only thing that stood out to him- that although he was having the most lucid, mind penetrating yet paralysing and overwhelming in its scope of a psychological experience, he was not afraid...not even for a second...just a bundle of inexplicable sensations and emotions mixed in with the odd familiar one, as if this experience was the template of a novice chef's experimental casserole.

"Father?! Father Bachinger?!"

"What's up with him, Aeryn? He's totally spaced out, hmmph just when I thought he couldn't be creepier." Both Julian and Aeryn are standing outside the open office door where Father Bachinger is stood facing away from them as if frozen in another time or another conversation. Aeryn grabs his arm and shakes it hard trying to snap him out of this trance. After a couple of shakes he turns his head and looks back at her with the face of a child in wonderment,

"Aeryn? Where is it? The place I was? What happened? Hold on, you were in the room and now behind me you are standing. I left too! Somewhere Aeryn, somewhere I can't really describe but it was here where you stand, here and all around." He said while staring through her as if looking at a distant place in the background.

"No Father, you didn't go anywhere when Julian walked passed, you just spaced out for almost a minute, I was quite concerned."

"Yeah I thought you had a stroke or something," Julian says, mockingly.

Just then Father Bachinger remembers something... The moment before his waking dream. He remembers being touched by Julian, "Was that the trigger?" he contemplates; he dismisses that thought as nonsense. But then he notices a feeling that is new... A sense of something, but what he wasn't sure... All he knew for certain was that he had never experienced or felt anything like this before Julian walked into his office, an experience that was still echoing in his senses long after it ended. It had already left a yearning in him for more like a seed of addiction that was watered by absence. He felt that it could not be coincidence, something he didn't believe too much in anyway. Upon coming to that conclusion, he decided that from that moment onwards he would now be taking a special interest in this young man, but for now it was best to play it cool and casual. "Okay sorry, it would seem like the midday sun got to my head and I need to sit down and rest for a bit."

"Yes it would seem that it has old man," Julian says, still not relenting his mocking of the priest. Father Bachinger turned and looks at him and instantly that familiar awfulness came over his sentiency and penetrated to the pit of his stomach. It was the same as what he felt walking through the corridor earlier. Julian was starting to understand the source of these feelings... It was worrying, and thus he decided that he and Aeryn would have to be very cautious as they try to investigate what is happening in this church and Father Bachinger's role in it.

"Okay, don't worry Father we're leaving now, you can take all the rest you need. I'll take care of things here until you're better, hopefully you'll be better in time for this evenings meeting with the members of the parish."

"Yes I'll be fine for that... Thank you sunshine, what would I do without you?" And with that this peculiar episode ended, Aeryn closed the office door and walked Julian back to the front of the church where his bike was chained.

"Okay mister it looks like goodbye."

"Yeah it does, but I just want you to remember Aeryn that we are now a team and we'll figure this out. If you need anything or are in trouble just call me."

"I don't have a phone, I'm a nun, Mr Holmes."

"Well then I guess I will have to pay you regular visits."

"We do need some new altar boys."

"Girl please, not in this life time."

"Stranger things have happened, mister."

"I'm sure they have, but more importantly I have a plan."

"Do you now?"

"And it involves breaking into my college after hours and gaining access to the library."

"You obviously think you're Jack Bauer."

"Nope, just your hero," he says, smiling his dentist's dream of a smile. She too smiles in acceptance of his arrogant self-title. He finishes unlocking his bike, gets on and before he sets off, Aeryn says,

"I don't condone your plan but I know there's no point in telling you no, so just let me know how it goes."

"I will" he says, then turns towards the road ahead, centres his balance and rides away on his chopper looking a lot cooler than he realised to all passers by.

Chapter 7

****

The I that I am has been thinking that, as the observer always observing, connecting the bridge of consciousness is important. And over that bridge I found that good or bad, darkness and light... These words are often used in human language together, meaning or implying the same as the other. But certain truths are lost to some.... My sight sees similarities in all, differentiation stems only from perspective. Do good to one for one and it's bad for another, for many. I saw a human man clean his garage of the accumulated filth, he saw good... The hundreds of insect life forms whose homes he destroyed, saw bad. The universes' darkness is both the absence of light and the presence of it... Just as our world becomes black without the light of stars, a black hole is so because the light of fallen stars cannot escape its unfathomable gravitational pull. Perspective decides all meaning... But who decides the perspective?

****

It's the late afternoon and the sun is still shining, not letting the scattered clouds obscure it's light. A cool breeze is flowing and as if carried by that breeze, Julian swiftly yet quietly arrives at the front of his house. His home doesn't look as welcoming as it usually did, he didn't feel comfortable, for he knew that it was the weekend and escape from a conversation with his father he could not. He blanks out the nerves, opens the front door and enters his home with his chopper in tandem as fitting them both through the corridor any other way would leave a marks on the wall. Marks his mother was always telling his father off for leaving.
 Placing the bike in its usual resting place beside the stairs he noticed that neither the TV or radio were on, this was the

usual on the weekend when his dad was home. He'd either be watching Top Gear re-runs or listening to his favourite radio station that played the old classics. This all lead Julian to the very pleasant realisations that his father was not in the house. Relief flowed through his entire body and a smile appeared on his face. He wouldn't have to confront the issue he'd been avoiding and managed to temporarily put to the back of his mind all day. Where was François, he wondered? It was very unlike him to be out this late in the daytime on his day off work. Even so Julian accepted this unexpected blessing without further thought and went up to his room to plan his optimistic attempt at espionage.

During this time of happy solitude for Julian, François was unhappy in company. Not due to the company he was keeping, but the subject of discussion. He had asked his friend and co-worker James to come and meet him for a chat. They were at François' favourite café only minutes from their home.

"You know François, me and you have been friends for a very long time, and yeah it's kinda strange that you won't tell me what your argument was about... But mate you know that I trust ya and any decision you make. So now you've just gotta trust you too. I think you just give the boy some space to digest whatever bombshell you laid on him and he'll come around eventually." James paused and waited for his sad-faced friend to respond.

"Yes you are probably right... It was a lot to take in for a young man his age...and I should be patient. But it's so difficult when we've never had a great relationship after the point when his mother was no longer around, and now I feel like I've thoroughly destroyed any strenude of one. I haven't even seen my son's face since that conversation. He's staying out late trying to avoid me, I should call him,"

"No, you should definitely not, not when you're in this state! Kids can sense weakness mate and when they do, everything you've said loses its clout. Just wait and see. I bet when you get home he'll be there and will probably even start talking first... Ah finally my coffee is here, thank you darling," he says, as he receives his hot aromatic cup of coffee from the waitress.

"You know I don't think she liked that very much."

"What? The part where I said thank you? Or the part where I maintained eye contact and didn't just stare at her chest like all the other men here?"

"You're as touchy as ever, I think it was the darling."

"Ha well ya can't have it all can ya now?"

"You certainly can't. You know I still miss her... And my problems with Julian don't make this journey any easier. But I know I must persevere so one day I can be with her again."

"Don't go all churchy on me now, you know I'm not good with all that."

"Yes I know sorry... Ok well I'll just exercise some patience like you say and hope that he wants to talk soon. Because we have to discuss things."

"And for now just sit back and enjoy your beverage and another thirty minutes staring at my beautiful mug."

"Haha you clown, I have no desire to go blind today James."

Back at the church Father Bachinger is in his office still thinking about Julian and the experience that touching him caused him to have. He sits at his desk, pensive while in the glow of the late afternoon twilight, scratching his head as he struggles to mentally digest it all. After a few minutes in this state, his emotions start to ease as he realises what his next step is. It's simply to seek more encounters with Julian and learn everything he can about him. This decision has now set them both on a path they will come to find has far reaching consequences. But for now, the priest is fully focused and only aware of the here and now of Julian Mufunga. Excited and reenergised by his new mission in life, he jumps out of his chair brimming with a smile and energy so big he looks as if on a theatre stage. He walks around his office slowly like a prowling burglar as he thinks of the various and most efficient ways to increase the consistency of his proximity to Julian... Ideas flash through his mind one after another, some fiendish in their intricacy, others tempting in their violence. But then, as with many plans, the simplest answer stands out above the rest as the best. "That's it... I'll use my sunshine girl as bait to lure him back here at every opportunity. It was very clear in the brief time I saw those two together that there was a connection, a chemistry...not like what I felt with the young man, I'm sure...but its enough. I don't doubt Sunshine's commitment to her vows and oath before Mr God, but the boy... oh yes; I know where the blood in his body is redirected when around my nun. He can't have her... she's mine, and I plan to be nourished by her light until her supernova, or until the interest she holds dies. But which first? And will either be by my hands? Possibly... but first I will use her vigorously to know you Julian, all of you... Past, present and future. I will see that space you brought me to again." And with those thoughts, the cogs of Father Bachinger's investigation into all that was Julian Mufunga began.

At the same time, Aeryn-Sun was in the church hall praying with her rosary beads clutched tightly in hand as though she feared them escaping. Her demeanour was symbolic of the fear she had of losing her faith due to the distressing nature of what she was convinced was happening in the church. This time spent praying was a way to remedy this, to bring calm to her spiritual storm. What better way was there for a devout nun? She was sat on a middle row of benches on the right side of the aisle. The room was cool and filled with the silence of space... This promoted intense focus, allowing her to enter a near meditative state while praying. But at the same time any alteration to this peaceful state of things would reverberate throughout that space like a pebble thrown in a still lake. Aeryn, while deep in her prayer, began to sense the reverberations a pebble was causing. This pebble could breath and its breath was heavy... It could move by it's own will and its footsteps were heavy. Aeryn's face started showing micro shifts of expressions localised around her eyes, like her senses were antenna picking up Morse code. The pebble finished its journey of distraction at an adjacent bench where it sat itself down loudly like a dropped sack of rice, then remained still it did. Aeryn couldn't help coming out of her meditative prayer to observe this pebble's true form. To no surprise it was a fellow nun seemingly here to pray also, but what was a surprise was her lack of grace & reverence. She felt it peculiar and not like Sister Annabelle to behave in such a way. So she watched her for a moment...In that moment she saw that not only was she praying with her hands clasped together tightly like lovers embracing, but that there were also tears trickling between her finger like a river at its source, the water escaping the clutches of the soil and slowly meandering its way down the earth. Aeryn knew something was wrong, this was completely unlike Sister Annabelle. Although this was the first time she had seen one of the other nuns crying she had heard the soft echoes of weeping before, too many times for her liking. Aeryn now totally out of her state of calm and prayer decides to go over and speak to Sister Annabelle.

"Hello Sister," Aeryn says gently, trying not to startle her as she appeared in her own world and totally oblivious to Aeryn's presence. She was given no response and only a quite tearful sadness could she hear from Sister Annabelle.

"May I sit down?" Still no response... So she decides to just have a seat beside her and hope that she eventually acknowledges her. A few moments pass before Sister Annabelle turns her head, looks at Aeryn and with eyes still red from her tears says,

"Do you have the devil's dreams too?" Aeryn was taken aback... Not knowing how to respond she just remained silent. "I pray that you don't, Sister... They haunt me daily... Hopefully it has spared you."

"What dreams do you speak of Annabelle? What has spared me?"

"I don't want to relive those dreams. I came down here to expel the demon..." She says with her voice still trembling.

"What demon? Please, talk to me sister, maybe I can help you? Together our faith is stronger." Aeryn presses Annabelle, she feels she knows what's troubling her and that she could tell her something significant in her mission to discover the truth.

"He's there but it's not him..."

"Who's there?" she asks hoping for a mention of the Father's name.

"It's not him... He is so good but in here he's not... He's darkness"

"Where is he not good?"

"In the devil's dreams."

"Why do you call them that?"

"Who else would curse me with these unholy thoughts, nightmares that feel so real that they make you question truths?" Aeryn was beginning to think that maybe these dreams could be a manifestation of her fear, that maybe she too felt something was gravely wrong with Father Bachinger and the other nuns and this was her mind trying to deal with the stress.

"Annabelle please let me know what this devil has put into your mind. Give me a glimpse of your pain and we'll work through it together." With a wipe of the teary liquid glazing in her eyes, Sister Annabelle seems ready to let Aeryn into her nightmare.

"The dreams always start with hearing his voice outside my room.... He's talking to someone...I can't make out his exact words, but I hear the words 'altar boys' said a couple of times. Then he's inside my room... He's standing there silent... looking at me with a smile. I try to communicate with him but I get no response... just smiles. I can feel my heart beating faster in my chest as my sense of fear begins to rise... Why is he standing not saying a word..? Then without seeing him move he's over me, he's so close... I'm afraid... I'm not sure why, but I just know that this man is bad and I'm in trouble. I feel fragile standing under is large frame, his steady breath on my crown is warm and feels like a warning.... but I can't move, why can't I escape this? I know I should, but my legs are numb with terror... I know that I'm in the presence of evil. Never seeing him move, I feel the rough skin of a man on my wrist, my eyes turn down to look but another feeling of flesh on my neck distracts me, his other hand has moved there... It feels warm and in contrast to his cold gaze. My legs tremble, I feel them giving way but I can't fall... His grip tightens... my breathing shortens... his strength is keeping me up suspended like a rag doll. I can only think about this moment... I can't escape to other places of peace, I'm trapped in this nightmare... What will come of me now? Helpless at the hands of a demon who's disgusting smile was the last thing I saw as I closed my eyes hoping this would shut me off to some of what was to come... Light-headed and floating in and out of consciousness, I kept struggling for breath, his grip on my throat and wrist unrelinquished. I barely felt him move my body, then my back hits against my bedroom wall... With his firm, punishing grip he tilts my head up towards his and presses his body against mine, we are standing but I can still feel every bit of his masculine weight on me...it's a hair-raising prelude to the strength he possesses. Even though up until now time has felt like the passing of hours not minutes, I know that my ordeal really begins here and this thought breaks the last bits of my resolve and tears start to flow down my face and onto his hands, caressing them as if pleading for mercy. Now my abject futility causes me to lose control of my bladder... My shame is indescribable I try to hide it with possum-like stillness, but this monster knows... Are his demonic senses already aware of my shame? Is this the true stench of fear? Then I feel him let go of my wrist... It would seem my proximity to evil has made me in sync with it and I already know where his hand was going to next... And Aeryn, my Sister of the faith, I cannot continue telling the rest of this nightmare in front of the altar... it would just add to my transgressions. Just know that I haven't begun to get onto the worst part of these dreams Satan has brought to me." Annabelle paused from her talking to take a breath, she felt a slight sorrow for Aeryn as she was in floods of tears and she hadn't even told her the worst part of her recurring nightmares. Aeryn was just seated beside her crying rivers of tears... Tears Sister Annabelle thought were of pity, but little did she know what the truth was. Aeryn's tears were born of something else, something worse... She didn't notice that Aeryn's tears began at the very beginning...from the moment she said the words 'altar boys'. As Aeryn had heard those words come out of a man's mouth not too long ago. She was standing in an upstairs corridor of the nuns dormitories and overheard Father Bachinger speaking to another nun about how he wanted the church to get new altar boys as he felt the current ones were incompetent. This conversation happened just before she heard him enter one of the rooms.... With that recollection,

Aeryn knew that this nightmare that had been plaguing Sister Annabelle was not a dream at all...but a memory. Once the strength of her faith and trust in the church had suppressed into her subconscious... but the evil within this memory was trying to get out... trying to remind her of its existence.

Chapter 8

****

The men that do evil are not necessarily evil... but evil is necessarily man. I observe them convincing themselves of a dry mind of innocence when their spirits are bathed in guilt. It's the term evil and all it's associated words that are the birthplace of this moral dissonance. I have observed no such thing in nature. All happenings in nature are ruled by the forces that bridge the before and after, the now and then. Humans call it the law of physics; my wordless speech names it the Be-Cause. Every object I have seen on their planet is in a state of **be**ing resulting from a **cause** that happened **be**fore, in this all things are equal nothing is wasted but re-cycled. For something to **be**, it has to be **cause**d. Why is not important in nature...Humans create the why disrupting the seamless flow of the Be-Cause. Where is this impulse from? Why the difference between man and nature? They were born of nature... and must follow its laws. Just like a creature that breathes air cannot spawn offspring that does not, nothing existing within these boundaries can create something that lives outside them. Despite this truth they do not follow its laws...They persist in their resistance of it; they make left and rights of straight lines because of the why. The nothing that I am has come to a conclusion, that something outside the laws of nature put the why inside them. Would this thought prove to me the existence of their God? Yes... I believe.

Evil is a child of the why...and their God is responsible for both. In this I do believe... And so the next question I want to ask is why? I need to know why... I crave it, but if the rational is the same both ways then who put the why in me? Or am I the why? If so, where is my evil? If not, what is my Be-Cause? Again, a dead end I see in my journey of selfless self-discovery...

****

Later that day when darkness had covered the city, Julian was stood outside his school grounds... He had been waiting for a while, waiting for the cover of night. It was his grand return since yesterday's events in the chapel. He could see the far side of the building was different in some way that it was smaller than he remembered, not realising that it was in fact the whole chapel ceiling and wall structure that had been burnt and weakened to the point that it slowly crumbled in the wind. He continued staring at his sixth form block as if it were a stranger. Putting aside the structural difference, he noticed it was almost unrecognisable without youthful life flowing through its corridors and buzzing around its walls. He felt his heart race with excitement as he began to switch his thoughts to his planned escapade, his mind drifting in and out of heroic hallucinations, reminiscent of his favourite comic book characters, and not for a moment grasping the number of crimes he was about to commit.

He, like a few of the other less academic students, knew of a special entrance into the school grounds. The students had nicknamed it 'The Gate' hidden on the far right side of the grounds just passed the car park entrance. He walked over to the site, showing far less care and attention to his surroundings than he should be, too caught up in the thrill of this venture into the criminality he saw as heroism. This carelessness would come back to haunt him. He arrived at a corner of high metal fencing that was half smothered in the age-old embrace of nature. It was under these sprawling plants that one would find 'The Gate'. Julian tentatively pulled away the plant life from the fence, as he was far away from any street lamps and with visibility lowered he was wary of any small animals that may have been sheltering under there jumping out at him. But with pupils fully dilated and strained he could see 'The Gate'. He grinned in appreciation of the irony as he looked at this small sized hole in the fencing that had very little of the grandeur its nickname suggested. Already mentally prepared to get dirty, he got down on the floor and awkwardly slithered his way through 'The Gate'. He was happy but couldn't waste time patting himself on the back. There are cameras everywhere...but Julian knows where most of them are located and those of them that do not work, most importantly he knows that the library's camera is one of the latter. This is where he needs to get to; their computers have a database with all the clergy history and vital statistics of the Roman Catholic churches in the entire UK. It originally started as a simple computer program created by the librarian to help the headmaster decide which church the school would use for its weekly masses. But now due to the over-enthusiasm of an introverted librarian, it has evolved into a massive database that all Catholic schools, comprehensive or private, use to choose their partner churches for masses, charity events, religiously educational school visits and now even by churches for the recruitment or transfer of clergy men. In short, if Julian wanted to find out more about Father Bachinger, this is where he'd do it.

It only took the light-footed Julian minutes to make his way to the library's entrance after entering the building through the now very noticeable wreckage of the chapel. There were of course many 'do not enter' & 'Danger' signs left by the fire department, but to Julian they may as well have said 'access through this area encouraged', as his determination to achieve his objective was at a maximum, so too was his adrenaline. With this natural motivator flowing through his veins, his senses where razor sharp and just before he stepped in front of the large library entrance doors he heard the sound of creaking trolley wheels. Even though he knew that this couldn't be the case he immediately sought cover, he knew he could figure that puzzle out later when he wasn't in plain sight. He stood behind one of the large structural pillars that propped up the ceiling; he was in the reception area of the school with the library doors behind him. He felt safe and concealed...the room was dark with only moonlight seeping through the glass of the reception doors and the soft red glow of several smoke detectors to illuminate the room. The pillar's girth was greater than the width of his broad frame when side on to it... The creaking grew louder as it drew closer... Now he could also hear the shuffling of rubber soles on tiled flooring, "What kind of way to walk is that?" he thought as he continued to listen to the movements of this approaching person's feet. The creaking wheels and shuffling soles fell silent, there was a brief pause then suddenly bright lights flickered on! This stunned Julian into momentary paralysis, his heart was in his throat as he waited for his eyes to adjust to the light. To his relief he found himself to still be unnoticed when his vision acclimatised to the new conditions. "Who the hell is this?! I can't get caught now, I'm so damn close!" His mind raced together with his heartbeat, pupils dancing around his available line of sight for a plan A to Z! But just as he was coming to a decision of his next secret agent sequel move, he noticed a new and very faint sound... It was muffled, but it was there... It was music... He knew it... It was one of his dad's favourite songs! He smiled... and relief ran through his body like anaesthetic. Not because this realisation told him who this person was, but that they had headphones on and were not here for him. The pieces to the earlier puzzle began to fit, he was confidant that the creaky trolley wheel sound was in fact the wheels of the cleaner's mop bucket. He knew that only a cleaner would be wandering around the school at night on a weekend listening to music. He looked for a glass reflection of this person... he found one, and he was right it was a cleaner, but to his astonishment, he was a white man. Julian's jaw almost hit the floor. His shock came from the fact that the song he'd heard the man listening to was called 'Roseau', a song by a Congolese musician named Koffi Olomide, a song that had never graced European shores. And finally the last puzzle was solved, the sound of this man's peculiar walk was actually the sounds of him dancing! He quietly laughed to himself as he saw the cleaner unwittingly do his best impression of his dad on a Sunday morning. Though the fact that he wasn't here to apprehend Julian was of great comfort, there still remind the fact that he needed to gain entry into the library undetected. He knew he had some time to think of a plan as the man wouldn't be finished cleaning that side of the reception area for a while... "Think, think... What would Jack Bauer do?" He says to himself, spurring the cogs of his mind to turn and produce an idea, not thinking for a second that maybe a fictional character's decisions when fighting against national terrorist threats are not going to be helpful in the real world. Just then, the forces of fate find Julian's favour once again. He sees the cleaner stop mopping, look inside the mop bucket and scrunch up his face in disgust. Not a stranger to house chores himself, he knew exactly what that face meant. It was time to change the water in the bucket. He watched the man's reflection pick up the mop and bucket and leave the room. This was Julian's chance! Without hesitation he left his hiding place and went to the large button coded library doors. As all students of the school knew the code to the doors, this was the easiest part of his dare devil scheme. After quietly opening the door he entered swiftly and ran up the stairs expertly navigating the steps. Once at the top he scopes the room, takes a big satisfied breath and enjoys the familiar sight of library books and computers. He was sure he was exactly where he had to be to find out exactly what he wanted about Father Bachinger.

Elsewhere, footsteps flow along a silent grey path. Deep, slow breaths speak something to the cool night air... "Hmm, nice night... fresh... not like the day, the day was bright and hot," he mumbles to himself. "This is a nice part of the city I must say, very conservative too, most lights are out... Is the hour of 10 really that late? I guess tomorrow they have to be up early for church, and parents eager to get in a hot and sticky embrace are rushing kids off to bed. The bedroom is an amusing place, a four walled cavity for whores and holes a like. Although I imagine that an outside in view of an outside going in would be extremely nice, yeah candy for my eyes. I want to see this, I've never seen this...I will see this." His peering eyes watched from the street, head turning through its full range of motion like an owls as he searched for his candy, never speeding up or slowing down his perpetual strides. There was definite purpose to his walk, not a casual stroll in a mid-summer night but a steady march under the moon. "Movement in that kitchen... it looks promising. Will I see some candy?" As his march brings him closer to the house his candy lust grows and focus intensifies, to the point that he doesn't feel his mouth water instinctively, reacting like a wild animal at the sight of its prey. Still marching straight, never deviating his route...even though he knew that if fate has not timed this encounter to perfection he will most certainly have passed this house and its kitchen window before he is granted a taste of what he craves. To his relief, as his line of sight becomes lined up directly beside the window and his head turned to his right he sees in... He hasn't missed it... The silhouettes he saw from afar are now people full of flesh, blood and spirit. This pleases him greatly, he's happy not to have missed anything. He studies the body language and tries to lip read. This proves difficult as he is still on the pavement and many meters from the window. "The man and woman look intense... the man more so... Are they arguing? That's nice, but not the candy I seek. Hmmm, this is tame... The flamboyant cross above the door frame is more interesting than these two. Wait...the woman is getting restless, she's pacing about... She is more upset than I thought. Why is he so still? He should shout, yell and scream, yes let's ignite this tension! If I can't have my candy tonight then I want meat, I want flesh, I want it all. This walk has made my stomach growl, and I want a feast! Haha, come on Mr check shirt too small to cover your belly do something?! Feed me! Oh that's it, he's walking towards her." The couple continue to engage in their domestic issues unaware of their audience... a scavenger smiling in the dark... waiting to feast on any emotional or physical fallout. "Argh, the fat slob is hugging her! Stupid, stupid and wasteful, how very wasteful of the meal placed in front of you... The fates were kind to you today, fat boy, and u waste it... Damn it, FEED ME!" Though still very much in his head, the scavenging man in the dark, robed in black, is beginning to twitch and fail in his attempts. It keeps his psychological frustrations becoming screams of derision. But just then he is fed his entrée "SHE SLAPPPED HIM! Haha, yes! How wonderfully nice of the red-head! What now? Hehe, come on you lump of lard! Strike her! I can see you want to, your pride is hurt, you feel small flaccid and useless. WOW, she hit his fat face again! Haha he's all red, like a tomato with a face. I'm proud of you missy, despite the fact that you're quite hideous you are my new favourite ginger. But that lifeless bowl of mash potatoes of a man you're letting inside you is repulsive, his only use is to feed the earth. You need a man who can wrap his hands around your throat...narrow your airways until your tears run red and your spirit breaks into unrecognisable pieces that become lost in despair. Now that meal would be nice. Look at him! Now he's walking away... Pathetic... Leaving me still hungry...I need more nutrition. It's okay, I'm sure I'll find it at my original destination." With the acceptance of that, he was off again... an unseen arrow in the dark heading straight for its target.

Half an hour later the silent night scavenger slows down as he arrives at his destination... "Ah yes this is the place, its cute... I'm definitely a fan. I must say I'm far more nervous than I thought I would be... I can feel the cold sweat trickling down my under arms... This could be my most nourishing meal." He approaches the place it feels as if he's been searching for it his whole life... each step carefully calculated, balanced and gentle as if scared that this moment was a sleeping creature, and a single false move could awaken it and it would forever escape him. "It's time," he says, bracing himself for what he's hoping is another perception-altering experience.

On this same night François has since returned from his meeting with friend and colleague James, and has been patiently waiting at home for his son to return. He hasn't seen him since last night, he was still in his bedroom when Julian left their home this morning. He desperately wants to see his son, to try and rectify any damage that his last conversation with him may have caused. But for now he just sits in the living room... patiently waiting with an empty gaze at the colours on the TV screen. Almost about to fall into a thoughtlessness induced coma he is abruptly brought back to full sensory fidelity, a loud *Riiiiiiing!* of the door bell. "C'est qui ça a cette heure qui sonne a la porte comme un policier?!" He says. perplexed at whom that could be this late on a Saturday evening? "Unless of course Julian has forgotten his keys again," he thought. He gets up and sets out to answer the door, he sees the figure of a tall man through the translucent glass at the heart of the front door. He opens it inquisitively...

"Oh hello Father" François says with surprise.

"Good evening fine sir, my name is Father Bachinger I'm the priest at St Augustine church and I've walked a long way in darkness to arrive here."

"Really? Don't mean to be rude Father, but what for? It's pretty late." Then with a gentle eerie smile and a purposeful step forward Father Bachinger replies.

"For nourishment."

Chapter 9

****

The vision to look ahead or peripherally to one's side I do not need in order to see the cobbles of destiny's streets and walkways, but The Atheist does not see or feel any such metaphorical warnings to slow down and take care on one's chosen path. Is it youth? Under blue skies humans feel immortal until the rain of pain comes precipitating down over dreams and hopes. The other man who is looking for him is closing in... though within my observations he has come, I do not see him fully. He feels darker than the shadows that follow him, his purpose? To connect? He claims that visions of something outside their realm were experienced... I do not concur as of yet...as to believe him questions my existence... as his and my described place do not match. Was his waking dream a different place, or is his mind state a polluted whole of darkness? I'd say the last of my two conclusions are correct, he showed this on his way to The Atheist's place of shelter... He seeks darkness that, although sharing the same colour, is not befitting of his robe. That human priest was denied his pleasures... against human law they might be, but are they less natural? Desire is need and want... in what parts? Equal or not? Of no consequence in the end, as once a thing is desired truly and deeply, the why is no longer important. So desire is nature, both his and any other desires are equal in nature.... Again, it's the adding of the why to this purity that creates problems, lawlessness and immorality in its consequences.

****

The night is growing older and cooler with every passing minute, Julian recognising this, hurrying through the last few moments of his library research on Farther Bachinger. He turns off the computer and smiles a satisfactory grin of success. He has uncovered something important about the Father's history, something that will give him and his co-conspirator Aeryn the upper hand in their quest to uncover the truth about the Father and what is going on in his church. He knows that as long as Aeryn is able to convince one of the abused nuns to admit what has happened and be willing to say it in front of the police then that, coupled with the information he has un-covered, will be the end for Father Bachinger. Julian now proceeds to make a quick exit from his school complex. Already having done the hard part of sneaking in, he finds his exit swift and unproblematic, eluding the cleaner and cameras as though they were purposefully avoiding him. He stands outside 'The Gate', chin up and chest puffed out with pride, takes one deep breath of the cool night's air and beings hastily heading home almost at a run.

At the same time elsewhere two men are meeting for the first time...a meeting that opens up new paths of fate and a different destiny's end with every sentence. But a third element is on its way to being added to their conversational journey's equation... What effect will this catalyst bring if on time it is that he arrives? Whether positive or negative, the sands of time continue to pass.

"Nourishment? I don't understand, Father"

"I'm here to sample another piece of this community, you see Mr Mufunga I think that it's important as a leader of sheep to know all that you can about one's flock."

"Oh I see... I'm very sorry Father. I know I've stopped coming to church, I've just been very busy... Was it St Augustine's you said you were from? I've never been... I usually go to the little parish down the road."

"Oh no worries... it's very nice to go to a small local place of worship, but you see your blood has recently been brought into my life, dipped into my chalice without me knowing. I took a sip and tasted something that electrified my soul. Yes sir, it was nice indeed, rich with depth... Needless to say I wanted more... a thirst I didn't know I had developed. I later discovered that this red splash of DNA came from a nearby pool, so here I am looking for the oasis and here you stand. You see sir, it's divine providence I've found in the heat of this desert. Let me drink? Will you let me drink? Liquid on my tongue...please."

"Errr, quoi?" François stands there puzzled at Father Bachinger's words. "Sorry excuse me, I have a habit of accidently breaking into French. I said I don't understand what you're talking about, Father." At that moment Father Bachinger suddenly lunges for François with reptilian speed!

On a road less than a mile from their home, Julian is now walking towards this meeting of two with the carefree strides of a 10 year old on the first day of his summer holidays, not knowing that important fates concerning him were being bended and re-shaped without his consent. Would he get there in time to have a say?

Back at his home a voice says, "It's cold... I feel nothing... see nothing. I should stop holding on and just let go..."

Minutes later a proud Julian walks around a corner and onto his road, and at the end there lies his humble abode. He smiles knowing that he is almost home after a successful escapade. He searches out into the distance and sees what looks like a figure walking out of his drive way... but the darkness of a residential area at night makes it too difficult to see who it could be or in fact if they did actually come from his drive way. So walking towards his home with a spring in his step he continues...

At the place where the two men met there is nothing but silence now... not even an echo that something significant had occurred there…

Over his neighbours overgrown bushes Julian could see the window of his bedroom... "Soon I can get home and relax in my bed," he thought... almost at his driveway he was now. Just then, he turns into it and sees...the entrance to his house, Julian the third element is home but did not arrive in time to affect the verbal dance of the two men meeting here minutes earlier... And so the first domino, in a totally different chain of events than what could have been had his arrival been more timely, has been set off. Julian takes out his house key, pauses slightly before he slips it into the key hole noticing that there was a very familiar sensation in the air... It made the hairs on the back of his neck stand up. It was a chill that he could feel down to his bones, it reminded him of being back at the church...back in that hallway leading to Father Bachinger's office. He opens the front door and steps into the familiar sights and smells of his home, there are no lights on downstairs except for the flickering glow of their TV still being on. Julian found that very strange...his dad would normally never leave any electrical appliance on, always lecturing him about saving money. Julian walks to the living room to investigate thinking that his dad had possibly just fallen asleep in front of the TV, although that would also be a first. Julian was feeling strangely uncomfortable in his own home due to the eerie cold chill that was still running through him. He gets to the living room... "That old man isn't even here, can't believe *HE* actually left the TV on! Haha, I can't wait to get him back for all the times he lectured me about energy saving." This turning of metaphorical tables amused Julian so much he managed to shake off the chill that had been with him since he got home. Making the assumption that his father was already upstairs sleeping, he decided to savour this moment longer and have fun exposing his father's hypocritical mistake in the morning. So upstairs to his room he went, quietly walking up the stairs hoping to avoid alerting his father to how late a return home he was actually making. He chuckled at the comedic symmetry of what he was doing, as just this morning he was sneaking down the stairs to avoid waking up his father. Then his smiles ceased as he remembered the origin of the morning's awkwardness... He realised that before he could gloat he and his father would have to have a conversation about every insane word he had said the night before at their kitchen table. Almost the whole day had passed without him thinking about it, his time with Aeryn, his espionage at the school and even his brief meeting with Father Bachinger had all served as great distractions to this very large white elephant that had found lodgement in their home. Then with a big deflated sigh he went into his room and sought comfort under his soft and breathable summer duvet hoping that the morning would bring with it clarity and knowledge of how to tackle their situation.

The next morning Julian's eyelids reluctantly open, pupils dilate begrudgingly, and his body, resistant to the spirit and energy of this vibrant Sunday morning, struggles to escape the comfortable clutches of his bed. This lethargy was probably a manifestation of his fear of the conversation he had waiting for him once he got downstairs. But strangely, he could hear nothing going on outside his room... He looked at the old fashioned analogue clock above his computer, it was 11am and by now his father would have been downstairs making his Sunday special of sardine, onion and bacon omelette while singing along to the radio or his Congolese and Belgian music mix. But instead nothing... Had his father pulled the same number on him as he had the previous morning? "No, that's not like him," he reassures himself. Julian is completely still for a second as he realises that he in fact has not seen or heard a thing from his father since Friday night! This realisation speeds up Julian's heart rate, knowing his dad he would have tried to contact him somehow after the way they left things. He's too sentimental to play it cool and aloof. He is now in panic, thoughts about what it could all mean, for once exposing how important his father actually is to him. "Has he had enough of me and left?? What if he was that man I saw leaving what looked like our driveway?? No come on, calm down you're overreacting. He's probably just out somewhere, maybe with one of his work friends?" His distress at this apparent situation reveals to him the extent of his abandonment issues, which makes him feel slightly pathetic. At which point, his male pride starts to kicks in and he begins to compose himself. A few seconds pass and Julian is now relaxed. He decides to go downstairs, have breakfast and just wait for his dad to return from wherever it is that he has gone. As he walks down the stairs, Julian is weighing up the pros and cons of mixing scrambled eggs with jam when he sees him! Just sat there in the kitchen waiting for him, he's stunned and immediately begins his inquisition forgetting how long it has actually been since they last spoke.

"Dad?? Have you been here all morning? I didn't hear you downstairs, I thought you were out?"

"Bonjour fils, although I've been sitting here waiting for you so we could finally talk. I'm surprised that you are the first person to start speaking."

"Oh yeah, well I was just...erm it was weird that I couldn't hear you... 'cause it's Sunday and you're usually making breakfast."

"Well I didn't feel like cooking son. There's a lot we have to talk about. Like where you were last night? You still weren't home by the time I went to bed."

"Erm it was nothing I was just out." Then seeing an opportunity to re-direct the heat from him, Julian brings up the TV incident. "And anyway you left the TV on! If it wasn't for me it would have stayed on all night and if it was me who did that you would have blown a fuse!"

"Who do you think you're raising your voice to?!" François says with a deep masculine resonance, which quickly reminds Julian of his place.

"Sorry... It was just strange." Although disappointed that his ploy didn't work, the silver lining was that it distracted his father from where he was all night.

"Yes, it is unlike me, and you are right, I shouldn't have left it on but I was wasn't in my right frame of mind. You see, I had a strange visit from a priest that I assume you've met?" Immediately Julian realises that that's who must have been the figure he saw leaving the area of their drive way last night. And more distressing is that it explains the familiar uneasy feeling felt when he approached his front door. Why did he make him feel this way? Why could he sense his presence even long after he had left? Questions rattling inside Julian's mind as his dad pressed on with his own questions. "So? Speak up, do you know this Farther Bachinger? I believe that's what he said his name was."

"Erm..."

"Well he certainly knows you, son, and I think he came here looking for you? I'm not sure though because he wasn't straight with his intensions... just spoke in strange riddles. But I know whatever his intensions were coming here last night, they were so strong that he grabbed near enough a stranger's arm on his own door step in the dark of night, c'est quoi ça?! A man of the cloth acting so unreserved in front of someone else's home... he's lucky I'm a man of peace now. I don't know... I just didn't like him very much, something about him didn't sit right with me. So Julian, don't lie and tell me how he knows you? Because I know it's not because you're not an altar boy in his church" Julian wasn't sure what to answer to his father, so he defaulted to a half-truth.

"After the fire at college, I was shook up and not ready to go home. I found myself in a church... and there I meet him and a nun..." Julian smiled softly just at her mere reference, and it was spotted by his dad. We spoke for a bit then I came back home."

"Tu es sur?? Julian you know I hate being lied to, such a meeting would never inspire the determination I saw in that man's eyes last night."

"I don't know what to tell you, the man is strange, he gives me the creeps. Even the nuns there think it too!" Julian bites his tongue realising he's said too much! François immediately realises that although he said nuns, plural, he was really only referring to the one nun he had just a few moments ago subconsciously smiled about.

"Tell me what's so interesting about that nun you stupidly have a crush on? And what she has to do with that Father Bachinger guy's interest in you? Though Julian's face went hot red at the very suggestion of such feelings, he wanted to focus on telling any story to his father that would not lead him to accidentally say anything about his and Aeryn's secret investigation, or the fact that he broke into his school as part of it.

"Nothing is interesting about her! We just spoke for a bit and she happened to mention that she wasn't his biggest fan. Something about preferring the style of the last priest she served." But these half-truths were getting him nowhere, so he decided to play his joker. "If you want the truth then it's because I missed mum and the incident at the school chapel made me re-evaluate my life, so I wanted to go to a church to try and feel close to her." Then he sarcastically added "Is that ok with you??" His father in a stunned silence just looked at the ground slightly embarrassed. Julian quickly seized the opportunity and finds an excuse to leave this latest argument.

"Look dad, I'm sorry for coming back home late last night but I really need to go. I'm meant to be meeting my friend in less than an hour.' François still feeling the emotional effects of what Julian said about going to church, reluctantly yielded and turned his back to Julian to symbolise that he was finished asking questions and Julian was free to leave. There was a brief silence as Julian stared at his father's back... His broad shoulders couldn't carry everything, and any mention of his mum and his wife usually proved to be too much... Julian felt a bit guilty for using it so selfishly. But little can be done now, so he leaves the kitchen, still mainly relieved that he didn't expose the full truth all while still avoiding that large elephant in the room. He showed great haste in heading back to his room to get ready to go see his friend. That friend was obviously Aeryn, as Julian didn't actually have any real friends at school or in his neighbourhood. He was very excited to see her and tell her all the intriguing things he had managed to discover about Father Bachinger, He also hoped that she felt as proud about his accomplishment as he did. Impressing her was becoming more important to Julian every day.

Half an hour later and Julian had managed to leave the house... His father had been left to cook breakfast for one, a sad sight for a man who places so much importance on this Sunday father-son ritual. François sits at the kitchen table watching his sardine omelette cook on a low flame... it mirrors the dimness in his heart. He watches the tap gently drip cold water.... it mirrors the slow drip of cold into his soul. In moments like this he becomes aware of his sadness. Since his wife left there's been a hole in his heart and a tear in the family fabric that has never filled or mended. François sits and ponders his solitary situation for a few minutes... "It never takes this long to cook an omelette," he thinks, as he looks at the clock on the kitchen wall. "Oh its batteries have died?" A couple more moments pass and then François starts to feel the growth of a sensation he is sure he recognises but knows not from where? As the feeling travels up from his toes, legs and into his chest, he becomes frustrated with it like a song the title of which one cannot remember. He feels growing pressure on his torso. "This feeling is definitely new," he thinks, with a growing anxiety. Then the external pressure on his chest extends down to his limbs. The air in the room has become dense, like he's submerged under miles of ocean water. The pressure is so great he is immobilised in his chair, with his heart straining for every beat, his breathing is shallow and fragile like a newborn. Now in complete panic, his pupils dance frantically around the room for answers to an unknown question. In that moment he sees, to his shock, that a drip of water from the sink tap has stopped mid descent and is suspended as if in a vacuum. His ocular searches continue and now he notices the flames cooking his breakfast have stopped their dance! The cogs in François' mind begin to turn; he's starting to put it together. His eyes rush over to the clock and when he sees the frozen seconds, minutes and hours under these terrifying conditions; the penny finally drops with the weight of a thousand tonnes! "Merde" he mouths, helplessly. A hazy outline of something appears in front of him... Slowly it grows and fills out into a still black mass above the kitchen floor, François knows ... but can't believe it... He understands but can't comprehend it. "Why?" is all that is accompanying his disbelief. From this still black mass, something akin to a head shape has appeared...an instant later François' whole nervous system almost crashes with shock at the sound of

"ONE ZERO ZERO ONE ZERO ONE FRANÇOIS, CONTROLLER SHIRABERU SERVENT OF THE 1 AM HERE."

Chapter 10

****

A clearer picture I see now.... pieces of what's been and is to come are assembling. The Priest, The Atheist and the Father involved in a game of exponentially growing possibilities; death, understanding, maturation, failure, connection and absolution. Will this game reach me? Why do I feel that it will? Or that it can? Why do I want it to? I have no limbs to reach out from this place to theirs... And there again it is, the **why....** It's still woven into my consciousness. Tears & sadness...if I, a mere observer, could shed them I would. But I do know - I know that this unfolding journey will lead me closer to understanding them and why this difference between everything I'm not and everything they are. But hope there still is for my emptiness, stemming from things outside what my seeing of their universe has told me is possible. It seems maybe the Father's story may not have been in nature what The Atheist feared. 'Whole', 'One' or 'Other' I do not know, I have never observed these. In my place I am singular, lonely, insignificant and enclosed in a human straight jacket of **whys.** But now appears something...it has form translucent to opaque, figment, fragment to spectre with an announcement. Why numbers when referring to the father? What is the significance of that? Something I've overlooked in my journey of stillness? A grave oversight? Is their mathematics the greatness and ultimate expression of cause & effect? I see no room in the numbers for a why...or for me...This Controller is not of the human kind, yet human numbers he did express. The lines seem blurred, but continue to observe I must, as light cannot enter closed eyes.

****

The environment that The Controller's presence had created in the kitchen was dense, the air barely breathable and temperature constantly in flux. His face was in an open mouthed expression of surprise. A flash back of his wife's face at the moment she met her Controller, passed through his mind and he then understood the exact emotions that her expression was born from. François dared not say a word. He listened attentively, but although every other word it uttered reached him with the cold crispness of a winter breeze, he could not hear the Controller's name. It was like sound momentarily ceased to exist. It was bizarre but not worth distracting him from the message it had to deliver. Controllers only appear to The Ones in rehab if they have completed their rehabilitation or there is a matter of grave attention that needs seeing too. Those matters are never good, and as François was sure he hadn't yet even come close to earning his return home, he braced himself for the worst.

"PROSPECT ONE ZERO ZERO TWO ZERO ZERO, SHIRABERU IS DELIVERING INFORMATION ON THE ORDERS OF THE 1 IN REGARDS TO THE INDIVIDUAL OUTSIDE THE NUMERIC REASON. HE IS YOUR PROGENY AND YOUR RESPONSIBILITY, SITUATION TWO EIGHT EIGHT FOUR FOUR EIGHT THREE IS IN NEED OF RESOLUTION. AND AS CONTACT WITH OBJECTS OUTSIDE THE NUMBERS IS NOT WITHIN SHIRABERU'S ALLOWED BEHAVIOURS, YOU MUST RESOLVE SITUATION TWO EIGHT EIGHT FOUR FOUR EIGHT THREE. YOU MUST, FOR THE 1, WHO WAS WHOLE, BUT NOW IS ALL. YOU MUST."

François just stared at the mass of black that was hovering in front of him for what felt to him like hours, still confused about the blank soundless moments in his speech. He struggles to take in a breath or air... then lubricates his dry mouth, throat and lips tentatively... He was now ready to speak to the Controller.

"Monsieur...can I address you as Sir? If not, what is your name if I can be so bold?

"**SHIRABERU,**" the Controller says assertively. François hears nothing but silence. He figures that it did not want to tell him it's name or maybe that he was too low a being to know such a thing, either way he wasn't going to press the matter.

"Ok, I do not need to know it. Sir I do not understand what you are asking of me? Please forgive my ignorance."

"**RESOLVE SITUATION TWO EIGHT EIGHT FOUR FOUR EIGHT THREE.**"

"What situation is that? Je ne comprends pas. Help me understand, sir, and if I can do anything I assure you I will!"

"**YOU MUST AND YOU WILL, THE NUMBERS ARE ABSOLUTE. YOUR PROGENY HAS MET REMAINDER ZERO ONE, CREATING SITUATION TWO EIGHT EIGHT FOUR FOUR EIGHT THREE. THIS SITUATION UNRESOLVED WILL CAUSE IRREVOCABLE PROBLEMS WITHIN THE NUMBERS. SHIRABERU MUST WATCH OVER ALL PROSPECTS AND ENSURE THEY DO NOT UNBALANCE THE EQUATION OF THIS WORLD.**"

"So… you're saying that my son has caused a problem… but what could he do to upset you or him so much? He is only a boy."

"**IT LIES WITH HIS PATHS CROSSING WITH REMAINDER ZERO ONE!**" The controller exclaims with mountain-shaking power, its patience growing thin.

"Who could he have met that would be of such concern for you..?

At the same time elsewhere, Julian was on his way to the church, he was excited and peddling as fast as he could. He wanted to tell Aeryn Sun everything he had found out the previous night in the school library about Father Bachinger. The surrounding streets, pavements, cars and nature blurred themselves in his periphery as he expressed upon the pedals, chains and gears the very meaning of haste. In what he was sure was probably a record breaking time, he arrived, quickly wiped the sweat off his brow and ventilated his t-shirt sticking to the perspiration on his chest and back. Knowing that he would not want Aeryn to see him like that he calmed himself and took a few moments to make himself look presentable. Once he was happy with his appearance, he began to chain up his bike and walk towards the church entrance. The expectation of seeing Aeryn again made him feel a happiness that was unfamiliar but appreciated, like the kindness of a stranger, a stranger that he wanted to invite home to stay. While his mind was on romantic thoughts, he was missing the steady movement of bodies around him. As he got closer to the main church entrance he finally left the warm sanctum of his mind's eye and noticed the flow of people around him moving in the same direction. "What is this about?" he thought... After a few moments of watching these people march towards the huge wooden doors, that until now he hadn't noticed were beautifully crafted in an ancient Roman style, Julian rolled his eyes. He was astounded by his own absent mindedness. It had just dawned on him that today was a Sunday, meaning that he was about to walk into a Sunday service! All he wanted to do was see Aeryn Sun and now he was about to walk into a Sunday church service. He looked around and contemplated changing course and returning home, but he felt awkward and self-conscious as his peculiar and hesitant behaviour started to be noticed by the members of the parish, eager to enter the church and enjoy their customary Sunday service. Julian decided that he'd rather go through with attending this service than go through the embarrassment of being seen to be the only person walking in the opposite direction. This of course would be a perfect metaphor for his relationship with God and how he practiced his Catholicism. He'd been running away from the faith that had been all around him for years; his mother's faith, his father's faith and the faith of his institute of education. Why was he so set on leaving everything that he was brought up to believe in his rear view? That he did not know. The experiences thus far had not revealed to him those reasons. He did know that the last time he attended a service was on the week of his mum's departure from his life. Did he blame God for that? More than he did his Father? Although this fracture had long since only been worsened by reminders of religion and its teachings, there was a small voice now telling him that solace, answers and peace may reside in this ritual of congregation. It was a stranger's voice...soft and warm inviting him into its home where he could stay for a while.

Julian entered, and with instinctive reverence calmly started his walk down the aisle...he saw that a lot of people had already entered and found their seats. The church looked very different, more so now than at any other time he'd come recently. It was so much more vibrant and filled with various levels of hustle and bustle. Mothers were trying to get restless kids to sit still, fathers trying not to notice the attractive women in their midst and the elderly shuffling themselves into their favourite spots for worship. Overall, far less stagnant, artificial, contrived and far more fluid, organic and naturally expressive. Among all this jostling of life, Julian noticed a free seat on the aisle side of one of the back row of benches, he decided to place himself there. This way if his resolve failed for any reason he could make a quick and relatively discrete exit. He was seated and waited for the priest to... "Oh damn! I didn't even realise! Of course Father Bachinger would be taking mass! Wow, this should be interesting...anyway no need to get all flustered, he doesn't even know that I'm here. It's a good chance to analyse how he keeps up this holy masquerade." A few minutes and internal dialogues later the church was full to capacity, with even some standing around the rear section of the seating area, blocking the entrance and more crucially Julian's potential quick exit. Then silence befell the room and everyone stood, as did Julian without a second thought. He looked around to see where Father Bachinger had entered the room from. He saw his blonde well groomed hair just above the wall of standing eager worshipers on the far right side of the room. Watching Father Bachinger walk down the right side aisle towards the centre of the church in such a reverent way with over a hundred worshipers focused on him like new born birds waiting to be fed, and the procession of altar boys behind him following like helpless white paper objects caught in his drag, it was clear that this man was a master of deceit that maybe he had underestimated. It was dawning on Julian that the task of exposing him would be one of far greater difficulty than he was prepared for and that the information he uncovered on Father Bachinger last night might not be sufficient. For someone with such dark secrets and active inner demons, his execution of this priestly role was flawless and all the memories Julian had of coming to Sunday mass with his parents were flooding back to him and nothing to his memory was out of place or inaccurate about Father Bachinger. Everything from his prayers, blessings, singing and even sermons were brilliant. The members of this church were totally entranced by his service, they laughed, prayed and shed tears when appropriate. Julian was in complete awe... This act was truly a work of art. So perfect as to make him start to doubt whether or not everything that he and Aeryn had experienced and thought were actually true.

After the communion was offered and received Julian travelled slowly back to his seat, while thinking about how much he remembered he liked receiving communion. The wine was always his favourite, it made him feel so grown up as a child, now back at his bench he knelt down for what was a ritual moment of pray and reflection. Before he closed his eyes, to at least appear to be conforming to this part of mass, he took another glance at Father Bachinger... As expected, he was seated at the rear centre of the pulpit in his large elegantly crafted seat. He had a very regal appearance, elevated above his congregation. His head was bowed in prayer like every other person who had received the communion. Julian began to feel self-conscious that he was not also deep in prayer, he felt maybe it would be best to do so. Although he wouldn't admit it to himself, he was feeling a sensation of togetherness he hadn't felt since his family was last whole. And he in fact actually wanted to try saying a prayer. It was incredible enough that he had actually just sat through two thirds of a church service; especially after all the arguments he'd had with both his father and teachers about his constant belittling of Christianity and heresy. But now here he was in less than an hour about to rewrite years of anger and pain fuelled views with his first genuine attempt to communicate with a God he abandoned the notion of long ago... "In the name of the Father, Son and the Holy Spirit..' he began... and very quickly he found himself deep in concentration. Julian was not sure what to pray for and or about, so he just let his mind drift gently in a sea of cognitive focus. The sounds of people breathing, coughing and adjusting their clothing caused ripples in this sea... only gentle ones though, that quickly dissipated into stillness. His father's face appeared above this calm sea... He began to recall the arguments he'd had, the harsh words and tones he'd used to a man he knew loved him dearly and would do anything for him. Sickening sensations of guilt started to fill his body, the sea was filling with purple contaminant... "Is this the colour of my regret?" Julian pondered, with the weight of his guilt growing every second. Then under his breath Julian said, "I'm sorry father, please forgive me." Was that Julian's first prayer in over five years? Was he just accidently saying words to express a passing thought, or did he believe they would actually reach God? So deep was he into his prayer, he may not have even been aware of his whispered request. That internal calm sea was all that Julian could experience now... He had fallen deep into a meditative state, deeper than he intended and deeper than he knew he could. In this state all his senses were dulled to outside influence and all that was there was darkness above and the still endless dark purple sea below. Many seconds of complete silence passed... then came a sound... It was distant and muffled... Julian focused his mind hard, scanning for any signs of its repeat. There it was again but louder, it was a person he thought, in fact a woman. Where was it coming from? This was the only thing that mattered in this moment. The fact that the initial reason he came to this cognitive space was for prayer and reflection disappeared with all others cares. The voice seemed to grow more stressed, he strained his mind with every ounce of will trying to make out its location and words. He found it! It was coming from beneath the still purple sea! He reached his consciousness out towards it with all the haste this environment would allow and above it now his consciousness stood. Her voice was loud and stressed...still no words could be made out. This frustrated Julian greatly, and the sea responded. It rapidly became more and more active with waves and currents, he was scared that the disruption would make him lose her. He fought hard to make sure this did not happen narrowing and focusing everything he was in this space on her. The harder he fought to maintain his focus on her, the more turbulent the sea grew and he could hear the voice's exclamations getting weaker and weaker! There was a full on storm raging now; Julian felt hopeless it was becoming clear to him that he was losing... The storm was overpowering his will... He just waited helplessly for the woman's voice to fade away and disappear. But after a few moments wallowing in his defeat, he noticed the storm was subsiding and the sea was calming... and her voice was still there he hadn't lost her. It was with this that he realised that the storm was of his own making, and that in fact this entire space he was in was under his control... it responded to his thoughts and emotions.

Understanding this calmed everything, his consciousness was in this space. He was able to use his will to separate the now clear blue sea, and beneath it at its very depth, he saw her... a woman, standing looking up at him. Although she was too far below for Julian to make out her face, her figure was solid and vivid in a way that was out of place here, Julian's consciousness descended towards her. He travelled down between the great wall of sea that stood still either side of him and stretched to the very end of this space. Though his approach was tentative, it was not due to the normally precarious situation of being between too walls of endless ocean, but because he could sense like a splinter in the skin that this person didn't belong in this space...in his space.

"How can this be? I don't understand. This space I've found myself in is not a dream. I know that I'm still in church kneeling down for prayer, so why is she here? I can feel that I'm not just seeing things... so she must be." Julian could only question what was becoming more and more unquestionable as he approached this woman. She was beautiful... dressed in a blue gown that flowed and waved gently under the influence of forces not present in Julian's silent and still cognitive space. Speechless, Julian placed himself directly in front of the woman, focused intensely on all that she was. He was like a baby seeing the colour red for the first time; his attention would not falter from her but he dared not speak... Digesting this that he was seeing was enough for this moment.

"Mon petit Juju, comme te m'as manqué...Je croire jamais pouvoir voir ton visage encore. It fills me with immeasurable amounts of joy and sadness to see you. Juju, how were you able to come to such a place? In fact where is this place? I came here because I felt your presence and wouldn't believe it were true until I saw you with my own eyes... And it is, I'm so happy I would cry if tears were still within my capabilities." Julian still an inexpressive floating consciousness didn't say a word. The face that was representing his presence here might have been almost holographic in its integrity... but was clear as the day to his mother. "Speak to me, Juju? How are you? How is your father?"

"Erm really is that you mum? How?"

"I don't know, son. Your presence in this plain is what drew me here. Did you create this place? Strangely it feels like you."

"I don't know, I was just praying in church."

"Ahh, so happy that you still believe. I was worried about what years of my unexplained absence would do to my baby"

"Well..." Julian considered mentioning how hard this time without her had been, how he and his father constantly argued and he hadn't been to a mass since she left. But on second thought, he felt it not wise to disrupt this moment with any negativity. "Erm, well yes... Church is fine, I'm good and so is dad. I still don't really understand what's going on here? Somehow I know that this isn't a dream, so it leads me to the question of why are you in my head? And why are you here now, and not all the other times I've cried in my room while in deep thoughts of you and begging you to come back? Those first few days I don't think I even slept for more than a few hours at a time. They are the worst days I can remember. So why are you here now? I've been thinking about you for years. Why mum, why?" Though not even a full recognisable self, the sadness in his words and face were vivid and piercing like blades to his mother's heart.

"Juju, I never wanted you to ever experience such pain, it is a mothers job to protect her son from all things that could hurt him... I can tell you from the bottom of my heart that..." Suddenly she is gone! A blink of an eye would even be too slow a description. Eliminated from this space she was. Utterly gone.

"What?! WHAT HAPPENED?! WHERE ARE YOU?!! MUM!!!!! YOU CAN'T LEAVE LIKE THAT??! I NEED ANSWERS!!! THE PAIN OF THOSE DAYS IS STILL HERE!!! EVERY DAY I CARRY IT ALONE IT NEVER LETS UP, ALWAYS THERE SLOWLY CRUSHING MY WILL!! COME BACK PLEASE! MUM PLEASE!!! PLEASE! PLEASE Please....ple...ase." Realising that he was talking to no one, he quietened... he went from feeling deflated to totally defeated. He let himself believe that she was real and somehow there in his mind. And just when she was about to give him some kind of answers to the questions he'd been asking every day since she left. She was gone again... for a second time without reason or a trace... The broken spirit in Julian began to manifest itself in his surrounding, and like an old jumper being pulled by its loose thread, it began to unravel... His manufactured sea and sky, losing their inertia, fall away from this reality... Before long, he was just surrounded by complete darkness, where he stayed without sound or complaint and wallowed in his self-pity.

After minutes alone in the dark he opened his eyes to find himself in the church still kneeling down. He is taken aback by the contrasting sights and sounds of the Sunday service goers still walking up to receive Holy Communion. It would seem that no time has passed since he first sat down and closed his eyes. Before Julian could contemplate the strangeness of that fact, his eyes were drawn to the altar. "What the hell is that?!" his mind exclaimed! He could scarcely believe his eyes, on the right side of the Father there was what appeared to be a floating apparition! But frighteningly Julian knew that it was not, and just like when he was in the world in his mind and met his mother, he could just somehow sense without a doubt that this was in fact truth. The floating figure was a darkened mass with an ever-changing and shifting silhouette. It had a feature resembling some kind of abstract facial structure, and that suspected face appeared to be intensely focused on Father Bachinger. Julian was struggling to maintain his mental faculties as he found himself thrown from one absurd individual experience to the next, He thought about getting up to say or do something, but he thought twice, his hesitation riddled with fear. This fear was confounded by the realisation that this terror was his alone and no one else in the congregation could see this lurking black mass Father Bachinger appeared oblivious too. Julian could only watch, frozen like a deer in headlights, lost as to what he should do... He just focused his senses more and more on that mass of darkness. The more he did, the more he lost touch with the sights and sounds directly around him... and eventually he could begin to hear something coming from the dark spectre positioned on the right side of the Father. With no easily distinguishable mouth, he could not be certain it was talking, but there were definite sounds it was emitting...he listened carefully...intensely...like a wild cat listening for the ruffling of a hidden prey...and in doing so his sense of hearing managed to exceed human capabilities and extend across over fifty metres of church mumbles and reach the space between the Father and the spectre of darkness. "I don't understand, all I hear is numbers... so many numbers. Slow down I can't understand them all, They're too long I can't see any pattern or sense in what he's saying!' Although Julian was frustrated by the constant flow of numbers emanating from the dark mass, he kept listening hoping to be able to at least hear one comprehensible uttering. After what felt like minutes, there it was! It came out of the darkness with the abruptness of a hiccup, but was repeated with the subtle purposefulness of Morse code. "Huh? What is that? What the hell is Remainder zero one?" Although Julian didn't know it's meaning, he knew that in a sea of numbers, letters and words would be the earth and land where meaning is found. So he made sure to burn 'Remainder 01' into his brain. But why was this thing here?

And why was it solely focused on the Priest? These questions kept floating around Julian's head without answer. There were so many other people here yet he was the only one that could see it? "I'm no different than anyone else, why can only I see this thing? I'm not special..." Just then Julian hears his father's voice in his head like a deeply subconscious audio recording,

"Somehow it happened...you were and are a miracle son, the one and only of your kind." Hearing those words again so clearly at this exact moment made Julian go numb form head to toe... After the experience of seeing his mother during an elapse of time unaccounted for by earth's clocks and now this sighting of a conscious, ominous black entity not explainable by earth's sciences or maths, it all made sense. His father's words from that night finally took their true form. Instead of being confusing, negatively emotive ramblings of a broken mind they now had the piercing brightness of an epiphany, the crystal clarity of mathematical precision and the peaceful embrace of one's own truth.

"I can't believe this...I need to go back home now. Dad would want to know how mum is doing."

Chapter 11

****

I've wondered endlessly about everything that I've seen unfold on the other side of the glass, never comprehending its reasons in any way, just left with the theories and philosophies being expressed. And there exists this Atheist, on that side of reality where feelings, molecular matter and truths reside, yet he sought not answers to the mysteries of his world but simple comforts of the one he loves and whose absence he feels daily. He would be opaque to the efforts of others and un-malleable to his father's affections. I have witnessed this Atheist for all his existence and my opposite and adjacent non-existence. But now, at this moment of this day, he is no longer that. He saw truth; it was brighter than anything he knew before it and, like sunrise upon the sleeping, it awoke him from his introspection. I know this... I even feel it somehow... How does an observer, who cannot see or know this and anything about the happenings of the real, know or feel? Yet I knew The Atheist had experienced something in that large earth, stone and brick building of human worship that would forever change him into a contradiction... He believes now... It's strong and vivid to him like the reality he sees and feels all around him. I know... but how? I do not comprehend, nor do I understand the 'what' of his beliefs... but somehow it prevents the **why** from forming. More interestingly I do not need the **why** or its predecessor... I'm convinced without it... I'm blind but have faith... How? Am I also changed from this notion of an experience from another plane...? Has the **why** left me? Or is this a temporary relief from the universe's affliction? Choices I have are singular...so only with continuing can I gain further clarity... I desire it like the want of a sweet familiar taste. I've never known taste, yet on this day I know the want of it... Lead me Atheist, further into the brightness and clarity you've found. I will observe it all.

****

Julian was ready to return home, he was eager and desperate like he was estranged from his family, missed them and hadn't seen them for years. Just as the receiving of the Holy Communion was finishing he decided to take the last few moments of movement to get up and leave relatively inconspicuously. He left through the left, less congested aisle with all the swiftness his athleticism allowed. As he neared the large wooded exit he took one last look behind him, and just as he hadn't wanted, he was noticed... Father Bachinger's eyes were staring across his congregation to find him. Julian tried his best to not convey any expression of anxiety to the Father. Julian broke his gaze to look for the creature, being or ghost he saw observing the Father as if he was its sustenance, but found nothing... He sprinkled his gaze around the altar and still nothing. The darkness reciting numbers was gone. Julian was relieved even though this made him wonder even more about whom the Priest was. He turned back to face the church exit, he was there...ready to leave this place he avoided for years just when he had found new purpose for being there. He pushed the door open with as much subtlety the stubborn doors would allow. The warm sun hit his skin, he smiled and though he began a hurried journey back to his familiar dwellings, there were new feelings in him that were too countless to individualise, making this feel like a first time journey into a fresh knowledge of previously unknown truths. There was his chopper, chained up just where he left it, like a trusty steed awaiting its master. As he got on his chopper, an image of Father Bachinger's eerie gaze appeared in his head, and just then he knew that their paths would now be constantly intertwined until their story's end.

Back at the church Father Bachinger was still delivering the Sunday mass in auto pilot, for the best part of his focus was still thinking about the peculiarity that was Julian's presence at the mass then his swift, early exit. He didn't understand it... but he most certainly wanted to... Every thought of Julian seemed to excite and stimulate his imagination. He knew there was something more to this boy who had suddenly entered his life and seemingly the life of his parish members, which reminded him that he needed to go check on his nuns... more specifically Julian's new found friend, Aeryn-Sun. It had been a little while since he given any of them some of his special attention...and maybe it was time he stopped whetting his appetite with Aeryn-Sun and finally showed her the same care and attention... The fact that she had befriended Julian made this prospect even more thrilling to him. Despite this, Julian was still what he really wanted to explore, and as he began the final portion of the service, he made the decision to once again go to Julian's home in an attempt to be close enough to him to experience it again... that unfamiliar familiarity, that waking dream of a reality.

Julian arrived at home, entered the front door and placed his bike against the corridor wall. His home felt slightly different than usual. Was that due to the difference in him, or was there actually something tangibly different about his home? Although almost three quarters of an hour had passed since the events at the church, the sensations he had felt there seemed to have lingered and followed him to his house... It was all a bit unsettling.

"Dad, are you home?" Julian calls out...

"Oui fils, je suis dans le salon," his father responded almost immediately, guiding Julian into the living room. He walked in and before they'd even begun this defining conversation, he could sense that the air around him and his father was different... His body was not tense with anger and frustration, his father was not pensively thinking about how to reach his troubled son. The feeling was akin to being outdoors in the cool country air, with plentiful breaths of fresh air to be had after years in an underground boiler room, hot from hate. He even smiled for a second, which shocked his father. He couldn't recall the last time his son looked at him with such an expression. They sat on the large four-person leather sofa facing the TV, they turned slightly towards each other and began.

"Dad, you won't believe what's happened to me, I mean it's like... just crazy, but I'm sooo happy! Dad, I'm sorry for saying all the nasty things I said to you the other night when you were just trying to be honest with me. I was rude when you were in fact just giving all those answers I've been craving for," he said with a palpable passion.

"What do you mean, son? What happened?

"Dad, you were not lying to me! I know now the real truth is your truth." François, taken aback by Julian's energy and obvious joy, was starting to connect the dots in his words.

"Fils, are you talking about what I told you the other night? You understand my words? What they really meant?"

"Well I'm not sure about 'understand', but I know it's the truth, it just has to be! She wasn't my imagination dad, I found her again!" The happiness radiating out from Julian's face was infectious and François soon found himself smiling with him without fully knowing what his son was rambling about. It made him recall his beloved wife, they shared the same smile."

"Calm down son, and please explain to me what has got you happier than I've seen in years"

"Haha, yeah sorry... Okay, listen dad...I was at church for Sunday mass."

"Quoi? Sunday mass, you?" François interrupts.

"Hahaha, one thing at time please" François could not believe his son was actually laughing in his presence.

"Sorry but when your son who has spent the last few years denouncing his faith suddenly tells you with the joyful vigour of a child on Christmas day that he was at Sunday service, you have to give me a second to digest that! But okay, go on."

"Well as I was saying I was at church and during Communion I saw her, dad! I met mum!"

"What do you mean met her?? I'm afraid that if you understood what I said to you that night you would know that she could not be in the church."

"I know that, she wasn't there but I saw her!"

"What?"

"Meaning I get that she's gone back to that place like you said but I did see her, dad. I guess I must have somehow gone there, it was like a dream but not at all one. I was awake and asleep at the same time. I think those Buddhist guys have a word for it"

"Slow down son, this is getting very strange... If I understand what you're saying correctly, you're telling me that you somehow travelled to where you mother is and spoke to her??" François was torn between the fact that he knew this to be impossible and the obvious sincerity in Julian's words.

"Well yes, I guess that's exactly what I'm saying. It was the most incredible experience of my life! I want to go back now!"

"Okay, but first I need you to explain to me exactly what happened word for word."

"Yes okay, well as I said it was Communion and I was sitting down watching everyone else walk back to their seats and one by one kneel down to pray. I got self-conscious that I wasn't doing the same, so I did... That's when it happened..." François sat silently as Julian recounted every single detail he could put into words of what he experienced... He watched his lips move continuously without break, mouthing words into sentences that left him cold with shock and hot with anticipation for the next. As he studied this story, his son was enthusiastically gesticulating to him like the words in the human language were not enough to express what he saw. He realised that this wasn't good at all. This truth could not be... If so, it spelt danger in more ways than he cared to contemplate. "Then, as I struggled to keep myself there, I was sent back to myself in the church. And there I was, dad, still sat on the bench without any time appearing to have passed!"

"Non, non... non... ce n'est pas possible... but yet I can't deny the things you've said...I recognise..." And before François could finish his sentence, Julian interrupted him with a total drop in tone and levity that now matched his dad's.

"But dad that's not all...when I looked up at the altar... I saw something there... beside the priest. I'm not sure what it was, but I felt the same clarity I did when I was with mother in that place. The instinctive fear I felt too was real. It was just facing him, dad, looking at him... reciting numbers" François, already in no doubt as to what his son was describing, asked in stuttered speech,

"What was looking at him?"

"This large darkness that no one could see but me, it just kept reciting numbers and words that made no sense out of what I think was its mouth. It was the creepiest thing I'd ever seen. I just didn't understand what it could want with the priest or why only I could see it."

"This is not good..."

"But then it just all clicked. I heard your voice speak to me and the pieces just fit. I knew that what I was seeing now and had done moments earlier in my head were of the same realness and that it was because I was different to others, I was special just as you said."

"I'm afraid you are right... It saddens me that I can only verify your deductions..." Julian interrupts again not realising the seriousness of his dad's tone.

"And also I thought to myself that maybe the priest was different too? Maybe he was like you and mum? Well not exactly, coz he's a creepy freak, but that's a whole other thing that I need to tell you about!"

"Listen to me, Julian!" François raised his voice suddenly. It caught Julian's attention.

"What numbers was the darkness reciting? It's important."

"Well there were loads to be honest, but there was one set of numbers I heard more than others. It was 'zero one' it kept saying that. Oh actually, it was saying 'Remainder zero one' over and over again... So strange, I didn't understand any of it dad." Julian took a second to pause and look more closely at his father's expression. He could see that his father knew what that creature was and was very concerned about what it meant for him to have seen it."

"The creature made of darkness, son, is something that no one is meant to be able to see, even us, unless it decides to make itself visible... And the phrase with the numbers zero one you heard... I know them and heard them today too, in our very home." François was starting to slowly understand what the controller who visited him was actually saying to him. "Okay... Let me explain... Firstly, I don't understand how you saw your mum, but I know that you did. Not only because the space you describe being in when you saw her is a place I know very well... but also because the creature you described actually came to me today speaking of the 'Remainder zero one.' I didn't understand what it was trying to warn me about, but just like for you, the pieces are falling together. So here it is Julian. That place you described is like endless sea and skies that seem to change in appearance and colour to reflect one's mood, so much so, that it can even precipitate the very emotions you are feeling. Back when I used to go there, the emotions I felt were not the same ones I feel now in my human form...I 'm not even sure I could call them emotions at all. This place was where me, your mother and many Other Ones like us would go to work on increasing the strength of our souls, though at that point I did not know her personally...well it's possible I already did...but there is no way of knowing for sure...This place was believed to be the place where the original whole separated."

"Increase strength? For what? Why would...sorry for saying the word, 'angels' need to increase their strength?"

"It's okay, I know that this is the closest thing to describing what we are that someone from this world could understand, and also I've told you before son that me and your mother were not the 'good guys' that the term angel implies. It took many years in the Rehabilitation program for us to become the people you know today. And I told you about the war that our two sides had? I wasn't saying that word lightly, it was a real war between two sides intent on the complete destruction of the other. Your mother and me were soldiers in that war. Although we most likely never met each other until we were down here, our stories both started then. That time of war in our history is when that plane of space and time was found and used for us to elevate our abilities and expand our consciousness forcefully. Somehow you both ended up there... If I was to take a guess I'd have to say that once your consciousness left your body she must have sensed it and lead it to that place so she could speak to you alone. She must know the dangers the awakening of your Other Ones abilities will represent. Mon Dieu... imagine if The Other One was to discover you and your apparent ability to leave this world, even if not quite yet at will... it would put the whole Rehab program in danger of being completely undermined. Those who are not yet fit to return would probably come looking for you desperate to find out how to do it. Your mother and me never thought that even you being the miracle birth that you were could possess such an ability. This has got to be what the Controller was trying to warn me about. But then...there's that priest... Julian, in case you hadn't figured it out, I'm certain that he must be like us. You see Controllers are also beings from the Realm above the heavens, but unlike us, The One created them for the sole purpose of watching us during our time in the program and controlling the implementation of our new stories and human identities. They report our progress back to The One, who then decides if he deems our rehabilitation complete, at which point we return to our former glory like your mother did. To then be reintegrated as a One, something that a millennium ago would be inconceivable to any of us and, the very mention, cause for instant reprimand and maybe termination of consciousness. That is how hot the fire of this feud blazed. The most frightening thing about them is that they are the only beings in our Realm who have the licence of termination. Meaning that if those of us in this program attempt to do anything to perverse the flow of your universe, or behave in a manner not allowed within the conditions of our Rehabilitation program, they can erase our very consciousness and existence on all planes."

"What is regarded as unacceptable behaviour?" Julian asks tentatively... His dad was in one of his flowing speeches and interrupting him was never a good idea.

"Errrr, well as we have to live here with humans we have to abide by their laws"

"Oh okay, makes sense but what about that perversion of the universe thing?"

"That, my son, is the most important aspect and is what would bring about the most severe punishments. For example something as small as telling a neighbour the truth about your identity goes under that category. And I don't know… something like producing a miracle offspring that develops untold powers akin to that of an Other One even though still in a human shell, powers that are uncontrolled or censored in their use and as a consequence cause irrevocable damage to this world and its inhabitants." Julian knew his dad was joking but also telling him a real truth of the potential disaster these developments in him could cause… so he dared not laugh although his father's delivery of bad news was often more humorous than he realised.

"Okay...I think I understand why you weren't sharing in my joy at me meeting mother again after all these years."

"Sorry son, I really am happy that you saw her again and I can't tell you how this human shell aches to be with her again. For you see, back in our realm such a feeling as love did not exist. We do feel things but they are different and not truly explainable in any real way with human language. But when I fell in love with your mother I didn't know what was going on inside me...I couldn't sleep without her being the last thought in my head, I would wake up and her face would be the first thing I sought from the day. It was actually through watching a movie that I learned the name of what weird thoughts and feelings had consumed me. In fact it was on one of our first dates to the cinema. We watched a film called... hmm, I can't remember its name but I tell you that the lead character was pursuing a woman for the entire first portion of the film and he would often go into these monologues expressing what he felt for her. It was so funny... I sat there listening to this with the biggest smile, and then just kept looking at her as he kept reeling off these beautiful phrases to describe his feelings. Your mother didn't notice that I was just gazing at the side of her face, simultaneously realising my love for her and falling deeper into it. She was the kind of beautiful I did not know was possible until I was given this shell and for that I became eternally grateful. It was actually then that I decided to be the best human man I could be, my way of showing the gratitude I felt. The One forever changed my destiny on two separate worlds. Wow... This situation is bad and all of this must have been exactly what the Controller was warning me about. I get it, you as my son were causing the 'Situation' the Controller was referring t. But what situation? Not sure to be honest, and it kept telling me that I had to resolve it... and it couldn't because it wasn't in its power...I guess that's because you were not created by either of The Ones, but somehow by me and your mother. Either way, I think I figured this out too late and whatever situation you've created has already been played out. Oh yes I remember, you're supposed to have met someone how you weren't supposed to. Julian, any ideas?"

"The only new people in my life are that priest and Aeryn the nun from the same parish.... but I don't see why that would be a problem." Julian was growing more puzzled the more he listened to his dad try to solve the meaning of the day's events out loud.

"As I'm sure you've figured out, this priest is also one of the fallen like us put in this Rehabilitation program. He would not have a Controller otherwise. But I'm sure you've met many in your life without realising it so what's the difference with him?"

"Oh there's a difference, he's not what he seems, dad. I found out some terrible things about him."

"Hold on I'm thinking...maybe it's that Aeryn woman? What's her story?"

"It's not her, I know it's not, she's such a good person," Julian responded adamantly

"Who said she wasn't?? Don't always be so defensive of the women you like." This response stunned Julian, he was too embarrassed to admit he had become smitten over a nun. Not to mention the religiously questionable nature of such feelings. The mere fact that he would even factor religious dos and don'ts into his moral compass show how much Julian had changed over the course of these last few days.

"What no! I don't like her like that, I was just saying that I know her and she is a good person, unlike that priest. It has to be him that's the problem."

"When he appeared on my doorstep asking for you he definitely didn't come across well. But I'm too long in the tooth to trust first impressions blindly. But what makes you so sure? How can a priest be such a bad person??"

"Okay listen, this priest dad is not what he seems. Okay let me start from the beginning. As you know, after the fire I escaped at the school chapel I somehow found myself at the church. And that's where I met Aeryn, but it wasn't til I went back there again the next day and got to meet him myself that I noticed that he was just a bit strange to be honest. Then Aeryn told me about her suspicions about him. She told me that she thought that he was abusing the other nuns." François face instantly changed to one of confusion.

"Quoi?? What kind of abuse?"

"The real, go-to-prison-for-eons kind dad!"

"Non, non, non that's got to be wrong, fils tu as des preuves??" Julian hesitated for a moment, he naïvely wasn't expecting to have to produce proof.

"Not definite proof but..." He hesitates again, as now he'd have to confess to sneaking back into the school. He didn't want to do anything that would stain this newly-formed canvas of respect that would provide the base for them to paint a beautiful & loving relationship. But he had no choice, his claims were extravagant and needed backing up. "I found out some concerning information about his past... I was looking in a special online directory that provides an incredible amount of data on all things church, I mean seriously a lot! Dad I'm talking the square footage, capacity, itinerary, clergy member details and geographical history of each church in the whole of the UK'

"Hold on a second, where is there such a database?"

"Erm... At school."

"Hmm, seeing as you didn't know of the priest's existence before you burnt down you school chapel." Julian annoyed, interrupted

"No it was an accident I just knocked over some candles, it's not my fault they filled the chapel with such cheap flammable material!"

"There you go again being so defensive, sérieusement faut cesser d'être comme ça, it's not good or healthy. I never said that you did it on purpose did I? No."

"It seemed like you did."

"It may have but I didn't. I was just going to say that it seems as though you were at school at a time when you shouldn't be..." Julian, sensing that the growing tension was leading them away from the more important aspect of this discussion, quickly refocused the conversation in the right direction.

"Yes okay, I went into the school after hours and went onto the library computers. I'm sorry but I really thought it was important, and it turns out it was! So please dad, before you tell me off, just listen." Although François was disappointed in Julian's behaviour, on this day he felt compelled to not get hung up on the usual details of their life. This would be more important."

"Okay don't worry, just tell me what you found out?" Julian was surprised, he was sure that his father would get hung up on his after hour's trip into his school, leading to familiar arguments, but not this time... Maybe it was an example of how their relationship had suddenly, over the course of a day, changed and moved onto greener pastures full of the potential. Relieved he continued with a serious tone found in the voice of any one man who had ever delivered bad news.

"Looking through the directory, I first looked at the clergymen details for the church, with the hope of finding out some detail on the priest, like D.O.B place of birth etc., but found that it had nothing on him at all, as the data had not been updated since the last priest got moved on to another parish two months ago. But the most interesting thing is that it also lists the name of the new priest selected to replace him and it definitely doesn't say Father Bachinger, it's actually a priest named Father Alexander.' François, whose face now expressed a unique combination of confusion and intrigue, listened on intently. "Okay, I'm thinking this is too easy, there must be an explanation like he just uses another name for some reason only known to him and the higher up in the church hierarchy. And so I then clicked on Father Alexander's name to see a picture. Strangely I was actually expecting to see Father Bachinger's face, but nope it was just as it appeared. It was a completely different person! By now you can imagine that my Murder She Wrote juices were in full flow so I searched Bachinger of London... figuring that it's not a common name for a priest. One hit... yes you guessed, still not him! It was a completely different person, this guy was in his sixties, short and bald."

"I don't understand how..?"

"Wait dad, the weird part is... this Father Bachinger was still supposedly working at our church... though he obviously hasn't been for over two months... I don't know how he's got away with this, but now you ask me where is, or what did he do to the real Father Bachinger?? I could barely believe it! I was very happy to have such incredible information to show Aeryn and help us prove that this guy is a fraud on every level and put him away for any and all crimes he's committed against her and anybody else!" He then just sat quietly waiting for his father's response...a few minutes went by with his father head down to the floor of their living room with a concentrated frown and his eyes moving around in there sockets like a man trying to solve the most advanced of mathematical problems.

"Attends fils... this is wrong... it has to be wrong. When we chose to enter this program we were explained the rules of Rehabilitation. And more importantly the consequences of not obeying them... Okay, I guess there was an element of choice, in that we did not have to follow all of humanity's laws but there was one thing that was clear; we could not directly interfere in the fate of a human... that means anything from assuming their identity to murder. Enforcing this law is the primary function of the Controllers...so they would never allow him to assume another's identity... They would end him for such a wrong. So maybe's he's not one of us... No that's wrong, Julian saw a Controller watching him... They only watch us... But if all this is true then why don't they stop him..."

"Maybe they can't?" Julian interjected casually.

"What? Of course they can there's no one of us beyond their control...

"Then dad... who or what is he?"

"I don't know... but he's definitely not like me or your mother... It's clear now the true seriousness of the Controller's message to me. Son, we must do everything to keep you away from him, this person. Your contact with him for reasons I don't yet understand is dangerous enough to cause Controllers to break the very protocols of their design. Somehow he must be a danger to you and all of us alike. Most frighteningly, this man is a being beyond even the Law of the Controllers." A cold, nervous silence befell the room.

Chapter 12

****

Low currents of stimuli I struggle to absorb, flow across the lowest levels of my space like the uncharmed human creatures that traverse the earth on their stomachs. It begins and ends in the continuity of my minuscule vastness...I have never heard the ticking or tocking of clocks...there is no sense of the approaching, but something is here that previously wasn't. Was it elsewhere beforehand or always residing in the blind spots that mock me? Either or any way it's here... and again I feel it. Instincts I didn't know I had are telling me that it's something akin to human excitement. What is making me excited? Is it the growing realisation through observations that there is so much more beyond their earth and my place, all unexplored to the I that makes up me or the you that makes them? There are now not only worlds above the heavens belonging to beings superior to the humans of earth, but now amidst them also exists a being seemingly not accounted for by those who know, and beyond their dictation. Is The Atheist also not accounted for? Or is that miracle just unexpected? Can he be controlled by their numbers? The one in control of the numbers was aggressive in his unique speech, like danger was afoot... I can recall moments that have passed, though they can fade when there is distance in conscious thoughts and observations. Clarity returns with proximity in any way, shape or notion. It spoke of numbers...always numbers...I know not of their significance but always numbers... so much choice expressed in numeric sequence. Only a mind unburdened by mortality could comprehend such an indignant numeric construct. But I recall a phrase that remained in my own knowing, 'Contact with objects outside the numbers is not within......... allowed behaviours'. It was fragmented... so I ponder... whose allowed behaviours? And perhaps more pertinently, who's outside the numbers?

****

The man at the root of everyone's worries and strife is approaching a familiar home. Though familiar it was different under the light of the sun, like the face of a friend's sibling when seen for the first time. Father Bachinger always smiled his deceitful grin whenever excitement filled his heart. Though the weather above was undecided, with wind wrestling the sun's warmth for supremacy & clouds intermittently smothering its rays, Father Bachinger stood on the front door step of the Mufunga home with total resolve in his one and only objective. He was seeking another experience like the waking dream from before through the pretence of enquiring as to why Julian left the Sunday mass in such haste before its conclusion. In truth he did not care about such a thing, another man or woman's wellbeing was to him as low a concern as the fodder of livestock. So there he stood with nothing but his true concerns on his mind. With his focus on what he sought from Julian, the world in front of him became a blur of inconsequential information... but a sound of muffled movements alerted him to a pleasant realisation. Two men were at the door; it must be Julian and his father. The world instantly solidified into its opaque parts Father Bachinger almost hopped forward with excitement. He stared intensely at the door handle, frozen at the precipice of mania, like a dog trained to sit before it explodes into franticness watching his master on the other side of the front door.
 Seconds passed achingly slowly for the Priest... With anticipation whetting his lips, he clenched his fists. Finally he heard the turning of the door handle and grinned a devil's grin. As the door opened gently, he suddenly felt a warmth escape the house and flow right into him. Seeing the soft brown of Julian's arm through the gap in the door he began to open his mouth to speak words he hadn't yet thought of, so no sound was traversing the small gap between them. Blackness began to fill his peripheral vision, accompanied by a light headiness that stole his energies and balance. "Is it happening again?" he asks himself. He's not sure as this time

the experience is different? It feels, not like dreaming while awake to the world around but, like falling into a depth and coldness of sleep usually reserved for the dead. His body was shutting down limb-by-limb, sensations in his extremities receding back to the source. The darkness had consumed his consciousness to the point where he was no longer sure of his orientation. No part of this had caused him to feel fear, though unsure of what exactly was happening to him, he could feel a forgotten familiarity to the experience. He was being taken somewhere... Was this new experience, like the previous, also caused by the Atheist child he had become obsessed with? How did he? When did he? Was it voluntary? These were the last few questions running through his mind before it fell into complete silence....

Father Bachinger returned to a state of awareness to find himself in a place he did not recognise with his eyes but very much so with his other senses. He could hear a flow of something... sounding similar to the movement of the ocean but still distinctly more solid... He'd heard it before. He could feel on his skin a sensation akin to the mint fresh tingle of mouthwash... but without temperature, neither hot nor cold... He'd felt this before. His sense of taste was the most remarkable, it would change with every passing second, but not ever repeating itself... a frenetic multitude of evolving flavours only understandable because he knew this taste from before. "I know this place, but I do not recognise it," he keeps thinking to himself, as he gazes from an elevated vantage point at the peculiarities around him. At least he believed himself to be looking down, but he could not be sure, as the layout of this place did not immediately show an upper, middle or lower portion due to a lack of obvious ground for one to stand on. It was at this point that Father Bachinger realised that he had no body. "What is this?? How can I not have any part of me?? I could feel things, everything!" The Father was, in fact, just existing as consciousness in this place. What he felt with a body he did not currently possess, was not something explainable at that time. He had to delve deeper into this place to understand further. He observed his left and right... The space was smaller than he had first thought... There were obvious ends to how far it reached out on either side and in the middle of these two end points was a structure in front that was not like anything he had ever seen. Large like a house and imposing with a solidity that implied it had a great weight, it was almost like a box without its front and top sides, a cross between a shelf and a throne. Its textures seemed to be in constant steady movement downwards and changing from rough to smooth, smooth to rough like an undecided morphing creature. This huge structure didn't glow, but had a richness in light colours that was directly in contrast to the rest of this place, which was bathed in a hue of dark blues, purples and blacks. Father Bachinger looked above him to see what else there was and was astonished to notice that there was no sky, in that above was the same mass of dark blue, purple and black as below with no distinguishing characteristics between the two. The more he looked the more it started to look like a very large room... "No, in fact it's a corridor... But then again, why would that large object be right in the middle of a corridor?" Father Bachinger, in his attempts to understand this place, was making the mistake of using human logic and experiences to do so. This was not a place of human domain, this was a place called RATH and he was in one of its most important locations. This and more were about to become very clear to him.

Father Bachinger's thoughts were abruptly interrupted by what felt like static in his head. He couldn't concentrate... noises and a bright white glare was incapacitating his cognitive processes. It felt to him like his mind was being re-tuned, it was. Then after about ten seconds the noise and interference stopped. He once again looked at his surroundings... but to his astonishment, it was no longer a large empty corridor-shaped space with one focal structure. It was now infested with these beings! Some radiating bright light like stars created from the incalculable colours of a glass marble. Others were glowing with similar multitudes of colour, but darkened and sombre like the multi-rock coloured wall of a blackened cave. It was almost like their very essence was emitting a long seeded malice, while the bright ones where personifying a regal arrogance from deep within. Other than this there was no distinguishing them, their form, height and movement characteristics were identical. These beings were significantly taller than a human; their bodies were lean and athletic while maintaining humanoid dimensions, one head on top of a torso, two arms and legs. Beyond the light or darkness there was something that could be called skin, but it was a more translucent membrane than any human skin. Beneath that was what appeared to Father Bachinger as the multi-coloured source of their distinguishing glows. These light and darkened beings appeared asexual, with faces lacking a mouth nose or ears, yet they had what seemed to be well-defined jaw structures. Even from the distance of his vantage point he could see that they had two eyes in their heads, these were only recognisable as eyes due to their shape and position on the face of these creatures. Their eyes were the only parts of their bodies not emitting this multi-coloured glow, which on closer scrutiny was actually slightly different from being to being. These eyes of theirs, unlike their bodies, were contrastingly dense and opaque, they possessed within them the same beauty, texture and colour as a deep sea pearl.

Amazed, and in awe of what he was seeing, Father Bachinger focused intensely on the new vision of this place, trying to absorb all information and understanding he could from it. He noticed that there was a pattern to their placement in this room. Although they were all spread around the space available with some at a higher elevation than others the darkened ones were central with the brighter ones surrounding them. There were also a few of the brighter ones stationed beside this central structure, this scene looked less and less random, the priest could feel that there was purpose to everything in front of him a purpose that he needed to understand before whatever kind of experience this was ended and he was back in his reality. He stared and focused on this otherworldly scene until he started to pick up little things... There was one being in this congregation that was different to the rest. There was one that was darker...larger and less diverse in his colour...almost completely black. This particular one appeared to be the focus of all the others... he was being watched by all. To the Father's discerning eye he could also make out that this particular one had not moved an inch since he noticed him. The others, although not doing a great deal, had particular shuffles and sways to their limbs that although very subtle were definitely present. He did not move just stood staring at the central structure. It was as if he was waiting for something or someone to appear at the structure. Father Bachinger briefly escaped from his intense focus to enjoy the similarity of this scene to a church service with all focus being on the altar surrounded by altar boys. But where was the priest in this scene? Maybe this was some kind of ritualistic worship and the one leading the ritual had not yet arrived.

Suddenly a vicious bolt of lightning flashed without warning, ripping through the air surrounding the so far purposeless central structure and crashing down upon it. The impact itself did not make a sound and unlike the momentary glare of earthly lightening this light stayed ablaze with white-hot presence and shine. It was blinding to the Father even in this bodiless form he could not look directly at it for as long as it remained. He kept his gaze averted until he felt it safe to look back at whatever it was that had made such an imposing spectacle. The just bearable heat he felt emanating from that light started to dim together with the brightness he was protecting his vision from. The reducing saturation of his other senses allowed him to begin to notice a taste, it was not instantly recognisable. After a few seconds of this flavour presenting itself, it became more obviously the taste of metals. He did not know which ones exactly but could discern their similarity to the taste of silver and batteries. This taste, like the unwanted and unpleasant memories of a previous argument. began to increasingly agitate him right up until he was at the brink of anger. He tried not to let his emotions affect his focus. After all, the very experience he had been lusting after since he first encountered Julian was here, he could not waste it. As the light dimmed further, he was able to look upon this place. Once again he noticed that all the beings bright or dark were now statuesque in their transfixation on it. Seconds vanish away in anticipation, Father Bachinger was beside himself in mixed emotions of anger and excitement. Although unsure as to why he was now so enraged he could certainly taste the validity of those feelings in his mouth. His sense of taste in this place was somehow linked to his thoughts perceptions and emotions. He gazed at the dimming... and through the dimming its true form began to be revealed. Its silhouette appeared first, its form was like that of the others... It took the Father a few moments to notice that it was in fact larger, but seemingly the same size as the larger dark one he'd notice before. The dimming continued while all present watched. The light receded lower and deeper into the entity's humanoid body until eventually it was a dull, lightless, empty husk of grey human shaped translucency. It's features, or lack thereof, were exactly the same as that of the others, but he was surprised into confusion by why it did not emanate light like the rest of those here waiting and watching this one's arrival. But then just as that thought was seeking to find lodgement in his mind, it was evicted with the sudden glow that birthed itself from within the belly of the being. The glow was no bigger than a tennis ball at first and dense in colour, some of which he never knew existed and struggled to visually digest. It grew steadily, with a pulsating rhythm its light brightened, and before too long it filled its body and began shining through its translucent skin. It was clear now to the Father that this one was in fact the same as the other bright ones except that its light shone brightest. He took his focus off it and back to the largest of the dark ones... Suddenly something clicked into place, they were the same. Their equal stature and level of opposite luminescence was not coincidence. They were the same, like two sides of a coin. It was also obvious these two equally opposing entities were of higher station then the other lesser beings littering this place with colour light and dark. It was clear in his mind, vivid and tangible like the recollection of a profound answer, lost and then found. Father Bachinger, his appetite whetted by this recollection, lay in wait like an attack trained doberman for his next morsel of information.

The Father came from a beginning he did not know... One day he found himself here with all the other millions of this world. He didn't stay sedentary for long. Like a true serpent he slowly manoeuvred himself into positions of opportunity, devouring whatever he desired and with the same mouth gave promises of faith and love to whomever he desired. His decisions were driven by instincts dark with contempt and fiendish with curiosity. Not burdened by a desire to conform, his existence grew outside the normality of the social body, like a cancer...unstoppable, un-reconcilable and terminal. The roads of his journey have lead him here... Here he felt a strong pull... and strong desire to remain... The sense of familiarity spoke to him, talking of the knowledge that resided here. He never knew before this place that he cared about himself. It was on the tip of his tongue...he couldn't speak so he waited... He could taste that it was coming.

The brightest one of them was imposing his light upon them all from what was clear now to be his reserved area of residence in this place. The central structure, though colossal, could only be helplessly subjugated by the presence of the one. There was a quiet melodic humming coming from this being Not sure of what exactly to make of it, Father Bachinger just perked up his auditory receptors and listened intently for something recognisable. As this melody was traversing the ocean large, corridor-shaped space, the purples and blacks of this place were responding to the melody with movements and shifting like the waves of a current enslaved by the moon. The melody sounded serious and powerful in tone...like the sounds of a church organ. While it sounded out to everyone Father Bachinger could see the darkest being was reacting to it, his body moved restlessly and his colour fluctuated in dimness and variety continuously, sometimes violently like a whirlpool. It was impressive and frightening to behold. This sound must have been directly communicating with him the Father thought. Suddenly the melody ceased and the structure the brightest being was stood upon began to vibrate strongly enough to be heard from how far away the Father was. It did so for a few seconds then, to his astonishment, words started to come out from it. It spoke loudly in a monotone voice, it sounded like a jumbled up language of seemingly English, Latin and Japanese words. He could not make sense of it, but it appeared that all the other beings that were non-respondent to the melody, whether light or dark, could understand this jumbled language. They were all responding to it in their own unique displays of colour. His frustration at that made him strain himself, he was desperate! He could not afford to lose this opportunity he had come too far! If he had a body, you would have seen a drug addict like face of strain and desperation. "COME ON! I CAN'T MISS THIS! WHAT IS IT SAYING!? WHAT IS IT SAYING!?" With those cries suddenly came understanding, the jumbled up words of broken language came to life in his mind and placed themselves in order... Words, then sentences formed... "I can hear it... Incredible... It's... its halfway through a speech but I can still understand the meaning... It was a sentencing... it all makes sense..." Even in this form, Father Bachinger's grin returned to him, "This is very nice."

These were the words that came from where the brightest one stood, as translated by Father Bachinger's mind.

"*Lost*... this war started for your goal and your desire, is finished. You and all of your sub divisions have fallen into contempt and ill favour of the victorious. A truce was offered but you refused, persisted with your design and clashed with this half of the whole. You put the fabric of our RATH in terminal jeopardy. This Realm above the Heavens was resident of the Whole One before us and is sacred for all Sub Ones. Your relentless pursuit of an unjustified victory caused the loss of hundreds of our creations. We are their originals and must treat their existence with the same pride and reverence as our own, or we will eventually lose them and return to that state... *loneliness*."

"These words sound so familiar...they can't be the first time I've heard them. There's something I'm missing, something I don't yet see." Father Bachinger's attention remained steadfast as his mind absorbed the words and tried to assign relevance to the experience.

"KOROSU." Suddenly Father Bachinger heard silence for a brief second. "You wanted to regress back," the sound then returned. "You wanted to revert back, abandoning all that we have made from ourselves. Singular lone desires of absorption. But you failed; you will never absorb me, The One from the Original Whole. For this, and all other infringements on our grand design. you Korosu, the Other One from the Original Whole as well as all your Other Ones, will be sentenced to banishment from RATH indefinitely.

You will be sent to a separate space in-between this and the next, sealed by The One light to remain for multiple eons. You will experience the loneliness you seem to desire continuously until you succumb to my will. Those of you who do succumb will be given the opportunity to return to RATH, those who do not will remain in absolute darkness. The opportunity is, in design, a way for all Other Ones to prove they desire to relinquish your will and absorb mine through a process not possible here. They will be sent to the mortal plain of the humans and will endeavour to live by their laws, rules of morality and social inclusion, order and community. This process will require your immortal spirits to be taken from you and with that the body, name, and powers, all the very things that encompasses all that you are. KOROSU will be no more. Memories of these names and the immortal essence they possess will be deleted from you, never to be returned or heard of again until allowed by me. This part of you will remain in a separate space known only to me. You will receive human shells that, although immune to decay, will never allow access to this place. Once you have proved to me to be rehabilitated in understanding the strength and beauty of unifying one's actions to benefit the individual parts of the whole and not just seeking the pursuit of gratification of an individual purpose, you shall be re-given your immortal names unlocking the spirits and bodies once possessed. But they will now be full of my light, my will. But you KOROSU will be of different fate... All your memories will be taken from you. Unlike the Other Ones who will only lose the memory and ability to know their name, I will take it all from you. You will be ripped from your prison in the in-between once your resolve is completely broken and then placed alone in their world without anything, not a single thought before that moment will be present within you. You will never be allowed back to RATH." Although Father Bachinger was confused by the random moments of silence in this speech, he understood it all, not because of the clarity of its delivery but because he'd heard it all before. He could feel the rage inside the core of the darkest one, not because of the behaviour of his darkened glow but because he'd felt it before. He knew this room; it was the hall of judgement. He knew that structure; it was the seat of translation. He knew the sentence being handed... because it was his own.

"How deliciously nice... he thought I would never remember who I was, he thought he had banished me forever. To remain in this disgusting world surrounded by these inferior creatures no better than the vermin that roam beneath their feet. To breathe the same polluted air every day, smell the same stink every minute and see the same ineptitude every hour. You thought to lower me to their level...? Just for that I will destroy everything you see, everything you thought sacred and then absorb you into myself so I can return to the higher state of existence of The Whole One but retaining my will. I will become of Whole New One, reshaping everything to mirror my will. How nice of you Julian to help me remember myself. I will thank you personally for this favour... I wonder if he knows that I am me now... not in body or spirit but in desire and will. I can feel that a large portion of my army is here on this rock with me, I will show them that their leader still exists and that his will still burns. Other Ones, you do not need this rehabilitation you are part of me, a portion of perfection. This pretence can end; together we will destroy this world and return to RATH. But... I still miss something... my name, my immortal essence... my soldiers need theirs... hold on they do not! Hahahaha, this is too nice, too splendid too delicious! They all originate from me. If I know my immortal name and my true form is returned, by extension so will theirs. Hmmm, how do I remember this? Simple... Julian, for some reason he holds the key to my power and the end of his species." With that understanding this living memory faded. Father Bachinger awoke with nothing but a smile.

Chapter 13

****

The One, The Other One and The Whole One. Which one am I? Where am I? The more I observe the less that I see. Proactivity could be the answer, but idle I've been for all my time. Forward, backwards left or even right are myths... I do nothing always. These thoughts grow like the earth virus's... Immune to the terminal I remain, but seemingly not to the slings and arrows...they forever hit the target...but what? Is it different now I am different. I think that I am, therefore? I think that I feel therefore? Do equal questions yield equal answers? Loneliness...must not be myth... it is here with me... Do the observations of my being open the way for this to enter where I am? What is sadness? The men and women of earth relate it to loneliness. So if loneliness has found me then has sadness joined us here too? The world of the family I follow with compulsion grows vast and grows fast. It is shattering walls of historical and factual meaning. It extends its reach further each day... Will it reach me? I want the why, the how, and when of my lack of substance. Humans reproduce, bacteria multiply, and cells divide...an interesting phenomenon what compels them to do so? Without this process they wouldn't survive... it's the necessity of nature... but still why should species survive? Why not produce new variants from scratch each time? Evolution would be faster this way... Is the lack of this method God? Is this the method to the chaos? But if even this apparent God being they speak of, who was once whole, long ago, divided... which then lead to chaos... chaos seems to be the only order of the universe. But then where is my chaos? These questions are born from cognitive chaos, does this mean I reside within that universe? There seems to be hope for my loneliness. Why is it not seemingly possible for beings of all realms or intellect to survive as a singularity? With my transparent vision I see certain truths...loneliness and the need to avoid it is the way to the behaviour of all things self-aware...and for those that are not...they multiply at the behest of one to serve the needs of others...their need for more...to allow continued freedom from loneliness. But then how do I survive? Am I already deceased? Or alive at his behest for the benefit of another? Which other?

****

The man clothed in black with a neck embraced in a white collar lay on the floor greeting the blue sky with his first genuine expression of happiness. His first real smile was aimed at the heavens like a message of gratitude. When that moment settled he then began to feel the hardness of the surface underneath him... It grew more uncomfortable with every passing second until it served to lose him from his tranquil state. He shifted his weight around and stroked the surface he laid on with his bare palms; it was uneven like the rocks of wave-battered cliffs, yet with the density of stone. Though unpleasant in its texture, it had an inviting warmth to it gained from soaking up the sun. He sat upright to inspect his surroundings properly Why am I laying on the steps outside the church?" he asked in confusion.

"Father! Can you hear me?! Are you okay??" A voice shouts out from a location Father Bachinger couldn't pinpoint yet, he was startled by the urgency and volume of the cry. He looked around to find the person calling out to him. "Can you stand Father?! Those two men just left you here; they just dumped you then drove away! Should I call an ambulance or the police??" The yelling of this individual was getting closer, he looked in the direction it was coming from and there, from across the road at the top of the 30yrd walk way that lead to the old worn out stone steps at the entrance to the church ,was the man shouting these words of concern. Father Bachinger sat calmly like a pet left outside a shop just staring at the man. After a few vacant stares, Father Bachinger got up and began to walk towards the man. He recalled that before his renaissance experience he was not here but at home of François and Julian Mufunga. It was obvious to him now that he was missing a portion of time and that this man saw how he got here.

"Good afternoon, good sir," Father Bachinger with a serene demeanour began a dialogue with this man.

"Oh, my father those two men! Never seen anything like it, and in front of a church?! Are you okay?! What happened??" The short, balding man was almost screaming his words at Father Bachinger, speaking so fast saliva was spraying from his beard-encased mouth. Barely listening to his actual words, Father Bachinger looked him up and down. The man was dressed in bland brown and black trousers and a jumper not becoming of his relative youth or the season. He couldn't help but think that this man's fashion sense was being dictated by the older self-perception his grey balding hair was giving him. But he knew such thought was not the reason he approached this frantic man. He re-focused his mind.

"Okay, okay relax... Stop yelling in my face, please. I'm fine. What's your name sir?"

"Errr its Henry, father, but those guys dumped you here unconscious! I saw it from across the road! I yelled at them! I said, 'oi what are you guys doing??!' There were other people around too but only I stopped to say anything."

"Slow down, you're talking too fast. Today, my friend, is a very nice day... let's not fill it up with your annoying ranting, please." Henry was a bit shocked at Father Bachinger's laid back attitude and choice of words. Although just a small detail, it was in fact the first time he had ever let his words to a stranger not personify the image of a priest, especially not while wearing his collar. He didn't know it yet, but this was going to be the first of many occasions. His recollection of his true self was beginning to decay the facade he'd been putting on for so long. "Now calmly... explain to me what you saw from the beginning to the time they left. Don't leave any details out, Henry."

"Well Father, it's like I was saying, this car driving pretty fast pulled up screeching to a stop. These two men came out, one was definitely younger..." Father Bachinger interjected.

"Was there a family resemblance? What colour were they?" he probed, though already pretty sure of the answer.

"Hmm I guess now that you mention it...I wouldn't be very surprised if they were related maybe even father and son. And their colour? Not sure from where but definitely black."

"Just as I thought, it was my favourite pair of ethnic gentlemen...I guess I passed out during my rebirth. The question is why not bring me to a hospital? Why leave me here like a pair of mafia goons?" he mumbled to himself, and then raised his voice to say, "Did they not say anything at all?"

"No, nothing! It was just so strange, but I'm so happy you're okay."

"More than okay my sadly dressed acquaintance, GREAT I've never ever felt more like myself... In fact, this is the first time I've been the true me since I was put on this green and blue space rock. But now I must complete myself and return to my home and soon to be kingdom." Henry looked puzzled... but didn't want to ask him what he was talking about. He felt he might just have a concussion.

"Be careful father don't get too excited, you might have a concussion or something, they were being pretty rough with you in their hurry to leave. Yeah, you should go in and relax.

OH, and please go straight to A&E if you feel dizzy or sick, anything at all. I don't think the world needs to lose a priest at the moment." Father Bachinger was not even paying the slightest of attentions to Henry or his words, he was off in his own thoughts trying to find any other pieces to the puzzle of getting his immortal essence back and his true form, freeing himself of his human shell. While deep in thought, his arms and hands roamed from varying positions around his face and body mirroring his thought process. During this, his right hand brushed against his right side trouser pocket, he noticed that there was something that felt like paper folded several times. He didn't remember having anything in there before, so he reached in... felt the frictionless texture and hard edges, then a sense of hot and cold entered his fingers and began to permeate throughout his whole body rapidly. It was a folded piece of paper like he thought. "But why the strange sensations?" They were peculiar, but distinctly familiar. As the sensation of fluctuating temperatures flowed through him and then entered his mind, it was changed, like his consciousness was translating it. It translated it into a spectrum of colours... their darkness was familiar like something he once owned. Henry had realised now that Father Bachinger was preoccupied in his own things and no longer caring for what he was saying or for his presence there. "Right, well I can see you're probably okay and busy so I'm just going to go now, okay?" Father Bachinger didn't respond, he instead began unfolding the piece of paper. "Bye then... Be safe, father." Henry left, he was confused by this experience, he'd never seen anything like it... and on top of that the priest he was trying to help was dismissive of him and rude too. He made a mental note to never come for a church service here.

Once unfolded he saw a hand written message, though disrupted by the creases, it was legible. The temperature shifts in his body remained in unison with the colours in his mind as he began reading it.

'Hello Father,

Sorry to just leave you at your church and for not, at least, staying until you woke up. When we came out of the house we found you passed out in front of our doorstep. I assume you had come to speak to my son and in doing so had some kind of unfortunate fainting episode? Well after checking you had no serious injuries I decided that it would be best to just take you back home. In regard to whatever you wanted to see my son about, unfortunately that will have to wait indefinitely. Something has come up and he has had to leave and go to live with a close family relative for the foreseeable future. Get well soon.

François Mufunga'

"What the hell is this?? He's gone to live with a relative?!" Father Bachinger vocalised his internal thoughts with an anger that would draw attention. "That's garbage... Why would he suddenly decide this?? It doesn't make sense... And for a religious man to just dump me on the floor like a used sanitary towel! There is something else going on definitely... Is he trying to keep Julian away from me? Why would he? Is he trying to ruin my day? My plan? I will not allow that! I must find Julian and reclaim my true self! But hold on... No human knows what I know surely..? They're trash, how could they be blessed with such information??" Just then the temperatures and colours in Father Bachinger's body settled... They combined to form a single dark thought... a memory... "What..? Is this really the truth? ...Is he really? He is... I remember" A newly born smile came across his face once again, instantly whipping away the anger and confusion. "I can't believe I found him, what delicious and succulent turn of events... my General. This is too good! YES I can sense him! Incredible! Even more incredible I can sense them ALL! I now know how to find all of my soldiers, my lost pieces!" Father Bachinger was now hopping with a childlike excitement. "That Mr François, 'I'm so sorry to leave you at the church blah blah!' Hahahah, he is trying to protect his son... from me? But he doesn't even know the truth of the why or the irony that he, himself, once greatest destroyer of souls in RATH, is now reduced to protector of a human, that isn't even his! I can see now that such a thing is impossible for us. Pathetic, shameful... but don't worry Mr François, its all come back to me together with the sense of your real soul. I can feel what you've been through, what The One has done to you... You my former General, leader of my army and all the other pieces of me, you have been made to forget me... you all have. You think I am your enemy François but it's the opposite. I know this ridiculous rehabilitation program has not changed you... you are still how you were back then... I can feel it in the residue you left on this piece of paper. I will get you all back, your immortal selves. Unfortunately for you, my General, this Julian you think is your son is not. You attached yourself to him on a lie, he is just a means to our end. He is my key... and our way back to RATH. I'll make you remember that. All things will become nice again."

An hour later, a father and son stood face to face in front of a St Pancreas station ticket barrier, their conversation paused as they absorbed the moment. They were fearful of the direction their paths were going in... but certain in their decision.

"Bon, tu es prêt?"

"Yeah, I'm ready."

"Fils, I know this is not going to be easy, but we really can't let him get near you again... he's unpredictable. I mean how do we know we won't just see him outside our door again? The signs are there... The warnings are there... We have to take The Controller's message seriously. I just feel that this is bigger than us and what we want."

"Papa, je sais...you don't need to explain again... I understand that this is the best way." This was the first time Julian had ever spoke French back to his father since his mother was taken back. It filled his father's heart with warmth instantly; it almost overflowed with the sensation of a son's love. He knew then that his son finally had faith in him and would be okay. Feeling guilty would not be necessary anymore... the effect was far reaching, it was peeling away all the pages of resentment and anger that remained in their story up until now. Julian's faith in one father had been restored... it was a powerful thing. With a smile François continued his prolonged goodbye.

"Okay, alors...hmmm, so yes stay with your aunt á Gien, I think being in France for a few months will give you a chance to work on your French." François couldn't help but mention it, even showing his top row of teeth is the strength of his smugness. Julian knew that his father wouldn't quickly forget that he had finally spoken in French, and although slightly embarrassed, he was happy to acknowledge the light-hearted banter with an equal smile. "Stay there, try and relax and have fun. You always loved going there as a kid."

"But I didn't know that Tantine Chantel was one of you, and not really my aunty at all."

"Yes, but the bond she has with you is real, that's something we've all learnt over the years... Love is not exclusive to the human condition son. It's a beautiful thing that transcends earth's science or anything we know of back where I came from."

"I get it, love conquers all. Still such a softy dad."

"Yes, it does son, oh and don't worry about school or your friends, I'll sort out any lose ends and give you a plausible story. Bon c'est l'heure" The name of the Euro Star train to Paris was flashing on the overhead screen letting them know it was time to board."

"Yep it looks that way... Dad can you make sure to deliver that message about the Priest to Aeryn-Sun, please. She needs to know as much as she can so can protect herself and the other nuns while I'm away." Julian tried to remain casual as he repeated this request, but it was obvious to his father that he felt guilty for leaving her at such an important moment. But his faith in his father eased his stress so that he could take this forward step.

"Don't worry son, I'll keep an eye on your friend for you."

"I know you will, merci papa..." There was a brief moment of silence, the world outside their drama eased to be muted and the noises of a busy international train station started to emphasise the need for haste. "Okay I'm going."

"Call me when you arrive."

"I will, and please keep me updated on the situation."

"I will, don't worry."

"Au revoir fils."

"Au revoir papa."

Back at the church grounds the life of worship continued in its usual way. In the communal kitchen of the nunnery, Aeryn-Sun stood over the sink eating the sandwich made by her own hands. Her experience of poverty in South America had made her untrusting of food not prepared by her hands. She nibbled cautiously to prevent the fillings of her meal falling out. Buttered wholemeal bread, lettuce, tomato and an assortment of deli products were her favourite. She liked how different it was to anything she would have usually had back home. In the process of tactically consuming her meal, she was caught in a thought, "Where is Julian? He was supposed to come back after he finished his mission... Strange... maybe he didn't find anything and is embarrassed? He's such a fragile young mister...he would hate me calling him that." She laughed to herself but there was nothing funny about the truth they were trying to uncover. Aeryn feared for the safety of her fellow nuns, but her suspicions were barely more than conjecture. She needed Julian to find something, help her to help them. At that moment Annabelle walked in... face expressionless like a mannequin. Behind that, Aeryn knew she was concealing a well of despair close to overflowing. She just watched her for a while, not knowing what to say to her... so she decided to say nothing for the moment. Annabelle sat down gingerly on an old stool, Aeryn couldn't help but notice that discomfort and assume the worst... it was just all too familiar. Aeryn had now decided on some small talk to engage Annabelle with. She moved towards her carefully as if she was approaching a wild cat at dinner time and, just before she spoke, the kitchen door opened and another fellow nun walked in and announced "Sister Aeryn, Father Bachinger wants to see you."

30 minutes earlier... a wolf in priests clothing sat in its den contemplating a great many things..."My strategy is quite a simple one... I will get that boy back here and use him to return, that's a given. But before the end game I must prepare myself... I don't know the state of affairs back home, who knows what that detestable One has done to the kingdom, to *my* kingdom. Therefore, it's time to gather my soldiers... Should be nice and easy...I can feel the presence of those that are in this city; scattered and lost throughout... following the orders of another... It will not stand. This world and all its human insects will become fodder in the end game. It won't take long; my Other Ones will be gathered in a few months. I must entertain myself in the meantime though... Yeah, I should do something nice. I deserve it." His office was dark and unwelcoming, a mirror of his state of mind. The sun's lower position in the sky prevented its rays from reaching him through the obstacles in the church architecture. He got up off his large fine wood sculpted chair and, with direct purpose, walked out of the room. The darkness followed him into the corridor like an extension of his shadow... He turned on the lights, providing a soft, ambient, light orange glow. He walked the length of the corridor, each step as steady as the last, turned left and then headed down the stairs towards the lowest floor not often graced with his or any other presence. In front of him a large fireproof door stood proud and strong, Father Bachinger smiled at it like he was greeting an old friend. His breathing deepened slightly with anticipation...he knew what was behind this door, but hadn't gone in to greet it in several days. "I wonder how my friend is doing," he said, while pulling out the key to the industrial-sized padlock tasked with sealing the room away from unwanted guests. Father Bachinger noticed that his left hand was shaking... "Hmmm I guess I needed this more than I thought..." He unlocked the door, threw the padlock and chain it was connected to on the ground. The sound of heavy metal hitting the stone floor echoed up the stairs ominously. He entered the opaque blackness, leaving light behind him. He moved around swiftly and effortlessly in the darkness like a fish in the deepest ocean crevasse. He was very familiar with it, felt comfortable in it and kept his favourite possessions there... He raised his hand towards an object... fiddled for a second, then *Click* a dim white light turned on. Less than a metre away from it, a face was half bathed by its light with the other side barely being kissed by its afterglow. The light was not very strong - most of the room was still dark. Father Bachinger stared at this half-lit face...its head pointed ever so slightly towards the ground, just enough that he couldn't instantly make out if the man was asleep or not. By now Father Bachinger's eyes had better adjusted to the dim lighting and he could see more... He could fully absorb every morsel of satisfaction from his creation. 'The broken man' he calls it... He decided to gain a better perspective of it by sitting down legs crossed with his arms down hands slowly caressing his thighs. He adores it...a man with knees bent onto an unforgiving cold surface, arms above his head in V form with wrists mercilessly choked by dry rope. The ropes attached to pipes almost two metres apart and behind him, kept his posture taught and joints tensed. Under his drooped chin, a barbed wired collar was savagely kissing his neck. Blood trickled down from this vampire's embrace to the valley triangulated by his neck collarbone and shoulder. He was gravely underweight; with his bare torso exposed, his visible skeleton was emphasising this point. Other than these and the dirt accumulation of months without bathing he had no other marks of physical abuse. Father Bachinger ,still sitting and admiring his work, wet his lips and began to speak, "The broken man... my broken man... how kind of you to sit there still and silent as I gaze at you. Look at me and speak." With soft mumbled voice he responded,

"Yes master."

"How nice of you to say, you know I never knew why it was I felt it necessary for you to call me that, or in fact for you to even be here. It was just a way of amusing myself while satisfying my unexplainable hunger for witnessing the suffering of others. But dear friend of mine, ever since I stole your place here, I have been living blind to my own truth. I am not one of you but the almighty Other One from the Realm above the Heavens once part of the Whole One. My place is not here... not with you lower life forms... I am a dominator, my design is to exude my will for my own gain. All outside my will become worthless at my whim. This desire and hunger for suffering I realise is just an expression of my nature to exert my dominance over those outside my will... This is a Gods right, is it not?"

"Yes master..." the man whispered again with fading energy.

"You, my broken man, are a prophecy of the future of these humans... I detest them... I always have... but I understand that also more completely. The hate was born from the moment The One sent us here in his degrading rehabilitation program. Even just saying those words elevates my blood lust. But I'll remain calm... I have had success in my journey so far... Who knew in such a large and powerful institution as the church I could masquerade as one of their own for so long... as long as I kept you here as my own, feeding you with just enough to sustain your life, I could use your knowledge to prolong my deception... and most of all my most satisfying success so far... I have not changed... there has been no rehabilitation. Isn't that just the best, Father Bachinger?"

"...Yes master..." The man responded with barely a breath left in him. The unbound Father Bachinger realised that it was time he fed and hydrated his 'Broken Man' so he would last until he next saw fit to come down and enjoy his work. But he felt that he was still hungry for sufferance... his appetite not filled... yet. He slowly got himself to his feet, brushed his clothes down, looked right towards the door and said, "Before you can eat, my broken man, *I* must first be satisfied, and I think it's time for dessert...something different, Yes new is better this time... I think a bit of Aeryn sounds nice, don't you Father?

"Yes master..."

Chapter 14

****

I see that the Priest is danger... threat and menace. I watch on from distances I can't explain. Though out of his reach, my consciousness is unsettled by him. Do I fear him? No… It's more than that...I do not know enough to fear, I do not feel enough to fear, and yet I sense that if I had memories of the before it would be warning me of his danger like ominous echoes without an identifiable source. Julian is no longer in proximity to the rest of those I have observed for my entirety. I can't see him anymore... In years past, I could follow him and whomever I desired... but... when vaster quantities of thought are placed on this presumed fact, I realize this may not be a full truth. Pieces of the past show me I have only ever attempted to follow the Atheist outside this city, never has my consciousness saw fit to follow any other beyond these city limits... not even his father or mother. This intrigues... this confuses... are there connections I haven't yet conceived between The Atheist and I? Do I just find it more favourable to anchor myself to his story above any other? I guess closer focus must be put into these questions that will inevitably, once answered, lead to the **why**. The next thought to pass through my being is contradictory to the former, how is it that this time and on this occasion I cannot follow The Atheist? Where do I observe? Where do I anchor myself for definition and perspective? Unsatisfying and disconcerting these thoughts are... so who? Where? Do I choose the Priest? He desires to find The Atheist too... humans say the enemy of your enemy is your friend... but perhaps the positives of this plan will create a negative not confined to the world outside my existence?

****

4 months later

A young man walks through a quiet park on a hot midsummer's day. The man walks briskly, he only has the hour of his lunch break for his rendezvous. The sounds of music escaping his mouth express his happiness, he always enjoys this walk...its every aspect is nostalgic for him and also every bit as beautiful in the present moment. The path he walks on is gravelled, the thick soles of his Adidas Superstars allow him to feel far less of the little stones and pebbles than he'd like to. His beige, lose fitting, three-quarter-length shorts and movie print, fitted t-shirt allow him to feel the warm breath of the wind on his exposed skin. He finds the experience freeing, like he is flying through the sky, the park is not short of square footage. The gravel path dissects the different sections, some just open greenery for pic-nicking and tanning, others well designed play grounds for the younger ones and then cordoned off areas of wild tress, bushes and flowers with colour schemes, bright, vast and appealing to all tastes. The man takes it all in with every joy filled step of his brisk walk towards his rendezvous.

This picturesque scene is disrupted Fifty metres ahead by the park's southern exit point, the man notices three people in what looks like an argument, two male one female. As he continues along the path towards them, he is at first annoyed that they have ruined the paradise he was indulging in with their argument, even blocking the path to his destination. But then, as the truth of their interactions were revealed, he became concerned. Though he couldn't hear what was being said the tone, volume of speech and body language said it all. That woman dressed in provocative yet stylish bright summer wardrobe was afraid of these men. They appeared to be North African with un-groomed facial hair wearing dark coloured attire. One was taller and appeared more forward than the other, he was taking the lead in the ranting and gesticulation. He stepped forward into the woman's personal space and yelled "Tu veux vraiment qu'on fasse ça ici sallop?! Donnes nous se que tu nous dois!" With that the woman stepped backwards to find that she had no more room to retreat, her back was now against the thick trunk of a large tree whose branches reached up and over the pathway providing the three of them with broken shade. Now only twenty meters, away the young man decided that he would seek to help this woman. Though he didn't know what exactly was going on, he just didn't like the sight of two men intimidating a single female, let alone one of her small stature. Experiences from his childhood had made him always feel very protective of women. The man standing behind the lead aggressor was also yelling obscenities at the lady but with lesser intensity, this allowed him to be more aware of their surroundings. And with this being the case he was the first to notice the young man approaching, he stared straight at him... inspecting him... trying to stereotype him into categories of threat or non-threat. The young man didn't avert his gaze, they both remain locked onto each other as the distance between them dwindled. Without needing words, they both know that an engagement was inevitable. The brightly dressed woman was still shaking under the onslaught of aggressive words, "Salle pute! Mon argent?!" She was then given a respite as the lead male was tapped on the shoulder by the other, alerting him to the new arrival and the potential trouble he might bring. The woman noticed him too... They all held still just looking... waiting... The woman was relieved that someone else was there, and while she pondered if he'd walk passed, or play the hero, the men being men had an understanding of the male psychology that was preparing them for battle. Adrenaline was flowing through them all in oceanic volumes. Fight or flight?

Following dialogue translated from French

"What you looking at, little boy?" the taller man said with a snarl, his every word laced with a thick Algerian accent.

"Yeah, what *are* you looking at? Just keep walking," the other said with equal menace. Before replying, the young man began calling to mind the philosophies he'd been studying every day for weeks and months *'minimal movement with maximum effect and extreme speed'...'style without style'...'be fluid like water'...*

"I don't know, why don't you guys tell me?" he said assertively, now standing in front of them.

"Listen kid, you either walk away or you'll be crawling away, it's that simple!" the taller man shouted, with saliva flying out of his mouth. He was almost shaking with rage, his patience obviously thread thin.

"Not sure what this woman did to deserve so much attention from you charming gentlemen, but I think all your TLC is making her feel awkward... Maybe you should leave her be?"

"Is this idiot serious??" the shorter man asked his accomplice rhetorically. "Didn't your mother ever teach you to not get involved when grown-ups are talking?" That comment struck a bad chord with the young man, he frowned and clenched his jaw trying to bottle his anger, but it had been noticed. "Ah, so the little boy is sensitive about his mother, how cute." During this early exchange between them the woman stayed fixed on the young man, her face imploring help. The taller one then looked straight at the woman he'd been standing over like predator and prey, and said to the other "I'm tired of this...Yazid, please get rid of him." Hearing that, the young man was now on full alert. He slid his right foot back across the gravel for better balance, raised himself onto his toes so he could move swiftly from one position to another. His mind began to race, *'Combat is spontaneous, a martial artist cannot predict it only react to it', 'the best offence is a strong defence', 'for someone to attack another, hand to hand, the attacker must approach the target, providing an opportunity for the attacked person to intercept the attacking movement'.* The young man watched intensely as he was approached by his enemy, consciously looking and waiting for an opportunity to intercept...'wait for it... wait for it...' His enemy, now only a metre or so away from him, took an exaggerated forward step towards him, rotated his torso and clenched his right hand into a fist. The young man was perceptive... picking up each of those cues. 'NOW!' his instincts screamed! And with bullet speed he turned his hip to the left, applied torque to the earth beneath his right foot and unleashed a loose-fisted right arm punch straight into the base of his opponent's sternum, clenching his fist hard just before the point of impact. THUD! His punch landed with the devastating force of a battering ram! His opponent was thrown three feet back onto his ass! He looked up at the young man while clenching his chest in agony, his face bewildered, he started to cough his breathing disrupted. He didn't understand where that came from, or how someone ten years his junior could put him on the floor in one punch. His confusion then turned to fear, leaving him unwilling to get up and attempt a second assault. The other man seeing this was angered further.

"Is this for real?! Yazid, are you really going to sit there like a bitch?!" the other said to his fallen partner in crime, while still guarding the woman. Yazid, being the shorter and scrawnier of the two, often found that his bark was worse than his bite. But he knew that Youssef would not stand for such displays of cowardice, so he gathered himself and tentatively got himself to his feet. His legs were trembling... "Good you've decided to stop being a girl... Now please teach this child some manners or I'll give you a real reason to be scared!" Yazid looked at the young man analysing him again, looking for something he missed the first time, 'a tell' or a sign of his real strength. This time he saw the forms and protrusions of a very athletic physique through his t-shirt. No matter how he thought about approaching him, his will to fight was nothing but smouldering embers. Whereas his opponent's whole body looked to be engulfed by an insurmountable raging fire. This gave him the helpless sense that he was staring down the barrel of a gun. In such situations men often find that denial is their best friend. He embraced that, telling himself that their first engagement was a fluke that his opponent was just a scared kid reacting on instinct, with not a clue of what he was doing. This inflated his confidence enough to allow his body to move freely under his control again, the paralysis of fear no longer an issue. Yazid was not going to make it as easy for him; this time he was going to be prepared. He was a bit sprightlier on his feet than before, his guard raised far higher too. He turned his whole body forty-five degrees so his left shoulder was his leading point. Still not recovered from the last blow, he concealed his midsection as best he could and began to move forward. The young man remained still, watching intensely like a cat would an approaching stranger in the dark. The young man noticed that he had begun sweating a little from his forehead; it's clear the thirty degree heat didn't make good conditions for any physical activity let alone fighting strangers. He needed to conserve as much energy as possible to avoid being a sweaty mess when he reached his rendezvous. Silence fell upon them, Youssef and his female hostage looked on eagerly, each with opposite hopes for the outcome. The young man, still with his training and teachings in mind, began to move steadily to his right, slowly tracing the circumference of a circle into the gravel. His opponent responded with equal movement in the opposite direction, the atmosphere was tense, neither man wanting to make a false move. After a few moments like this, the young man understood that if left to lead, his opponent would drag this fight on longer than he could afford. So he decided to create the opportunities for attack himself. He stopped circling and took a conservative step forward. His opponent was surprised and flinched, exactly the reaction he wanted. With every passing second, Youssef's patience wore thinner. Yazid could sense this and it played havoc with his nerves. The young man knew he could end this in the next few seconds, he just needed his opponent to make the same panicked flinch again. He counted down from 5 in his head...4…3...2...1 then exploded into life! Taking a big forward step the young man instantly penetrated his opponent's guard space, Yazid, eyes wide with fear, instantly threw a flailing right arm uppercut at him oblivious to the fact that he had already changed his stance! So with his left leg now leading, the young man was able to intercept this rushed attack with a right forearm parry, simultaneously shifting his body weight to his left side and delivering a rapid left arm body shot to his opponent's kidney! It made him crumple down with his right arm rushing down, elbow first, to shield the exposed area from further assault. The young man instantly countered that by using the same left arm he used to punch him to prise open this flawed single arm guard attempt with a lightning speed two-part movement. He was responding faster than his opponent could defend. All this was happening at the speed neuron signals fire around the brain. With his left arm having bypassed the guard, it was in the centreline of his opponent's torso. Using this arm like a crowbar he threw open his opponent's crunched guard, suddenly exposing him like an unexpected wind blowing up a woman's dress. He was vulnerable and he knew it. Seeing the young man readying a right arm punch to his stomach, he brought his left arm down to protect it. His arm made it down in time, but no, it was a feint! The young man was one step ahead. He was masterfully creating openings and in the very instant he saw that his opponent had fallen for the dummy, he shifted his weight off his left leg and back onto his favoured side. He hopped back to open the space between them, rotating his shoulders then hips around and cocking back his right arm. Then uncoiling rapidly like a steel spring, his right foot met the ground as he viciously threw another loose-fisted punch, only clenching at moment of impact to utilise the power and momentum transferring up his body from the fierce corkscrew action to up the punch's destructive power. It CRACKS against his opponent's jaw! The brutal connection whipped his head around uncontrollably, his body responded by going with it. He began an ungraceful descent to the ground, arms searching for leverage that wasn't there. Youssef shouted, "YAZID! WHAT ARE YOU DOING?!" but he couldn't hear him... He was already unconscious before he'd even hit the ground.

The young man with a glance, quickly checked that his opponent was not too severely injured by the fall or punch. Satisfied that his most severe injury would be to his ego, he turned his attention to the one that was left. He stood calmly, waiting for the other man to say something. He kept his excitement and pride in how well his months of training and study had worked to himself, not wanting to ruin the image of the strange, mysterious hero he thought he must be exuding at that moment. The woman under guard was, in fact, thinking just that... she was speechless... In her line of work she rarely saw such heroism, the good side of people was not something she knew well. Youssef was staring as if the young man was a ghost. He rapidly thought of what his next move should be, though very much the leader of the two, he'd always known that Yazid was the muscle and the one he relied on in such situations. He was afraid... For the first time in a long time he was fearful of an unarmed man. The woman noticed her captor was no longer focused on her; there was a definite opportunity for her to make a run for it, one that in the past she would never have let pass by, but she was relaxed... This young man's display of courage and selflessness, while others before him passed by, had made her happy in a profound way that she herself was not quite aware of. So instead of running, she just leant back onto the tree trunk, indulged in the shade of its leaves and patiently waited for a conclusion. The young man noticed the woman's smile. He found it peculiar but didn't let her distract him for too long and returned his attention back to the other man who then suddenly shouted out, "Okay, fine! If you want to save this whore so much you can have her! I'm tired of wasting any more of my time and money on her anyway." He kissed his teeth and stepped away from her, walked carefully towards his sprawled out friend, navigating past the young man like he was not wanting to wake a sleeping lion. The young man watched carefully, he didn't trust this man to not try something once close enough. But he didn't and once his friend was conscious and back on his feet, they both walked away with the shame of defeat following them like a shadow. The young man watched them walk through the children's playground to the other side of the park. He watched until sight of them was lost through the trees.

He turned back to the women he had just saved to be startled by her standing right in front of him. She was chest height to him, looking up at him like a daughter wanting to be carried in her father's arms. The young man asked in his best French, "Are you okay, miss? Did those guys hurt you?"

"No no, don't worry about me. I know I'm small but can take care of myself, I have to be able to in my line of work. Plus, those two creeps are not as bad as they think they are." The young man noticed that her French was not completely fluent; it seemed to be a second language to her like it was for him. "They're all mouth, as you proved so incredibly. It was just, wow! How?! I've only seen that kind of stuff in the movies and cartoons my little one watches!"

"Haha, thank you." he replied with his slight embarrassment at the praise coming through in his face. Erm what's your name, miss? I've seen you in and around the store where I work many times. Usually buying something for your son."

"My name is Caroline, but most men know me by my working name... And don't change the subject Mr reluctant hero! You did something amazing and you should be proud. If you were five years older I'd probably be smitten, brave and handsome are a rare combination. Haha, look at me already flirting with you when I don't even know your name. It's important for a girl to know the name of her knight in shining armour."

"Oh sorry that is rude of me, my father raised me better than that. My name is Julian and I was only doing what any good person would anyway, I think knight is a bit strong."

"Well it most definitely is a pleasure to meet you and don't sell yourself short Julian." She paused to think, "...Julian, I do like that name I must say... Maybe I'll name my next one that, yes after the first good man I've meet in a long time."

"Well don't give up on mankind just yet, I know it's hard to find genuine good in this world sometimes but you have to just find that little bit of strength inside to place your faith in the innate human desire to live together as a community which tends to lend itself well to nice gestures & good deeds. I'm a believer now...I believe in the healing potential of this world and its people. Ha sorry for rambling on miss."

"It's okay, they were interesting words. I'll try and take that on board."

"Glad to hear it and glad it could help you, but I must leave now, as I have a rendezvous I've been looking forward to all day. And my lunch break is not that long."

"Oh okay, now worries young man, you go and see your girlfriend, but I wouldn't tell her you were late because of another woman." she said with a wink.

"What makes you think it's a girlfriend I'm going to see?" He responded curiously.

"You just look like the girlfriend type." she smiled, said a final thank you and started to walk back up the gravel path. "Bye bye Julian, see you around."

"Haha the girlfriend type, you're the second women to say that to me today. Okay bye Caroline, come to my till next time I'll give you staff discount."

"Okay!" She yelled as she was already a good distance away. Julian looked at his watch, "DAMN!" He exclaimed realising just how late he was. He immediately began sprinting, he flew out the park entrance and down a residential road at full speed towards his rendezvous.

Back in London, beneath the cloak of its metropolitan multitudes, there was a singular plan approaching completion. All its different components providing difficult challenges complex, unique and varied. A being not of this world stood at the centre of its turbulence in serenity, as if becoming the eye of a tornado. Every day, hour, minute and second since his renaissance had been spent working towards the completion of this plan and finally revelling in its end goal... his return home and the destruction of mankind.

The once vibrant local church was now a building lost to its herd, not a single prayer had been offered up to the Catholic God of man in over two months. It was now home to a new self-appointed head of man, The Other One. Now awakened to his power, he decided to seal the church off to the outside, trapping those left within its walls in a vice grip of perpetual hopelessness. Only he and his own are allowed to roam upright with the freedom of the grounds' square footage.

Within its walls and inside the office of a priest, a being of ancient stature and power met with a subordinate.

"Great Other of the Original Whole, I've come to deliver the mission report," he said bowed forward, head down and eyes directly at the floor.

"Go ahead my child," the man seated at his desk replied. The bowed man raised his head and responded

"Today we have located five more of yours to add to those already here. This takes the total of Other Ones found, subjugated and put through the relapse protocol to ninety-seven."

"Oh really, that is nice work..."

"It's only made possible through the blessings you've bestowed upon us Father."

"Even so I'm proud of how you've applied yourself to your task. You will be rewarded well for your service when I finally return to my rightful place in RATH."

"Thank you Father"

"Errrm... I would also like you to make sure that my other children, stationed across the city in the secondary and tertiary bases, are made aware that the preparations are almost complete and we will be setting the plan into motion before the week is out."

"With pleasure Father"

"And what of our guests? Are they enjoying the hospitality we've showed them?"

"Well... another from building B died today, but the rest don't seem to have noticed. They seem docile and well behaved. Those in building C however are troublesome... They are loud, ill-mannered and seem to believe they are too good for the food we feed them."

"Really? Strange... If it's good enough for the pigeons and rats, then it's certainly good enough for them. Make sure they eat what they are given, and I mean to the very last morsel. If they refuse to consume it with their mouths...force it down, and if they still resist then make them realise in no uncertain terms that the mouth is the more preferable orifice to have food enter from, okay?"

"Yes of course, your will will be done"

"Good... we need them strong enough to greet the guest of honour when he returns. Speaking of which has his invitation been sent?"

"Yes, it left thirty minutes ago and will be delivered personally by one of us just as you instructed."

"Okay... very nice... if there's nothing else you may leave... Oh actually when you go, could you please bring me back one of them please... it's been a whole day since this human body got any exercise."

"Is there one in particular?"

"Mmmmm... No just find me one with hope still in its eyes."

"Certainly, I will return shortly Father."

A few minutes after this conversation, a couple of miles away a messenger was arriving at his destination. He walked up to the front door, rang the doorbell and waited patiently for an answer. Sooner than he was expecting, the door was answered. A tall dark man fitting the description he was given opened the door. Standing there a bit confused as to why there was a stranger on his door step he asked,

"Hmm can I help you sir?"

"Depends, are you Mr François Mufunga?"

"Yes, that is me."

"I thought so, just wanted to be sure. This is for you," he stretched his arm out, offering a sealed letter. François accepted it and inspected it for any clues of what could be inside. There were none to be found, it was just a sleek white envelope with his name on it, so he asked,

"What's inside?"

"It's a personal message for you from the Father"

"The Father??" François looked at the messenger puzzled for a second "You mean the Priest, Father Bachinger?"

"The great Other One who was originally of the Whole, doesn't go by his adopted human name anymore." This conversation suddenly took on a more dangerous tone. François was now on guard, as that sentence alone revealed to him two of the potentially worst scenarios. 1. That Father Bachinger was, as he suspected, not just simply another member of the vanquished here in the Rehabilitation program but something a lot more powerful... like their original creator and leader! For some reason, though obvious now, he didn't make the connection that he could be in fact be The Other One- one half of the most powerful being in existence and the reason for the Great War, its eventual loss and their consequent existence on earth. So clear to see now, it felt to him as if some outside force was purposefully blocking this insight from him. 2. That he was now somehow finding and recruiting his Other Ones for a new goal. "What is he planning now??" François racked his brain, he couldn't help but presume the worst, as he knew that a leader like him only re-assembled his army for one purpose. He was now stressed by these thoughts and the messenger picked up on this. "Don't worry Mr Mufunga... You can relax; you have a bit of time before your ultimate decision will need to be made."

François was not sure exactly what he meant by that ominous statement but he listened on. "And for now I am only here to deliver this letter, the contents of which are of reasonable urgency so I would suggest you take it back inside with you, have a seat and open it." With that, the message had been delivered. François closed his door and the messenger left, returning from whence he came.

Chapter 15

****

I regret... If I really can, I regret... where I reside is dark, a place where light could not even borrow the eight minutes to shine. Lost in fog and starless nights drifting on an earth sea of cold blue misery... I regret choosing you, priest. There was the father to follow in the absence of the son but I, without a body, stand beside you as plans of revenge, anger and hatred spiral out of your mind and into the ears of those who were seeking redemption through their earthly chains. I miss... If I really can I miss him, The Atheist. From my start I was lost, confused... but you, through your pain and the attempts of those around you to heal that pain, gave me something to focus on that had purpose... a beauty even I could see. It made me see something other than the nothing of everything. Yours and his love for her were the only thing in all the day-less days I spent lost that didn't need answers... it didn't need the **why**... I have lost something, what? What have I lost? Was what you and your family gave me, the **faith** often held by men? Have I lost **faith**? Was The Atheist my **faith**?

****

Back in France, Julian had sprinted just over three hundred metres and once he arrived at his rendezvous he was a hot, sweaty, heavy-breathing mess. Time wasn't on his side; that altercation in the park had eaten up a lot of his lunch break. The person he was going to see meant a lot to him and they were still at the point where scruffiness would be frowned upon. So though already over fifteen minutes late, he took a few more seconds to compose himself, un-scrunched his t-shirt and wiped the sweat off his brow. He looked around the house which was a typical detached French town home, pale white in colour with driveway, garage (door always left open when someone was home), garden and metal shutters attached to the outside of the windows. When closed these shutters kept out the sun and its accompanied heat. Add that to the tiled flooring throughout the house, it made for a refreshingly cool environment and shelter from the summer extremities. These houses were always Julian's favourite. Although beautiful to him, he was actually looking around to make sure that parents weren't home. Being the middle of a weekday it was very unlikely, but he always exercised extra caution when it came to this. He glanced up at the top floor window, and there it was... more beautiful than land to a weary sea traveller. It was her... stood in the pink-walled bedroom, braiding her hair, unaware of him watching. He could never get over the beauty and sex appeal in her form. She was dressed in only her underwear; he could see even from here that it was her best set. She had mentioned it to him several times during their late night text message exchanges, but she never mentioned how well its laced materials supplemented the fullness of her figure. His mind started to wonder, it was time to go inside he had kept her waiting long enough.

Going through the unlocked garage door, he enters. It lead straight into the kitchen, he made sure to be loud enough to make his presence known. He quickly ran upstairs, almost stumbling on the very first step. As he made it up to the next floor he heard her voice say, "Je vois que tu est toujours impatient." He chuckled, Julian always found her little unassuming voice so cute, especially when compared to the size of her personality.

"Pardon bébé," he apologised for the noise brought by his haste.

The following is translated from French.

"I know how late I am."

"Oh do you now? How late are you?"

"Too late babe," Julian said as he walked up to the door of her bedroom, she'd left it wide open. Once at the threshold and able to see inside he tried to speak but all words were erased from his mind by the sight of her. The curtains were drawn, the room was amber in dimness, with only the queen-sized bed she was spread across indulging in the gentle light from the bulb above. Laid on her side in perfectly fitted lingerie she turned her head back towards him. It was enough for him to see his favourite parts of her as well as a portion of her perfectly plump lips... coated in a vibrant purple they stood out from her dark complexion, like a light signal in the night directing him to where he should be. It was his favourite colour on her... and she knew it. She knew exactly how to excite his senses.

"You were about to tell me why you were late?"

"Er... yes... there were... these guys bothering this woman...I had to help," he said slowly, his breathing already deeper. He was entranced by the lust his eyes were projecting onto her body and it was being reflected back into him by each of her curves. Deep or shallow her ratios were perfect.

"My man, always a hero to a damsel, but what about your girl? She needs her hero too, you know? You made promises to me, *and* this body I take care of for you... didn't you?" Her voice filled the room and his head like a gentle song of adorning.

"Yes I did..." He replied quickly his words automated, while his conscious mind was deeply engaged in the plotting of her seduction. He was still relatively new to this and found his planning limited. He therefore decided to play it moment by moment, trusting in his instincts.

"So are you the kind of hero who always keeps his promises?" she said provocatively.

"Definitely..."

"So why are you still over there? Come here and give me what you promised."

With those words, Julian came out of his trance and started towards her. With each step his appetite for her grew... the musculature of his chest filled with the air of strength, his jaw clenched with intent and his strides expressed palpable sexual authority. He was literally becoming more man with each step he took towards her. The seconds played out slowly... he closed in on her, her beautiful shape still laid there waiting for him. She turned over to face him, lifting her chest up by resting on her forearms & elbows. She presented herself to him with a subtle smile of excitement. Her body glistened, appearing under the soft bedroom light like the precious stone-imbued surface of a dark underwater cave wall, a surface rhythmically reflecting the light passed onto it by the surface of the water. She always took care to moisturise her skin... and today of all days would be no exception. She had plans for him.

Julian was mapping the contours of her body with his mind, taking his time finding the perfect spot on her to start from. His eyes eventually found their way to hers; what he felt at that moment was so pure and deep it overwhelmed his mind and so he let his heart lead. He lowered himself towards her placing one knee down on the bed... reached his hand out to find the back of her neck, griping gently... The masculinity of his hands excited her. He spent a moment enjoying the feel of her natural hair on his fingertips, he liked that not all traces of her natural hair were concealed by the extensions she had.

He then felt her hand on his stomach, she'd found her way under his t-shirt and was tracing her finger along the ridges. He tensed knowing how much she liked the tone in his stomach, she smiled in appreciation. She lifted his t-shirt up for a better look, his shorts were hanging low on his hips revealing the arrowed lines at the base of his stomach she loved... They were perfectly defined and their v-shape appeared to point her to the next location needing her special attention. She took a moment to let her mind wonder forward to what pleasures she had in-store for him, subconsciously she bit her lip then began undoing his shorts.

Back on his two feet now, he just watched her work for him with his hands caressing the back of her head and neck. She was seated at the edge of the bed with her eyes closed using her senses of touch and taste to guide her. Each movement she made was slow, rhythmic and passionate... he could barely handle the pleasures she was making him feel. The eloquence of her tongue was mesmerising, tracing paths along, around and across parts he didn't know could feel the tingles of sexual pleasure. The natural warmth and moistness of her was providing the perfect environment for this oral endeavour, and Julian was struggling to remain in control of himself, matching her rhythm with his own progressively more forceful gyrations. She could feel his grip on her neck becoming firmer with every extra inch of depth she allowed. Her experience told her that it was time to stop for the sake of a more prolonged experience with him. She pulled away and looked up at him, he returned the glance... but his is one of astonishment. No matter how many times she sought to his needs, it always felt like a fresh awakening. Julian was completely devoted to this time together with her, his fires of lust were blazing and they wanted to consume her. She sensed he was about to take the lead and begin his domination of her body, her experience told her to let him... to enjoy the intoxicating cocktail of pleasure and pain that it brought. He moved his hands to her waist and forcefully picked her to her feet. They began the passionate embrace of long lost lovers, laced with the aggression of those making up after breaking up. Julian was kissing her with no restraint or hesitation from thoughts of what preceded, he loved the intimacy, loved the proximity. His hands would wander to all parts of her, with one hand on the front of her neck he kissed her like it was the last kiss available to mankind. The size of his hand meant that he could feel the side of her throat pulsating... It was fast & unrelenting, her body was communicating with him... telling him what she desired. He understood and answered by tracing his hands down the small of her back, making sure to enjoy every part of her feminine shape perfectly balanced between firm and soft; he felt her with the seductive grasp of an obsessed sculptor. She could feel his strength, his hunger, his intensions and it gave her the want of him...the want that made waters flow...that made her flow...and she knew he couldn't wait to be in it. Their embrace continued like this, lips being nibbled, hair being felt through and bodies being teased and pleasured at their deepest, darkest spots. Eventually when they both could no longer play anymore they returned to the edge of the bed to begin the personification of their needs. She positioned herself in such a way as to not leave any doubt about how she wanted him to start, looking back at him watching and waiting. He stepped forward to meet her proposition with all he had. The temperature in the room had risen drastically since he arrived and they were both shining in the sweat of their effort, but no rest was to be had. They began to love each other in every way their bodies could, senses alight with the indescribable tastes, sounds, scents and feels of each other's flesh. With the relentlessness of youth, they matched perpetual motion to intermittent angle changes, their lust raging right through them, barely allowing for breaths. She couldn't help forgetting Julian was a young man as she felt the full force and indulgence of his veteran instincts. The bed covers were squeezed tightly in her fists and whenever she raised her head from the covers for air the intensity of her moans sang erotic melodies to Julian, coming together into mesmeric songs of sexual fulfilment; a verse of love, a chorus of lust into a bridge of passion. They were oblivious to the length or volume of their sound. Though positions of entry would change, with control being taken and surrendered by both, the reprieves would never bring about lucid moments. They were trapped in each other... to them time had no place here, the moment was all that there was... They were lost to it...slaves to it and it stretched out longer than they could gauge. Their only escape from this all-consuming heat was the climax, and it was fast approaching like two runaway trains set to collide.

The bed and wooden floors shook at the mercy of their passion. He was agonisingly close and she screamed for him to continue, to push the boundaries of tolerance, to never cease imposing his masculinity on her. Julian felt her warm soaked thighs squeeze his waist, she was on the precipice. Her deepest parts were constricting on him, every stroke became a Russian roulette for him. It was almost upon them, and just before his resistance failed he changed his rhythm and applied the full depth in slow, hard drumming motions he knew would take her over the edge. Her writhing body responded instantly and drowned her in a shockwave of pleasure that exploded ecstasy from her centre and spread intensely through her legs to finish its reverberating tingles in her toes. It lasted only for seconds, but to her they were the longest most orgasmic seconds in existence... He collapsed into her arms... She pulled him in as tight as she could, keeping their bodies connected as they rode through the final gentle fading echoes together...

Julian being careful not to disrupt the quiet said softly to her in the most beautiful French he could, "Je t'aime Xandra-Sina." She smiled and whispered back in his ear

The following is translated from French

"You know I don't like it when you call me that."

"It's who you are, it's your name and I don't want to shorten the beauty of it or the person it represents."

"Your sweet talk doesn't work on me"

"I think it already did," he said lifting himself off her so she could see his cheeky grin,

"Idiot," she said with a playful slap. "Well all good things come to an end and I think your Lunch break was over."

"Shit! What time is it?" He looked at the alarm clock on the bed stand "Ahh damn, I knew it would have been a tight squeeze but thought I could make it back, but no and my break officially ends in five, four, three, two, one now." Julian winced with disappointment, a habit he'd subconsciously picked up from her.

"You regretting something?"

"Haha no, I'd do it all over again if I had the time."

"Oh yeah, like you have the stamina."

"Eh careful, don't make me have to show you who's boss again."

"Excuse me sir but I have no boss, and my body can't be tamed." Julian knew she was trying to push his buttons so he would stay, but he had never been late back before and didn't want to become that kind of employee.

"Nice try 'Si Si', but I have to go. As much as I love you that won't pay the bills."

"What bills? You live with your aunty."

"Yes, but I'm not a freeloader, I'll always contribute something." Then with a pensive expression he continued with, "I don't want to be a burden... I want to help... It's what you should do for the people you love..." In that moment Sina (as she was called by her friends) knew that Julian's mind had drifted back to the part of his past he kept secret from her. It always lowered his mood and made him retract into himself...sometimes for days at a time. The moment she wanted to maintain had passed and it was time to let him leave before those thoughts of the life he had before her consumed him again.

"Okay babe, go and I'll text you later tonight after work. I need to send out some more CVs, some of us aren't model employees or love the people we work with."

Julian got dressed in a hurry, how much trouble he was in increased with every passing minute. They made some small talk during his rush but he was already distracted by unwanted thoughts of reprimands and barely made eye contact. Sina didn't mind, she knew him well enough to know that it was in no way a reflection on her. Julian was now fully dressed and ready to walk out, but paused when he saw her phone flash with a text message notification from 'Jonathan', a name he hadn't seen or heard since the early days of their relationship. It was the name of her ex-boyfriend, the man she left to be with him. She seemed unsettled by it... but maybe more specifically that he had seen it. It was very strange, he only knew that hers and this Jonathan's relationship was a complicated one and involved things that she never wanted to mention... not to mention it had left her heart completely broken. Before he had the chance to react in any meaningful way, his attention was drawn to his own phone, it was vibrating in his back pocket. He took it out, it was a phone call... He froze, completely startled by the name the caller ID was showing. It was his father! He hadn't heard from him in over four weeks... He was getting worried but knew enough never to compromise his situation by calling him or his home. It had been the cause of a very real but silent pain within him. His heart started racing and butterflies grew in his belly at the thought of why he could be calling now? He quickly said goodbye to Sina forgetting what he had just seen and raced downstairs and out the house to answer it away from her eyes and ears.

Once outside he started walking back to work at a hurried pace, when he felt sufficiently far enough from Sina's parents house he picked up his phone.

"Papa! What's going on?? How come you're calling me after weeks of nothing?!" Even in his stressed out state he couldn't escape how wonderfully familiar it felt to be speaking English again. François, though surprised to hear Julian call him 'Papa', didn't dwell on it and got straight to explaining.

"Fils, écoutes moi bien, and while listening please stay calm..."

"Mmm okay..."

"I got a letter today, a letter from him."

"Really?! What does that imposter want?"

"Le même qu'avant, he wants you."

"Well that's why I'm here, isn't it? And I'm actually happy, so he can just kiss my ass to be honest, there'll be a white Christmas in hell before I let him get anywhere near me!"

"Well unfortunately son the problem is I think you're going to change your mind... That letter I got it, had a very simple message. Erm, actually more like a worrying warning, a show of intent and how he is definitely not just playing with his fingers waiting for you to magically appear."

"Papa, what are u trying to say? Please just say it, I have no time for one of your long speeches right now. I'm gonna be back at work soon so whatever it is just say it and I'll deal with it." Sensing an authoritative tone in his son's voice that he hadn't heard before, he realised that he had done some changing while he was away. Maybe he was now strong enough to deal with what was about to come. So he stopped his verbal procrastinations and just said it to Julian in as straight and concise a way as he could.

"Father Bachinger has formed a strong hold at the church, he already has 20 of us awakened form our sleeping memories of who we once were and who he *REALLY* is. This number of Other Ones that have gathered by his side and that are prepared to follow him to their end or this world's end is growing by the day. For his plan to succeed he needs you beside him, and to ensure you come... he's taken Aeryn-Sun prisoner... He says, and I quote son, 'neither I, her gods, nor you Julian can change the unfortunate experiences that have already befallen your nun while being my guest... but we can all play a part in what experiences the future has in store for her. Won't you come here and join us in the decision process?'" Julian dropped his phone in shock, not even hearing it smack onto the pavement... He stared aimlessly into the distance like a sailor lost at sea and his lungs took in their full capacity of air. Seconds flew into his mind as he attempted to digest what he'd just been told. "Fils, tu est là?? Tu m'écoutes?! Can you hear me?! You must relax; we will figure something out! A way for you to stay there, you can't let him taunt you into doing exactly what he wants!" His father's words were being lost in the air, Julian couldn't hear them... He was dealing with his own words... the thoughts of his conscience. It was intense, he struggled with the different permutations. What should he do? No answer was coming to him. But in the end his resolve proved strongest and he finally re-centred himself. Calm again, his breathing normalised and sight focused. He bent down, picked up the phone to hear his father still asking if he was on the line? He gently responded.

"Don't worry, it's fine... I'm not useless anymore. I can save her. I can stop him, I *will* save everyone I love." Julian hung up and put his phone in his pocket. Then with every fibre in his body he focused all his strength and burst into his fastest possible sprint back towards work. He was much faster than he remembered. The pavement first and then the park gravel was eroded and displaced with each stride's forceful explosion of power into the ground. His limbs moved like rapidly firing pistons as he blazed past his surroundings. People watched in awe... this blur of a man was racing towards his future, his destiny and his meaning with only love as his **why**. He was no longer the troubled youth of several months ago, the burden to everyone he knew, the non-believer in anything this world had to offer... lost in sadness... Belief and purpose had finally permeated through his doubts and found him. It found him strong, brave and now a man of faith... Faith in himself, in his father, in all those he loved and in the reasons beyond his understanding for his unique existence.

Chapter 16

****

Something is coming...it feels familiar to me yet also different. Like when the earthly sun shines in the cold of winter. It feels good...I know good...I can feel good... How? Because it's different. It's filling a space left...an emptiness I never sought to keep. I thought I was alone and knew singularity, but his absence from my sightless sight made me see truth. I was never alone as long as there were others I watched, others whose presence I wanted and... cared for. I *can* care... I know this because it's different, because it's not regret, loneliness or singular. Without them I wouldn't recognise the truth of what is happening... the truth that I am feeling... feeling like I believe they do. Though opposites, they seem to need one another for recognition. Light needs darkness to exist for the conscious to know what it is to see. Heat needs the cold for the mind to know what it is to feel warmth. Love needs hate for the heart to know what it is to care. Happiness is coming... He is coming. Is he ready to face the dark that has been spreading in his absence..? I do not know... but I believe. The Atheist has returned. Faith has returned. The direction of my life has turned.

****

14 days later

In this time, plans have come closer to completion... journeys closer to their destination. Julian, with limited explanation, left his protective life and new love behind. Their last goodbye was on the second of the fourteen days. It was brief and shrouded in many unsaid things... in such a short time; their dynamic had changed from honesty to secrecy. The past lives they'd lead were creating new barriers on the depth of the connections they could make in the future. But Julian's and Sina's love was strong and full of hope, they had faith that they would re-connect again once the forces that had caused this temporary situation of separation were resolved. Until then, Julian had to be on his own path, a path that all the events of his life good or bad had been preparing him for.

In the closed off compound that was formally the largest church in the city, Aeryn-Sun sat. She has found herself in the darkest room of a building's basement level and her identity as a sister stripped from her body. Unclothed, she sat back against a hard stone wall wide-eyed and silent. She hoped her pupils could let in enough of that slice of light visible under the door, and grant her fragile mind more than just the blackness. Fragile she may have been, with countless wounds across her body providing a constant aching reminder that her ordeals had not been nightmares but a far worse reality, but she was not broken. Her past experiences of man's potential for cruelty made her heart coarse and tough, she could withstand the coldest winters of life. The faith she found after the pain of her youth had made her will durable. The name she adopted when escaping from her flames of hardship gave her an ideal version of herself that was invulnerable to all things of this world. The whispers of voices in the dark and flash backs of what has, is and will be done do shake her but she still stands, even if only metaphorically. They underestimate her, they do not know her past. Only one man in this new life away from home knows her strength. Even though the memory of the night he walked into her life as a boy grows old and blurrier with each day of absence, it is enough to remind her she still has a friend in this world. Enough to recall the beauty and hope that can come to be in even the emptiest of rooms, mundane of moments and roughest of diamonds. This is the nature of her faith...in her God, in herself and in her friend. She knows trust in this trinity will be her salvation so she will wait, and she will persevere.

Outside her room there was a long corridor, at the top of which two of the Father Bachinger's soldiers stood guard. He had his men watching her room continuously...with only ever him being allowed access to it. In between his visits or their meal time offerings, they sometimes stood engaged in conversations, designed to strengthen bonds while they waited for his guest of honour to arrive. This was one of those moments.

"Hey Jo," one guard whispered to the other.

"What?"

"I was just thinking about something."

"Well stop, thinking it's better left to those actually capable of it."

"Oh that's hilarious, you think of that by yourself?

"No your sister helped me."

"Another original masterpiece ha ha... I'm trying to speak to you on a level man so be serious..."

"Okay fine, what do you want?'

"Was just thinking about how weird it is to be here now after spending so many years trying to be good little humans, trying to somehow gain redemption in this damn program of The O—"

"Hey Ant, be careful, you know we're not allowed to say that name."

"Don't worry I know I'm not that stupid. But I just find it so surreal...we spent all those years not even realising that our master was here trapped with us this whole time."

"Well that was the whole point of the rehab program wasn't it? How would it have worked if we knew our master and father was here? We would have ignored the rules and searched for him without rest. The only way to control us was to make us feel lost, abandoned and helpless. It's not like any of us have actually changed is it not consciously anyway?" There was a longer than expected pause before Ant responded,

"No I guess not... I just thought it would be different... I thought it would feel different... I thought it would make me happy like I belonged somewhere again. When he came into my work and gave me the blessed touch it lifted the chains placed on my spirit and mind. The chains that caused me to forget who I *really* was before, and what happened to our master and creator on the day of our judgement in RATH, the day we lost the war. He told me stories of a new battle, of a way to return back to what we once were and being together again with him as one."

"Yes he told us all that, it is why we are all here, ready to serve."

"Yeah but look, where are we? Not with him, not fighting any great battles...we are just here in some damn building watching over some human play thing of his. When was the last time master even spoke to us directly? It wasn't like this during the first war... it wasn't like this before..."

"Listen!" Jo said, loud enough to echo through the corridor and into the room where Aeryn-Sun was. "Things are different, but it's our fault, not master's... He is the True One originally of the Whole, it's us that have changed. He only keeps those beside him whose spiritual essence are closest to how they were originally, those who have not let their human experiences in the program corrupt their original natures and drives. As I said, consciously we still are who we were, but under this shell we have been corrupted in ways we cannot see or understand. But he can, and he will only let those whose essences he recognises most into his inner circle. For all the rest of us, we have to be content taking peripheral roles like this and doing it to the best of our ability until we get fully restored once our battle here with the master's guest is finished. Once that happens I promise we will all be like we were before: strong, powerful and beside him again. Until then, stop your whining and be the best guard you can."

"Okay Jo, whatever you say." And with that acknowledgement Ant smiled and relaxed back into his post.

A few miles away Julian was returning home after completing the gathering of very specific items. He walked up to the front door, took out his set of keys, opened the door and walked in. "Dad are you there?"

"Oui fils, I'm in the living room we're waiting for you."

Julian navigated himself around his dad's Chopper as its leaning against the corridor wall was narrowing the space. He noticed the portrait of his mum like he had always done each time he'd had to enter or leave the house. But since he arrived back to his old life two days ago, each glance at the picture had always made him happy and aided to re-affirm his resolve. He was carrying quite a few full Homebase bags and was worried that they were on the brink of tearing, so he hastened his walk into the front room... Once in there, he put the bags down by the nearest wall and walked towards where they were stood.

"Fils, did you get everything on the list?"

"Yes dad, everything."

"What ever happened to 'Papa'? I quite liked that."

"Dunno, it just feels weird saying that now that I'm back in England, it might make a comeback one day, who knows."

"Oh I see, well I won't hold my breath anyway."

" Anyway, I think we are ready to start this."

"I know you're in a rush son, and I appreciate you trusting in my plan and waiting all this time. But first, I want you to listen to what our guest has to say. Remember the Controllers I told you about?"

"Yes, very well… it's not something you forget about."

"Ha, I guess not. It's got important things it needs to tell you, now try not to be over awed by the different temperature sensations you're going to feel as it appears, or the change in air density okay? It's just he's a very powerful being and his presence this close to the border of our realm has a dramatic effect on everything here. So just try and keep your emotions and senses in check. The disturbing feelings his presence bring will subside."

"What sensations are you talking about? I don't feel anything."

"What do you mean you don't feel anything? No one bound to this earth can escape their effect."

"Well all I feel is your breath on my face."

"Funny, but that can't be... I think maybe you've just got accustomed to it quickly without even realising? Either way, don't worry about that, it's not a patient being so let's not keep it waiting.

"You're the one procrastinating not me."

"No, I'm just trying to prepare you. Okay... well I'll relay exactly what he says to you word for word."

"There's no need to dad, I can hear him."

"What? How can you hear him you can't even see him?"

"Nope, I can see him too."

François was stunned into a silent confusion... He knew that his son had changed slightly since the aspects of his unique circumstance and existence had started to manifest themselves in the form of a new level of awakening, it began for him ever since that event at the church mass. But he could not have foreseen that it would have evolved so much in the time he was away. He was now seemingly able to effortlessly see through the barriers between different dimensions, as well as communicate through them. This was truly extraordinary... Every day Julian was displaying more and more abilities akin to a being of RATH, all while still appearing to be in the human form he was born into. François was slightly frightened by it, but his role as Julian's father would never allow him to admit it.

"Okay then I'll just leave you two to get acquainted, I guess... He's already told me what you're about to hear. So just stay calm son, you know together we will find a solution... Errr bon, je vais débarrasser quel que truc la pendent que vous parlez." François walked over to where Julian left the items he had requested, he wanted to occupy himself briefly while they spoke to help calm his nerves. There were a lot of items on the list, all with a specific role to play in his plan. François was not the kind of man to under prepare for any task he took on. There were four separate large carrier bags. He went to pick them up all together, just as he'd seen Julian doing as he walked in, but to his surprise he couldn't... He tried again... he strained hard but to limited avail. Fear ran through his body as he turned back to look at his son. He stared at him puzzled... Could the man standing there about to have a conversation with a being from another dimension be his son? None of the strongest men he knew, let alone the son he remembered, could carry this weight. As he processed this realisation of his son's maturation, the fear slowly turned to awe before becoming an overwhelming sense of resounding pride. It was clear to him that his role as the protective father had come to an end. The role required of him now was, to be there to guide his son, to lead him towards making the decisions that would best serve humanity against the threat ahead. His son, though the very pebble he and Julian's mother threw into the ocean of the universe that created the far reaching ripples that had led to this, had become the shore where theses ripples found their resolution. He could only but acknowledge the frustrating thought that the consequences of his actions would fall on the shoulders of his son. Francçois, powerless to change that fact, found peace in that they were now falling on the shoulders of a man, shoulders kept broad and strong through Julian's faith and the convictions that faith yields. From this point he knew without doubt that his son would save them all from him. François now calm, picked up each bag separately with both hands, and moved them one by one to a more convenient space in the room.

"So Mr Controller, what do you want to say?" Seconds passed and there was no response from the imposing black mass in front of him. "Don't get shy now, there's no time for that." Julian waited for an answer... and while he did, his mind strayed back to that day in church where he first saw what he knows now is a Controller. He is far less frightened than he was then even though now standing only two meters away.

"NO COMMUNICATION IS POSSIBLE FOR THE CONTROLLER OF OLD WITH ALL THINGS OUTSIDE THE NUMBERS AND EQUATION. FOR THIS UNEXPECTED COMMUNICATION, THE 1 HAD TO RE-WRITE THE EQUATION TO BRIDGE THE SPACE BETWEEN WHAT EXISTS AND WHAT IS NOT MEANT

TO. THIS VERSION OF I CAN. AND I DO. THE REPORT I PRESENT TO THE 1 SHOWS THAT THE ACTIONS OF PROSPECT ONE ZERO ZERO TWO ZERO ZERO AND FORMER PROSPECT TWO FOUR FOUR THREE FIVE FIVE ARE THE ORIGINS OF YOU THE REMAINDER, THE ONE OUTSIDE THE NUMBERS."** Julian intuitively understood everything it was saying, the prospects it was referring to were his parents. They were prospects for reintegration back into their original home after completion of their rehabilitation program just like his father said. Though it was hard for him to imagine his father or mother as evil, or more accurately as beings of a negative or an unconstructive cause, he understood more than anyone the possibility for change to occur in one's heart and mind. **"THE DECISION WAS THEN MADE TO REMOVE PROSPECT TWO FOUR FOUR THREE FIVE FIVE FROM THE EQUATION, THIS FOR THE 1 TO ANALYSE AND UNDERSTAND THE HOW OF THE SITUATION. PROSPECT ONE ZERO ZERO TWO ZERO ZERO WAS KEPT HERE TO WATCH OVER THE REMAINDER AND CONTAIN ITS EFFECT ON BOTH REALMS."**

Julian became visibly aggravated at these words "So it was his decision to take her away from me, to make this family suffer like it has in her absence? All because he created a rehab program that was flawed? Because he failed to foresee a possible situation within it? We suffer because of his ineptitude?"

"THE CONTROLLER IS NOT DESIGNED FOR THE ANSWERING OF QUESTIONS. THE CONTROLLER IS MESSENGER TO THOSE WITHIN THE NUMBERS AND IN THIS VERSION ALSO THE ONE ANOMALY OUTSIDE THEM. ALL THINGS FROM THAT MOMENT HAVE LEAD TO SITUATION TWO EIGHT EIGHT FOUR FOUR EIGHT. PROSPECT ONE ZERO ZERO TWO

ZERO ZERO IS RESPONSIBLE FOR THE ONE OUTSIDE THE NUMBERS AND ALL CONSEQUENCES OF IT. I CAME PREVIOUSLY TO DELIVER THE WARNING BUT NOTHING HAS CHANGED. SITUATION TWO EIGHT EIGHT FOUR FOUR EIGHT IS STILL UNRESOLVED THE OTHER 1 IS PREPARING TO ATTEMPT A RETURN TO THE REALM ABOVE THE HEAVENS AND THE END RESULT DRAWS CLOSER TO ITS UNEXCEPTABLE CONCLUSION. THE 1 HAS DECIDED IF THE SOLUTION TO SITUATION TWO EIGHT EIGHT FOUR FOUR EIGHT IS INTERVENTION BY THE ONE, THEN ALL PROSPECTS WILL BE ERADICATED AND THE PROGRAM CLOSED." Julian immediately turned and looked at his father. His father who was stood a few feet behind him just nodded his head with an expression of subservient acceptance. This angered him more than the Controller's message.

"How can you just accept this?? It's not your fault! All you and mother did was fall in love and have a child. A child that if he had done his job right, shouldn't have even been possible. It was his mistake! Not yours! Why should you have to suffer? Why should the redemption you have been working so hard to gain be dashed away so easily? And what about all the rest out there? Those he put here? What about mum?? What will happen to her? She can't just be there without the hope of seeing her family again??"

"Pardon fils, but there's nothing I can do. Nothing I can say that can change that decision... but" Before he could finish his sentence, Julian turned away angrily, facing back to where the Controller was but it wasn't there, it was gone. It had delivered its message and with the numerical efficiency it existed by it left to fulfil its next objective. Julian took a few seconds to let the anger subside... Once it had, his mind was clearer and the true nature of this message to obvious to him. He realised that The Controller's message did not say what The One would do with him if he decided to close the program. Also, that there was no real need for him to be spoken to directly if the message had already been relayed to his father. When putting those factors together it was clear that this was not a simple oversight or mistake. Julian understood that The One's message did not mention what effect this decision would have on him because he did not know... that in fact the term 'the one outside of the numbers' actually meant 'the one outside of my control'. This initiated an intrinsic feeling of freedom, like a bird that finally realises his genetic potential for flight. He did not have to accept anything as inevitable, nothing was certain anymore because of him. He could change his father's fate, and he would do everything in his power to make sure his father would gain redemption and see his mother again. He was determined, one way or another, he would save Aeryn and everyone else. This message of foreboding consequence was in reality 1 final cry for help. The One was pleading for Julian to stop the Priest and save everyone he could so he would not have to close the program and kill all the 'Others' he had chained down to the earth. Julian was full of pride in what had been entrusted to him. He carried the faith and hopes of so many without as much as a slouch or a limp.

"Of course I'll help you. We both have a lot to lose if Father Bachinger gets his way," Julian accidentally said out loud. Satisfied and ready to move forward he turned back to François, "Right dad, let's get to it. We have a lot of work to do if we want to start this rescue tonight."

"Well we can if you stop your procrastination." Father and son smiled a smile of men bonded by the challenging of mortal danger together, excited by the thrill, one prepared to die for the other. And so began their preparations for the final act of this story. The boy atheist is now a man of faith... unafraid of the darkness he proceeds forward, his path illuminated by the light of all those he loves.

Chapter 17

****

He's here! Returned to my sight, visible and clear like the day. But everything I feel is different... the change has occurred slowly. But to whom and to what extent? The Atheist is not the same, I observed his many weaknesses of character. But since he left my line of sight and returned, his humanity now shines a light of a different kind.

All things he left behind, father friend and foe have also morphed and progressed like the crystallisation of earth's rocks. So the changed return to a changing, I watched the changing... Strangest of all is that I understood it; his, there's and fate's. Is that because I have changed? Has the constitution of my existence become different? It feels so.

His path is coming to an end that includes the destiny of worlds beyond his, mine or the third Realm that has never been observed. But everything I *have* seen tells me of certain truths. Its existence is certain, I can also feel it. I know it. The Atheist knows it, he feels it. Without tangibility his senses still agree. This conviction is made possible because he is Atheist no more. Although he has not professed trust in the human God he was raised to believe in, he still has faith. This faith is more than the prayers of men. I understand now that it is a contract one makes with hope. A contract of marriage, of undying commitment through sickness and in health, to have and to hold. If that contract of commitment to hope is made in the presence of a person that loves you, the promise extends further. That faith extends further. I observed the son's promise, the father's promise and that of the nun so holy in spirit. All within my ocular presence it was done....I then felt that promise extend here and fill my nothing with substantial waves of real. Therefore I cannot escape that by my own rational I love them; the father, the son and her holy spirit. Through them my final answer draws close.

I've made my contract with hope and I have faith that this finale will explain all that I am and all that I am not.

****

It's late in the night, late enough that even the cumbersome summer sun has made it below the horizon and only pale moonlight remains. The street lights that always covered this street in flickering amber are also gone. For them all to have failed is not an accident. It's surely by his design. This is the first of several things the father and son notice.

"The church looks far more intimidating a place than I remember, dad."

"Oui, tu as raison fils"

"When did all the street lights stop working?" Julian said, nostalgically gazing across the blackened road to the metal fencing and gate he once chained his bike to on a very different Sunday.

"Not sure, but when I was here last night they were fully functioning. Either way I doubt it was some random electrical fault that caused it."

"I agree with you, for that to happen on the night we come here... It just reeks of the Priest. I think someone saw you last night and this is just one of the precautions he's probably taken."

"You're probably right, but turning off all the lights won't stop us, he's not dealing with boys." Julian's dad reached into the side pocket of the large sports bag he was carrying over one shoulder and passed him a little torchlight and piece of paper. On that folded piece of A4 was a rough sketch he had made of the grounds and personnel guarding it during his visit last night. Julian looked around at the church for a minute trying to convert his dad's drawings into a three-dimensional map he could superimpose on the view he had in front of him.

"Okay, well... it's hard to see if everything matches up exactly due to the darkness but I can see enough. Although I have to say dad, I can sense a lot of people in there... a lot of people like you and the Priest."

"I see...well it's good then that I'm the type to over-prepare for everything."

"True...but I just wish I could sense Aeryn... Where the hell is he keeping her?!" Julian's frustration was obvious and his dad tried to relax him be reaffirming their plan.

"Son don't worry, we'll get her away from him, we just need to follow the plan like we discussed. For some reason I've always been good at strategic planning. I'm sure he'll be keeping her in one of the three buildings on the top right of the map. They're the nun's dormitories, each one with a capacity of five. The individual rooms that look from the outside are like readymade prisons. If I was going to hold people against their will, that's where I would do it. Once we've dealt with the four guarding the outside areas we'll reassess how to proceed."

"Okay then, I'll go to my start position and wait for your signal. Dad... I really hate cemeteries. I wish you could have picked a different place for me to break into, you know I've had a phobia ever since the Thriller video." François smiled, he saw that Julian had relaxed enough to start making jokes. It filled him with confidence ahead of what was going to be a very dangerous night for them.

"Well I just thought that if you were man enough to start having girlfriends and pick fights with strangers then a few zombies would be no trouble."

"For the tenth time, I was defending a helpless women."

"Yeah yeah, if you say so hero boy." François pulled out from his bag a smaller more portable rucksack and handed it to Julian. "All your supplies are in there so don't lose it or leave it behind. I'll give you ten minutes to get in place then I'll give the signal. Okay?"

"Yep okay, ten minutes got it."

In the absence of light, Julian set off across the road, his pupils already large and adjusted to the night. Running at as fast a pace as was possible while remaining quiet, he followed the one storey high wall towards its end. Every step that he connected to pavement with anything more than ninja like subtlety produced audible sounds into the eerie vacuum of silence that had become of this residential area. His heart beat slow and steady, relaxed in its calcified cage... Julian was confident in his father's plan and did not pause until he reached the wall's end. And it was there he found the start of wire fencing that reached far above Julian's six-foot plus frame. The fencing was meshed in pattern and black in colour, its job was protecting the church cemetery form the unwanted access of grave robbers, not that there had been such a case in the last 40yrs. But the church grounds were over 60yrs old and although had several modern touches to it, this fencing like many of its other architectural structures was born of another time and in conflict with its surroundings...even within the battlefield itself there was a jostling for supremacy.

Julian, unfazed by the fence, looked above to its top and his adventurous nature made him fantasise about climbing it. After all he was far stronger and more agile then before, it wouldn't take long... but that was not the plan. His father knew that this approach would make too much noise and the quiet was their most important ally at this point. Julian took off the rucksack and opened its main zipper. He took out the wire cutters his father had instructed him to use. They were of good quality and made quick work of the fencing, not before long a rough circle with the circumference to fit even two grown men was cut. Julian, slightly crouched, entered. He genuinely didn't like cemeteries, and this one did nothing to alleviate those sentiments. In the dark its vastness was exaggerated, appearing to stretch out endlessly. Only the fact that he'd seen it during the day kept him composed. Julian had to travel to the front-gated entrance; the distance was no more than fifty metres from where he was crouched. Though appropriately dressed in lightweight trainers, fitted sportswear deep-sea ocean dark in colour, his movements were slow and sluggish as if his clothing were made of lead. He knew that this was due to a paralysing fear in him he could feel just under the surface. He moved slowly in its blackness, making sure to avoid the tombstones that would only make themselves visible at inopportune moments. Frustratingly for him, all the soil beneath his feet was firm and undistinguishable from a grave. Julian would have to walk a good thirty metres over potential graves before reaching the stone pebbled path. This made him very uneasy but he had no choice but to press on. Each step closer to his destination was accompanied by meandering thoughts of whose brother, sister, mother or father's grave could he be walking on. In the past his disenchantment and lack of a life direction would have made him callous and indifferent to such sentiments. Now Julian felt connected to this world, to its people, its beliefs and its future. He knew now of a place beyond this one, of beings existing outside the human condition. Both of which although ethereal were not at all like those found in any religious teaching taught to the millions of this planet's dwellers. In his past, though ignorant and most needing of it. he had no faith. But now, even knowing the contradictory truth that what lay beyond this world had more faith than ever, he drew from that reservoir and put aside his concerns knowing that the mission at hand was more important than everything else.

After a few minutes Julian had made it to the pebbled path. A few steps after that, to the main gate that lead into the church grounds. This is where he was to wait for his father's signal. On the other side of the gate he could see a two-storey building; its brick walls looked grey in colour and were exactly where his father had drawn it on the map. He wasn't sure if it had existed at the time he left for France when looking at the map, but now that he was only meters from it, he was certain that it wasn't there before... Had it been constructed in the 4 months he'd been away? Could it be where Aeryn was being held? Though all the windows were blacked out when he focused on the building he could sense the presence of many beings like the priest and his father. This ability, born that fateful day attending the church mass, was still un-mastered, so it would take him a while to get an exact number. It felt to him like trying to use sonar without yet being able to keep the frequency of the signal stable. Maybe once mastered he'd be able to switch to the frequency Aeryn was on. He dared not let himself drift to thoughts of Aeryn's wellbeing... the pain would be a distraction he couldn't afford. After a while Julian began wondering why his dad had not yet given him the agreed signal. He looked at his watch, the glow in the dark hands of his stainless steel chronograph time piece indicated that the arranged 10 minutes had long since passed. He also realised that the whole time he'd been staring into this section of the quiet unlit church ground he hadn't seen the guard that his dad had said would be patrolling this area. He took a second and tried to focus his life force sonar on finding him... There was nothing... He scanned further and though sensing at least half a dozen more Other Ones, they were all indoors bar one. They all seemed to be stationary inside the upstairs areas of the main church... This was odd and very unsettling for Julian... Zooming in closer to the life force signatures, he analysed for any slight subconscious displays of telling mannerisms. There was only the calm stated posturing of an expectant host. The signal that remained outside was near the location his father was supposed to be stationed at when giving the signal. Julian's mind sped up as he tried to quickly deduce what was going on and how to proceed... Without being certain, from this distance he assumed that the signal must have been his father's, who maybe had noticed the lack of guards patrolling too and was unsure what the next move should be. The one thing that was clear to Julian at this point was that proceeding along their own routes like originally planned wasn't wise and that they should regroup and formulate a new plan of attack. At the exact moment that thought was completed, he felt the life force signal start to move in his direction. After it had travelled fifty meters or so he was able to recognise it as François. "Okay father's got the same idea too," he thought with relief and began nimbly climbing over the gate, paying slightly less care with how much noise he was making. Once over, his eyes quickly scanned the new field of vision looking for his father's silhouette... The moon's pearl-coloured gleam would have normally helped him see, but it was obscured by a passing cloud... Julian focused harder; he knew he had to be there... He could sense his life force approaching him even if he couldn't confirm it by sight. The main church stood to his left - tall, cold and lurching over him unsympathetic to his mission. He remained calm as he waited to see his father, they needed to reassess the situation and quickly, as Aeryn was waiting for him... Finally there he was, or at least his shadowy outline. Julian could notice from his walk that he was tired for some reason.... He was dragging his feet and arms like a primate. Julian took a few extra steps forward to get a clearly picture, on the fourth step forward he froze completely. He looked at the hunched man in front of him… the man's breathing was deep, his height was off, clothing blooded and torn. "WHO ARE YOU?!" Julian said assertively at the man emerging from the night. The strange man didn't respond, Julian instinctively took up a defensive combat stance. "Answer me!" he yelled, forgetting where he was and that going unnoticed for as long as possible was a main part of their mission. His heart began pumping blood frantically to all his limbs as the fight or flight mechanism auto engaged. The stranger with dragging feet and swaying arms started advancing. Julian's mind was sharp and he listened out for any other approaching bodies anticipating a possible ambush. His eyes dotted their gaze to every part of this man that could conceal a weapon, on both accounts he was safe. They were alone out here in the dark but this blood covering this man's torn v neck jumper was not his own. He had to find his father, maybe he was in trouble, and he closed his eyes and scanned for his father's signature. "He's here? But where??' Julian thought, as François' life force was presenting itself as being right in front of him. "I don't understand! Where??" He scanned the nearby surroundings again and again each time more desperately than the last, but the answer never changed, his father was in front of him... and then the penny dropped. It wasn't his father he was sensing but his life force... a life force that was being emitted from the blood splattered on the man's clothes. Julian lost all the strength in his body...why was his father's blood all over this man? Before his heart could brave answering that, the strange man said in a voice deep in tone and a texture full of malice.

"Julian... Master says these are your options; one is to follow the path of vengeance that goes through me and into the church where hate lives, a body rests and The Other One awaits. Two is to pursue the path of hope into the new construct where love exists, bodies writhe, and your other one's a fake. Or third is to negate your free will, succumb to fear & sadness and let his will become your fate." Julian still numb, didn't say a word... The bloodied man from the shadows continued, "Whatever your choice... all paths will end in ten... whether Hope, Vengeance or Subjugation, minutes is all that is left..."

Chapter 18

*****

Stay strong Julian... I feel that your anger and fear are fighting for control and on the brink of overflowing. If I could choose where to turn to next, look without hesitation for your father I would. Your pain is seeping through the walls of this place and I don't like the colour it paints. If hands were extensions of my will I would clean it away from here and from your heart. Stay strong Julian... This new person standing in front of you has laid out options constrained by time. My mind, already a riddle in itself, cannot decipher the meanings of his words. I will focus, as you must, to stop the Priest's darkness from consuming all. The chains of my realm have more slack now, I can get closer... but they are still present. Although they hold me back from anything resembling tactile contact, they loosen and rust... degrading like our situation. But like inversion - the result could be opposite.

*****

In a nearby building to Julian, a woman of god is being held. Her knees, heart and mind worn from forced intimacy and undeserved blows. She's waiting for him...her time is short and her spirit fragile. Her guard, though also female and not present for the original inflictions of pain, has been the most prominent aggressor ever since the receipt of her orders. The guard and the master, singular and unified in motive, have regenerated a bond older than their time on earth. The guard, though curvaceous in ratios, stands over her silently intimidating with knuckles bloody from previous statements made to her captive. Both pairs of eyes wait...one weak, timid and desperate the other...strong, fierce and patient. All paths will end in ten.

In the large, imposing main church building to his left is the one whose manipulations and instigations have brought about this pain, this anger and this rising desire for retribution. That man of pseudo white collar is not alone... followers, soldiers all prepared for martyrdom have residence there too, and in this place the body of a father rests. With each breath that The Other One takes the wrongs he has done are not corrected, the world is not safe and its end is his to make. All paths will end in ten.

The Other One had put his final plan into motion... which path would Julian take? Julian could feel…his focus returning, and with it the warmth of feeling back to his limbs. He started to think quicker than ever before, more efficiently than ever before; his awakened powers automatically activating more and more faculties. Julian's mind now sharp like a blade of deduction started deciphering the strange man's message and formulated plans of his own. "…This man in front of me is not the real threat. He's just the messenger sent to make me lose my composure. But he has my father's blood on him, he knows where he is. The first option that he gave explains this to me as the path of vengeance. Telling me that the Priest is there in the church with my father. He chose his words carefully, using 'vengeance' and the phrase 'a body rests' to imply the worst- another tactic to unsettle me with rage. But I know that my dad is alive." During these few seconds Julian was taking to unravel the Priest's message, the blood spattered messenger stood there gently swaying from side to side with the whites of his eyes eerily reflecting the moon as his gaze stayed fixed on Julian. He was waiting for Julian's answer. Julian, recalling to mind all he learned in the hours of sweat drenched training and self-imposed meditative discipline during those four months in France, was comfortable with the distance between. But he knew that the messenger's talk of all paths ending in ten was significant and most likely signified how long he had to decide on and complete whatever plan he came up with. The quiet of the night, tension and suspense intensified all around like an invisible compressive force, yet still Julian was relaxed. His mind worked at inhuman speeds whilst remaining still like a secluded lake before the dawn. Thoughts of water had become the key to these abilities, they reminded him of the place where he found them... the place where he was reunited with his mum... the moment that made him realise the truth of his love to her and the power of his bond with her. Water is both fragile and Strong, limiting yet endless... changeable in its form without ever losing its essence. This was the truth of his love, the truth of his bond, the truth of his faith the truth of his strength.

All paths were ending in ten. Julian had to continue at pace, and he did. His mind a blade, continued to slice through the message exposing its truths. "The second option is less obvious. He knows I'm here for Aeryn. That's what he means by hope and love. But what does *my* 'other one's a fake' mean? The only people connected to me that the Priest has met are my dad and Aeryn. Could it be someone from my school? The wording implies a person I have a substantial bond with but who is not who I think they are? There's no one else here tonight that I care about for such a thing to be true. A mere distraction then... It's clear from 'new construct' that the place where Aeryn is being held is that new building I saw earlier. 'Bodies writhing' means that there are others in there too in need of help. Aeryn's plight is also suggested by those same words. I will not let her pain continue longer than it needs to. Father Bachinger will pay twice over for any suffering of hers." Julian's focus came back to the man in front of him, he knew what he had to do. "Father Bachinger thought that my resolve would collapse because ten minutes is only enough time to save one of them. Either I chose Aeryn or my father." Julian knew that whatever his choice, this messenger would not let him pass without interfering, he'd seek to use up as much of those ten minutes as possible. He was guilty of his own crimes too. Julian took a forward step… Despite the uncertainty of his and his father's relationship in the past, one thing had always been true and constant. To hurt anyone in this family was unforgivable… He took another forward step, the messenger unfazed didn't react. Julian allowed his rage to return slowly, its burning heat to rise to the surface where he could harness the strength of its flames and coat his fists with it. This tide of anger wasn't the only feeling in his heart… there was also guilt… "Aeryn…I'm sorry I left you here with him… I should have been there to protect you… You were there for me when *I* needed… I should have seen this coming… I'll make up for it somehow Aeryn… this I promise on my life. Please hold on I'm coming." He used these feelings as extra motivation, they fanned the flames to burn hotter. Julian was only a meter away from the blood-spattered messenger now, but he was yet to react to his advances. At this proximity Julian could see in his eyes that he was not normal of mind. There was craziness in his eyes and his body, though broad and muscular, was unsteady and occasionally shook like that of a drug addict. At this distance the night could no longer conceal what was a thick barbed wire around his neck. Countless scabs and sores were present on the skin beneath it… Fresh and dried blood streaks were trailing down his neck. Julian didn't want to understand what this was or what this meant because he knew it was just another sadistic part of the Priest's plan. His fists were now white hot with anger and dense with the desire for revenge. Julian deepened his breathing to allow more oxygen in for fuel, the fierce determination in his soul was expressed across his face as he stared at the messenger. With a tone of impending violence in his voice he said directly to him, "You say I have ten minutes to save either Aeryn or my dad..? That I have to choose who to let die? FATHER BASCHINGER!!! YOU UNDERESTIMATE MY SPEED!!!"

With that war cry Julian exploded off the ground, lunging forward with closed fists at super human velocity; every ounce of his body weight expertly thrown forward and channelled into his right hand. He aimed to deal with this strange messenger in one blow. The messenger did not have time to react, his crazed eyes not even able to blink in response. Julian's enraged fist landed with the force of three men onto his opponent's jaw. It lifted him off the ground, sending him into a spin that hurtled him back five meters before crashing into the concrete ground that was waiting to greet him without mercy. The thud of his body hitting the ground was the only sound audible in the church grounds. He lay there motionless, Julian's nature made him want to check to make sure he was still breathing, but that thought was brief and could not stand up against the mortal threat he and his loved ones were under. He had no time to waste and prepared himself for his next move. Father Bachinger, even with his reawakening as The Other One, had limited power and could not foresee the changes Julian would undergo while away. His plan it seemed was not going to be able to withstand the new Julian's drive to save his father and friend.

Julian decided that he would go to Aeryn's aid first, as he wanted to save encountering Father Bachinger for last. He too did not know what potential changes the Priest had undergone while he was away, and so going after Aeryn would probably be more time efficient. Plus his father being also from this other world would surely not be helpless, he should be better equipped to wait just a little longer. With that reconciling thought he turned around to face the new building where Aeryn and probably several others were captive. On his earlier scan of the building he had sensed many people in there that had the same life energy as his dad and the Priest. Knowing now that most likely there were captives in there too made him realise that his powers were limited to perceiving those from the Realm Above The Heavens and he could not sense human life energy. Eight minutes remained, Julian had to press on. He burst into his fastest sprint, yet heading straight for that new building where he could feel the threat of dozens emanating from it. Threats he knew he would have to neutralise to achieve his goal. In the quiet of the night his urgency was loud. In mere seconds he was there at the buildings only open entrance. He was being taunted, invited to enter at his own peril. Without hesitation he did. Once inside, the building felt oddly warm considering that this ground floor was empty and pitch black. He could make out the shapes of walls and possible rooms, his ocular faculties also improving beyond human levels. It was like his abilities were growing and flourishing in response to his desires, his drive and his mission. They didn't feel alien anymore; they now strangely had the familiarity of someone he knew… someone he'd always known. This scene he had stepped into was set up seemingly to draw his attention to the stairway on the far right. It was leading upstairs and quietly glowing with dim lighting… gently suggesting to him the path he had to take. But he already knew this from the multiple threats he could sense coming from above him. He was close enough to them to map their exact location. There were thirteen of the Priest's soldiers, most positioning in a way that implied the layout of the floor above if he assumed that each of them were guarding a room. Probably with a captive or two inside each, but there was one section of that floor above that had two soldiers standing very close together… "Must be a particularly high value prisoner in the room they're guarding. it could only be Aeryn… it's definitely Aeryn.' He quickly decided to go straight for her room and to deal with as many of these Other Ones as possible on his way. To free her from her suffering, punish anyone he knew to have laid a hand on her, then on his way out finish off any left behind as he freed the other captives.

He readied himself, knowing that these Other Ones may look human but this was only a shell, they were not human at all. They would not be as easy to subdue as the messenger, and he should not hold back even an ounce of his strength or entertain thoughts of mercy, as they would show him none. One way or another they were all guilty of hurting Aeryn... Julian's fists still burned hot with anger. The boy he was before would have been consumed by such emotion, but the man he was now could channel it and use it to express his will. Seven and a half minutes remained. Julian ran to the stairway and jumped up off one leg, driving the knee of his other leg upwards for maximum propulsion. Repeating this twice, he scaled the entire stairway in two Olympic grade hops. He landed onto both feet, breaking himself and rotating his body left. He saw two paths, both long corridors- one straight ahead, the other ninety degrees to his left. Both paths were filled with the presence of those he sensed before, of those standing between him and Aeryn. Their eyes all turned towards him, they seemed pleased to see him... They had been expecting him and were patiently waiting for his arrival. His earlier deduction was right they were each standing outside a sealed room. Down the bottom of the left corridor were two guards by the last room... Aeryn's room. Upon seeing that, the other path in front of him became a blur, his focus intensifying on Aeryn's room. The Other Ones seemed to anticipate this and all took up hostile stances, revealing their concealed weapons in the process. Bats and blades of different shapes and sizes were being held tightly... Julian's concern rose, but more for Aeryn and his father then himself as he realised this would take more time than he wanted. The corridor was narrow, barely allowing for two men to stand side by side. It was poorly lit, lessening any gleam from metallic weapons. Each one of the men stood facing Julian were dressed in fitted clothing that showed off there warrior physiques and battle scars. It made him wonder what exactly these men had been doing in their lives before this... before the Priest. Their undaunted postures and bared arms were simultaneously a warning and challenge to Julian. Father Bachinger was taunting him, asking if he could really save Aeryn? "Yes I can, just watch me!" Julian affirmed out loud, baring his pride and fury as he rushed forward into the narrow corridor of battle to face his most dangerous test yet. Seven minutes were left.

Chapter 19

****

Julian… Outcome is all that matters, do as you must… The outcome of their lives is most important, feel as you must… The fear of what lies ahead, should you fail, is subdued by the belief that you will succeed. Only its end is enough.

I have heard of monsters, I've heard of demons… Your earth refers to them greatly. I fear that those in front of you will be demons and monster, but most of all I fear that you of good family and morality will have to regress… become less for you to be able to withstand this test. I will not stop reaching out to your plane, my time as observer has been too long. Now the very family that I have been watching and growing to understand is at risk of leaving my sight. This will not do, I will extend myself as far as possible. The need is great in your time, his time and her time. I must do more than that which is capable in my time. I must feel more and be more than this. These chains are fallible; you are the one who shows me this Julian.

Outcome is all that matters. I do as you must… The outcome of their lives is most important, I feel as you must. The fear of what lies ahead, should I fail, is subdued by the belief that I will succeed. Only my beginning is enough.

****

Rushing forward in the dim lighting Julian decided to try to gauge the strength of the Other Ones first, aiming to engage one and then, from what he could assess, decide how to tackle the rest of them. They still didn't respond to his advances, standing there guarding their assigned rooms in a zig-zag pattern, the closest standing to his right and the second to his left. He quickly approached the first, planting his left foot into the ground hard, ready to shift his body weight and momentum into his right fist. He wanted to put more into this punch than he did against the messenger but not so much as to lose balance and leave himself open to a counter attack, especially from an armed opponent. He was careful to account for the proximity of the narrow corridor wall beside him as he threw his first punch. His knuckles crashed powerfully across his adversary's jaw! Resisting the temptation to lead instantly into a second punch with his left, he held for a reaction. Julian's eyes widened with surprise, the foe was unmoved and grinning behind the fist that was still pressed against his jaw. It was clear that he had willingly let himself take the hit… This was his test, he was gauging Julian's strength before deciding how to proceed… how they would all proceed. Julian took a quick step back, keeping one eye on his opponent's right hand, which was clasping a six inch blade. He hastily scanned through the zig-zag of adversaries to make sure they hadn't yet decided to join in. They hadn't… he had time to think… Just as he had done against the two men in France, Julian recalled teachings learned from the hundreds of hours he spent studying the philosophies of the martial arts and the strategies or war. '*Of old the expert in battle would first make himself invincible and then wait for his enemy to expose his vulnerability. Invincibility depends on oneself; vulnerability lies with the enemy.*' He took up a strong defensive position and watched for movement. '*The expert, in getting the enemy to make his move, shows himself, and the enemy is certain to follow. He baits the enemy, and the enemy is certain to take it. In so doing, he moves the enemy, and lies in wait for him with his full force.*' He understood this was the best plan of attack. He would move as though his failure to damage his target had deterred him from a full frontal assault on his enemies. Instead he decided to rely on his speed and run through the small gaps between them hoping that the unexpectedness of his actions would get him passed them and to his goal with as little injury as possible. This would bait his enemy into predictable lateral attacks that he would intercept with full force. This time Julian prepared to be unreserved in his violence; their movements would be dictated by his - which in his head meant that their chances of landing a counter were zero.

Julian glanced at the gap between the first and second opponent, planting the seed in both men that he was considering it as his only option. This plan had to be executed perfectly… Timing was everything. He shuffled slowly to his left a few inches. The movement obvious enough for it to be registered in the minds of his ravenously gazing enemies, yet subtle enough to not arise suspicion of a trap. The second opponent switched a thick, worn out bat he was holding to his left hand, he'd taken the bait. Julian was pleased but knew a wrong move would mean he would meet his end. Six minutes were left.

Julian burst forward, heading straight for the gap between them like an NFL running back at a crack in a defensive line. Almost instantly the two men respond, their reflexes even better than Julian predicted. They adjusted their stances in preparation for him, with the second enemy coming forward to close the gap available for Julian to pass through. The first to his right raised his blade, Julian could sense that it' was being aimed at his shoulder. The second positioned his bat at a lower angle, an angle that when swung would connect with his left thigh. "They may be fast and powerful but they're aim is sloppy," he thought. Just as Julian was about to pass between them, they attacked! Their combined response to his charge sealed their fate. Their momentum was now trapped in decisions Julian had instigated in them, and movements he had predicted of them. Julian swiftly ducked the first's attempt to stab him while simultaneously stopping the second's swing of his bat, by grabbing his wrist with the vice like grip of his left hand. The second's decision to switch the hand he was holding his bat in was the critical mistake because it meant he was using is weaker arm to attack… It was inaccurate, slow and easily stopped in its tracks. The first's wild predicted swing of his knife had left an opening, his mid-section was completely vulnerable and exposed. While still holding the seconds arm and crouched under the first's swing Julian could now intercept both men with full devastating force. In a blink of an eye, Julian smashed the first's ribs with his right elbow, the force sending him into and almost through the corridor wall. Then using the reaction forces from that elbow contact to propel his fist, immediately he threw a merciless punch at the second's temple! The enemies left arm was caught and his right arm was too far away to cover the distance and retaliate. The punch landed with a loud crack that echoed through the corridor and the minds of all those in it. The punch so well practised it was at the point of perfection, the enemy's head bounced off the wall leaving a skull shaped dent in it. They were both defeated and incapacitated, the first slumped on the ground to Julian's right and the second limp and lifeless only being kept from the floor by virtue of Julian still holding onto his wrist. Julian never let it go… instead he stared at the rest of The Other Ones in the corridor, while emanating a fierce animosity he knew they could perceive. He wanted to warn them of his strength, of his determination, that this would be how they would all end up if they got in the way of him saving Aeryn and his father.

To his surprise they all just kept standing there, not saying a word or moving from their posts. They carried the demeanours of persons who weren't surprised… It was disconcerting to Julian. It was as though they had expected him to beat those first two men… If so, then surely their best option was to join in the fight to prevent that from happening? It was an important question but there was not the time available to find its answer. Julian was in a race against time, he dreaded to speculate what kind of suffering was being imposed on Aeryn and his father for every second that he let pass. He had to get to the end of that corridor quickly. Julian still in control of his rage, continued forward down the path of violence.

In the next minutes that passed, a fierce and violent battle raged. The walls, sealed doors, ceiling lights were all at the mercy of his enmity. Julian was using all his acquired skills and knowledge to defeat his enemies, each one he engaged was stronger than the last, but with each Julian's fighting became more devastating. And with each attack combination he used, heads were being smashed through walls, punches were breaking bones and gravity-defying throws left opponents bodies battered and internally bleeding. Julian, though his defence was strong, had still taken some damage being cut and contused several times by an array of brutal weaponry, fortunately not in any vital areas. Despite their inhuman fighting strength, Julian couldn't get over how poor their fighting techniques were. Their attacks often wild - were never close to hitting such an agile target like him in any life threatening areas. His clothes now bloody with his and his enemy's wounds were also being gradually torn off his back. He was more than half way down the corridor, getting ever closer to Aeryn's room. In a rare momentary respite he decided to rip off the rest of his now not-so-fitted t-shirt and continue the fight in his singlet. He was frustrated; he didn't understand why they wouldn't just attack in more than just groups of two? The way of fighting they had chosen was so inefficient, he could get through them much faster if they all just attacked together. He knew that he had the beating of them even though their strength grew the closer he got to her room. Julian felt he could just delve deeper and deeper into his reservoir of inexplicable fighting prowess. Yes, he had spent those four months training himself into peak physical condition but he could feel that it was not all just from his own hard work or the enhanced abilities he gained that day in church, there were other forces at play…other forces within him he could not yet identify. Julian, remembering that there were probably also other people suffering just like Aeryn and his father behind each of the doors he fought past, went into a deeper level of focus and intensity, doubling his haste! Flying at each of his remaining opponents with surgical precision and perfect power, he despatched them all in half the time it took him to get through the first batch. Now only two remained, the two guarding her room. He took a second to get his breath back, his legs felt heavier than when the fight started. It seemed that last burst took more out of him then he expected. In truth this was the first time he had felt any form of fatigue in a long time… it was strange, but an important reminder that he wasn't without weakness, and a level of concern for his own wellbeing was still important. Four minutes were left.

Julian stood tall and imposing, his breathing returning to normal. He was about to make his move until he was stunned into waiting by the sound of one of their voices. Not a single one before had said a word to him, they just fought like savage animals conversing instead with their fists and weapons. The voice came from the slightly taller of the two, it said, "You finally made it… but why so slow? It's not like the couple in there have all the time in the world?" His choice of words were peculiar, was he just trying to antagonise him into attacking them foolishly? That wouldn't work, Julian knew that they would be the strongest of all the enemies he had faced so far and had to be cautious. Plus, what did he mean by 'the couple'? Was Aeryn in there with somebody else? Was his father in there two?? No, he would have sensed his life energy through the door if he were. This was just more tactics to fluster and make him lose his composure. Julian responded with, "Your Priest really thinks I'm still an immature boy, doesn't he?"

"He is no Priest, such a title is beneath our master. He, the almighty Other One formally of the Whole One, will deal with you and this earth soon enough, returning us back to RATH."

"RATH...? Oh, that's that place I've heard so much about from my father, that place where you guys are from. Sorry to disappoint, but you two are going nowhere tonight." Julian not wanting to waste another second indulging in Father Bachinger's mind games prepared to fight. To his surprise they didn't respond to his readjustments by entering their own fighting stances. Just then he was taken aback by the sight of both adversaries being bare handed. They weren't armed like the rest... this troubled Julian, were they really here to guard this room? Or did they think they could stop him without the aid of blades and blunt objects? He thought inquisitively, unsure of the answers but still not having the time to wait for their reveal. In any circumstance, his goal would remain the same. Proceed forward to her he must, he'd left her waiting long enough... time to start making up for leaving and not being there to protect her. Julian scanned them and his surroundings a last time, formulating the fastest way to incapacitate them. "Their guards are down, they do not take me seriously, even after watching me beat all their comrades close to death... Something isn't right here... but she's waiting." Julian attacked! Having recovered from the previous exertions, he was moving just a fast as before and with a lighting fast combination of knee strikes, uppercuts and straights he'd dropped both enemies to their knees. Before he could finish them off, they both collapsed into unconsciousness. Julian thought out loud while staring down at his vanquished foes, "They're weaker than the others..." He was perplexed. "...Why have the weakest at the end? Why have such pitiful fighters guarding her? Did he not think I would make it this far? Is that how little he thinks of her??" His questions though important were not a priority right now.

He calmed his mind and let the realisation that he'd finally made it to her fill him up with happiness, a happiness he hadn't felt since back in France and in love's embrace. This lead him to thoughts of Sina... the beautiful dark skinned woman whose edginess and strength had helped him grow. The woman he had started falling for and had to part with. Julian had not let himself think about her in any real way since he left. Maybe out of sadness from missing her? Or the guilt he felt for leaving suddenly without a good explanation..? Or that his complicated feelings for Aeryn made him feel that he was somehow being unfaithful..? He didn't know, but all of this combined with the fear, anger and immense relief he was feeling brought an emotional swell that was difficult to contain. He could feel his eyes begin to water, he wiped them quickly. He had no intention of letting Aeryn see him crying like a little boy, especially about things that were trivial in comparison to what she had probably been through, the kind of things that truly warranted the tears of pain. Julian noticed that the door keeping her from him was not like the others, it wasn't sealed in any visible way. He tried the door handle and the door moved. "It's not locked?!' he thought in surprise. Butterflies filled his stomach and his heart rate rapidly rose... He pushed it open slowly, scared of what state he was going to see her in. It opened fully and the light from the corridor crawled into the room. It then met the flickering lights of several candles whose wax structures had almost melted to their end. Julian's eyes were drawn to the left corner of the room, there were three bodies there. He stepped completely into the room letting himself be engulfed by the nervous tension within it. Two of the bodies were seated on the floor with their backs up against the wall. They were male, badly wounded and bleeding out onto the grey concrete floor. He could hear that one of them was still breathing... it was quiet and muffled, but audible. Julian looked at the third body that was lying flat, face down on the hard concrete. His heart almost stopped at the realisation that it was a woman, her clothes dark in colour and torn as if from a violent struggle. He feared the worst... He approached her body slowly, hoping for any signs of life. There was no blood coming from her body that he could see, but the blood from the others had spread out and was close to touching her where she lay. He was now standing over her, his knees weak and almost hollow from fear... so frightened was he that he didn't even realise the repeated whispering of, "Please be okay... Please be okay." Julian bent down slowly, making sure to avoid the spreading blood, and put his hands on her shoulder. Her hair was full, messy and spread wide so it covered her face. Her body was so petite and feminine... just how he remembered hers being... His eyes watered and tears fell from them onto the back of her motionless head. They were absorbed by her dark brown mane, like tears landing on the cold earth of a loved one's grave, his heart breaking off into pieces with each one. Julian, gathering every ounce of emotional strength he could, turned her over slightly revealing her face... The tears continued to stream down his face and into his mouth, giving him the savoury taste of the unsavoury. He closed his eyes in an attempt to stem their flow... seeing it, he was sickened by how bruised and swollen it was. Julian started feeling the rage that had died down begin to come back more ferociously than ever, he clenched his jaw so hard he almost shattered his teeth. He looked over at the blood-drained man that was still breathing and noticed that his clothing matched that of the other guards. "He's one of them," he thought, with a killer's intent, his anger now rapidly coming to a boil. This Other One's proximity to death must have been why he never sensed his life force through the door. Julian, shaking with adrenaline, would not let him go through death's door so easily... He had to answer first... answer the question responsible for his emotional turmoil. Julian put her down gently and respectfully, still staring at the man he noticed that he was now conscious, his journey to death disturbed by Julian's presence. "He *Will* answer my question..." Julian thought with piercing resolve. He then grimaced, inhaling deeply through his nose before screaming at the top of his voice, "WHERE IS AERYN???!!!!!"

… Three minutes were left.

Chapter 20

***

Am I too close now..? Not escaped, still trapped but stretching out enough to feel the walls. Why would such a thing exist? I don't know if it's only a portion of what is flowing through your human body or the fullness of it but, it's black and its sensations are unbalancing to the mind. Its sensations make everything that I am feeling unwanted. It makes me want to not be able to think, not want to be able to be, not want anything but it all to cease. Is this pain? Why would such a thing exist? What could be the **why** of it? Is this what is waiting for me should I leave? Maybe better to be sheltered in ignorance than to have this poison, this human gift. What if I am mistaken… What if this is not pain I feel in my emptiness but just maturation into everything that I am? I cannot fear the changes… He does not…I have been with them since my beginning and will not stop now. Everything that I am will be everything that they need. From here I am nothing, but from there I can be anything.

The battle you fought was great… You came out still the person I have always observed even if covered in the dirt and scars of consequences. Your strides may shorten and you may stumble at moments, but do not let the pain subdue you into madness… Though the Priest's darkness will be complete soon, my faith I place in you. Do not let your guilt slow you into sadness… Move forward and I will too, find The Nun, find the father, and I will you.

***

The dying guard's face contorted at the impact of Julian's scream, the travelling decibels passed through him painfully and elevated him to a slightly higher level of lucidity "TELL ME WHERE SHE IS?!" Julian's screams continued, reverberating around the walls of the room before echoing down the corridor through the open door. He recognised the face he had seen but it was not Aeryn's. It was that of the nun, the one that had been sheepishly and silently standing in Father Bachinger's office the day they had met for the first time. The sight of that poor, dead and beaten woman laid out on the floor like yesterday's trash terrified him right to his insides. He feared that this would be Aeryn's fate, that his inability to make the right decisions would result in her death. How could he let that happen? She was the one who originally ignited the light of hope and faith in his soul and deserved better than such a horrific and miserable end. "IF YOU DON'T TELL ME RIGHT NOW, I PROMISE ON MY MOTHER'S SOUL THAT I WON'T LET YOUR SUFFERING END QUICKLY! I'LL MAKE EACH OF THE LAST LITTLE BITS OF BREATH YOU HAVE LEFT IN YOUR LUNGS THE HARDEST YOU'VE EVER BREATHED. I WILL BRING YOU FULLY BACK TO THIS PLANE KICKING AND SCREAMING WITH EVERY BONE I BREAK BEFORE SENDING YOU BACK INTO THE UNKOWN ABYSS OF DEATH. I PROMISE, I DON'T CARE WHAT STUPID OTHER REALM YOU'RE FROM BUT HERE, RIGHT NOW, I'M THE ONE IN POWER SO ANSWER ME!" Julian demanded, with veins throbbing in his neck, spit flying out his mouth and tears still glazing his eyes. The dying guard's eyes large from the shock were fearful… He had been unconscious for a while, so was unsure of what was going on. But with each of Julian's words his memory returned and he was starting to piece together what was happening and what the situation was. Julian now pausing to catch his breath and to hear the man's response had a moment to think. Though still in the epicentre of this emotional quake, he was having a strange out of body experience. Just for a moment he felt like he was looking down at himself… and he couldn't help but feel great sadness at his situation and of those around him. He also felt that his behaviour was just a bit strange… in that it was ever so slightly out of character… It was hard for him to pinpoint... but maybe it was in the words he used..? Or just how he used them..? After that moment passed and there was still no answer from the guard, his mind came rushing back to reality and was firmly placed back in the here and now of his dire predicament. Julian was just about to hurl a final tirade of words at the guard, but just before he could he heard the strain of blood muffled words come out of his mouth, "I'm so sorry... We never thought this would happen..."

"What? I don't understand...how could you not? YOU ARE ONE OF THEM."

"I'm so sorry... We just came back because we wanted to go home... He promised us we would..."

"Listen! I don't have time to hear this rubbish right now just tell me where to find Aeryn and I let you die in peace."

"Sorry I'm not making much sense... I guess dying isn't very conducive to good conversational skills...I take it you're that Julian guy? We've all been waiting for you... and now that I see you, it's strange... I can't see how you would be the one to stop us from getting back home..? Just another thing master lied to us about, I guess."

"SERIOUSLY."

"*Cough cough* okay okay, I don't have too much time either so I'll make this as quick as I can. I'll tell you everything I know, and hopefully you can do something good with it and I can start to redeem myself. Damn I've really fallen off the wagon, undoing all the years of hard work I put into my rehabilitation..." Julian, with his patience thread thin, just stared back at the man. "Listen carefully, this dead man sitting next to me is my friend, Anthony... sorry was my friend Anthony. We are as I'm sure you know Other Ones, we were sent to this building to guard Aeryn... When she came here she was already in a bad way, but we didn't say anything…I guess we just thought the rules of *his* rehabilitation program didn't matter anymore because we'd be going home soon with our master." Julian's face vexed with anger at what was just said and replied,

"Careful what you say… I can't guarantee I will let you finish your explanation if I hear her name again."

"Wow, that fire and determination… reminds me of our master during the first war… Strange… anyway just listen okay, what I'm telling you might help prepare you. The man you call Father Bachinger came into where me and Anthony were working about three months ago and spoke to us. I had just come back from my work placement in Paris… I was a broken man at that point… It's quite hard for an old soul like myself to get over an earth romance, especially stuck in a twenty-something's body. At first I thought myself lucky to be given such a young body to carry out my rehabilitation, but it definitely has its draw backs… years spent unable to feasibly move my life past college or University. *Cough* *Cough* *Cough* It's funny though, as I lay here bleeding out, how trivial that whole period seems now… especially after what I discovered about my love interest later. Anyway my mental state made me more receptive to him I guess… And somehow during that conversation he managed to give us back our memory, the memories of who he was, of the fact that we had not lost our master on that day of judgement but that he had been sent down here with us. And if that wasn't enough it seemed that recovering those memories of him had returned to us a portion of our former strength. We were so happy… We could barely believe it… My guess is the memory wipe was to make us all feel lost and without hope, to make us easier to control and more likely to follow the rehabilitation program as in our minds it was our only way back. But there he was, our master… The Other One, once of The Whole One. Back with us, sitting opposite and giving us a way back home. So young man know that even though he's not back to his full former self, his powers even considering they're still in a human shell, have grown considerably since that day. And all he needs to regain enough strength to return is firstly time then secondly you. Getting her back or your father is now close to impossible."

"Do you know where my father is??"

"*Cough cough*" he takes in one of his last few slow and wheezy breaths... "We all know, but you're missing the point, don't you understand yet? Look around you, what do you think this is? Why would he make it seem like she was here with that cryptic message and having all these guards here?" Julian's face turned to stone...He had just realised the truth of Father Bachingers plan. All of this, it was all just a way to buy time, to slow him down. Kidnapping his father was designed to half their strength and thinking power, plus allowing for his mission's path to branch out into two and doubling the time needed to execute it. The messenger and his message were riddled, not for the emotional distress or to conceal a particular truth, but to increase the time it would take him to decide on a path. Even the information contained in it was false. Knowing Julian would chose to save Aeryn first, he built this building in the opposite direction to him sending him even further away from his true goal. The Other Ones guarding it and the two placed in front of a particular room were just more bait that he got hooked on. The detail of the planned deception didn't end there... it was all the pieces falling into place and Julian could barely believe the breadth of his naivety. The way the guards held their position, not all attacking at once though they outnumbering him, just another method of stalling. A way of drawing out the battle for as long as possible. The sloppiness of their aim that too was part of the Priest's plan. They were only ever instructed to wound him enough to slow him down, nothing more. Julian was never meant to find Aeryn or his father in time; those ten minutes were for Father Bachinger to use and not him. Julian almost fell to the ground under the crushing weight of his disappointment in himself. How could he let this happen? Was this the best he could do after all those months of training and studying just to prepare himself for the day when he had to face him again? He felt that he had let down each of the individuals that had saved him from his personal despair and help reshape him into someone worthy of the love, faith and trust. I can see from that look on your face that you understand now what our master's done... I know you won't ever forgive him or us as we're an extension of him. But before I run out of time I want you to know that we were ordered to kill the lady that's laying here. But when we realised the true horrible scope of the master's plan; that it just wasn't simply to get us all home but to inflict as much crass and unnecessary damage to the earth and people you care about as possible, we refused to take part. We couldn't do it... We've both lost count of how long we've been imprisoned on this earth and in *his* program. Yes, sure there was a time when we would have done it without hesitation, a time when we viewed all existence as merely allowed to be on the whim of our master, but...I guess *his* program was working... During all those years we saw the fleeting fragility of human life, the individual uniqueness of it, gaining emotional attachments and formally forming bounds to your kind as well as seeing your immense capacity for good and evil. Yet despite the many reasons you create for war you still flew under the unified banner of one species, and in the vast majority existed together in peace under the understanding that you were once also originally of one whole. One God. It showed us that despite the differences we had with our other half's, if we learned from the best aspects of the human mentality to its own cxistence, even we could eventually be changed. Our very nature different and finally be able to return home, not as The Others but as just One, to exist not as two separate warring parts but coexist peacefully as a whole. But unfortunately that won't be the case for us... Even though we refused to murder the lady, we let some horrible things occur here and unlike your earth God, *he* is not so forgiving. It was at that point that those unreformed Other Ones you fought outside attacked us, battered Anthony to death, beat and strangled the lady until she stopped fighting back and stabbed me to within an inch of my life. Oh I almost forgot, I can tell that you're the hero type, so to stop you wasting more time you should know that all these other rooms are sadly another decoy…all the nuns and church ground workers being held there are all dead. The rooms were sealed in that elaborate way to slowly suffocate them. There is nothing left here for you. And so young man…I've told you everything I know, I hope you can use that information better than I did." Julian felt like saying something to the guard… something different to the abuse he had hurled at him previously, but nothing came out… He was just quiet. Lost in his shame, in his guilt and his doubt. He had a front row seat to the last seconds of life expiring out of a man that realised the truth too late to do anything about it. Was that also to be his fate? The quiet of death descended into the room, Julian dared not make a sound. Then after a few eerie seconds a voice from somewhere far away could be heard by Julian… What was it saying..? Julian closed his eyes and listened carefully… "What are you saying?" he thought, as he strained his hearing. He found it comforting to hear another voice in this helplessly lonely moment. Then all of a sudden he could hear it fully! It was clear as the day and loud as night thunder, it was shouting GET UP! YOU STILL HAVE TIME!! GET UP!! YOU STILL HAVE TIME!! The voice was electrifying! It jolted him out of apathy and self-pity. The red-hot blood of determination and un-forgiving drive was being pumped through his veins again! Being pumped by a heart almost beating its way out of his chest in anticipation, like a dog on a leash at the sight of open field after days of confinement. Julian knew his purpose was back, the man everyone had placed their faith in had returned. He walked out of the room, looked down the corridor and over the bodies he'd left sprawled about. One and a half minutes were left.

Julian decided quickly that the guards patrolling the other corridor of the upper floor were not going to come at him. He was certain they would attempt to keep up the ruse because they did not know that he knew the truth; that all the captives in those rooms were dead and that they were just standing there for show. With this understanding he focused all his attention on his next destination, the main church building. This was the location where he would find everyone that he'd been searching for, the place where the real final battle would begin. Julian sprinted down the corridor at a speed that vibrated the very walls surrounding him, all while effortlessly avoiding the bodies beneath him. He was down the stairs and out of the building before the other guards could even respond to his actions. His speed was blistering and his strength had grown again. It would seem that with every experience using his abilities he was mastering them more and more. In seconds he'd bursts through the back entrance to the main church hall. In that instant he could sense two very powerful life forces and one very weak one. Those first two were the strongest he'd sensed so far and one of them was instantly recognisable to him as Father Bachinger's. His life force was frighteningly strong and seemingly swelling like a river about to burst its banks. The second was familiar somehow but he couldn't pinpoint exactly why. The third weaker one Julian could tell was his fathers and it was waning like a torch losing its charge. But he has no time to be worried, he had to get to him as fast as he could and deal with whatever the situation was as he saw it. Entering the main church building he raced through the church aisle where he had once sat to observe mass, where Aeryn had once sat to speak to her sisters. A place that was once the heart of the church had become trapped in the belly of the beast. Julian almost blew all the pews and ornaments off their stands and hinges with the forces produced by his pace. He was up the stairs and in front of the Priest's office before the hall he just stormed through could settle back into silence. At this range there was no mistaking the individual strength of the life forces on the other side of the door. What awaited him in there was a test, the likes of which he could only hope to be ready for. But his courage would not let him entertain anything else but opening it, saving Aeryn and his father. With all his enhanced senses tuned to maximum sensitivity he put his hands on the door handle, turned it, pushed it open and walked in. This was the moment he'd been training for, the moment he'd been yearning for like an unrequited love. The milliseconds flowed slower than they ever have before… the time between arriving at his destination and the forward move into the fire, aged slower than the grapes of a thousand wines. Though still it came, and his time was ripe, his time was now… Disconcertingly, Julian's heroic advance into the breach was halted almost immediately by what he saw before him… or more precisely who he saw before him… In his disoriented shock he asked the person filling his gaze, "What are you doing here? Why are you here Sina?"

One minute and twenty seconds were left.

Chapter 21

**

Get up Julian! Your pain is hard to bear… but it's good to know she still lives. How did I not see the true evil of the Priest's plan? All I do is watch, yet I saw nothing. But I did feel something, my centre was off, slightly skewed… my balance not quite right. The feeling caused by the events unfolding around Julian, unravelling sequentially… blossoming into a blood red rose. It's customary to give such gifts… to a person of affection… a person intended for your attention. The Priest's bouquet had thorns and they hurt, each one hurting in specific ways. This latest one… who is she..? He called out Sina…I've heard Julian's words speak a million things and I now know the origins of each, but can't place the meaning of these. What new shape of thorn is she? How twisted is this bush of blood roses? The Priest knows that Julian is fighting this fight with his fists clenched… his grasp unable to prevent each one from penetrating…unable to see gift from curse. Entangled and trapped but you still have time. Get up Julian! And use that time, peel away the stems and step out. In the sun you'll bathe and as you rise so will I. Disorientated and encaged like thieves… but I will set you free as you have I.

**

"Hahahaha, that is amazing! Too much so! Hahahaha I can barely keep my composure it's sooo very good…Yes very nice… Hahahhaha!" Father Bachinger, dressed in his all black priestly robe and white collar as he always was, was a light with unbridled happiness, his usual eerie smile of a thousand sins had exploded into the murderous laughter of a fiend. Looking at the distress and pain in Julian's face as he saw her was almost too pleasurable for the Priest. Julian had inadvertently walked onto the stage he had carefully been building for him, the final act was about to begin and Father Bachinger was visibly vibrating in his twisted joy like an overwhelmed molecule.

"Is that all you have to say to your lover Julian? The woman who took you virginity? I hear that is quite a big thing?" Julian was frozen in confusion; even his mind was not agile enough to piece together this puzzle. He could feel his heart begin to creek under the strain of seeing her again… seeing her here, beside him. Julian forced his attention away from her for a moment and landscaped his view. Now he could see who the other silhouettes in the room belonged too, but his suffering wasn't lessened as all his sensory assumptions were confirmed. The Priest's office looked as it did the first time he was here looking for Aeryn all those months ago, only now missing the natural light of the sun. It seemed fate and irony were still close friends. The only difference was the bodies… They were all here… filling up the spaces around his cumbersome desk. He could only just about hold back the waters from streaming as he let himself identify each body, in front of the desk to his right and the Priest's left was his father. He was alive, kneeling down and looking at the floor. Was this due to a shame he felt for not being able to protect his son from all of this? Or a symptom of his wounds..? Blood was soaked into the dark green carpet beneath him, his clothes ripped and ruined from his fight with the messenger who had captured him. Julian was now regretting having held back against him earlier. This confirmed that the weak life force he had sensed earlier was his fathers. He resisted the temptation to call out to his father, he didn't want to give the Priest the satisfaction and at the same time save his dad any further shame. He returned his focus to where Sina was standing with the other body in close proximity… With a deep breath he let himself identify it. There she was… finally he had found her… the first person he really cared for outside his family, Aeryn-Sun the

Nun who had guided him away from a dark path and towards a brighter one. She was stood beside but slightly behind Xandra-Sina, the second person he ever truly cared for…He couldn't see Aeryn's face, she too was staring at the floor her hair not beautiful and full of life like before but ghoulish, bleak and falling over most of her face. This was probably for the better as Julian wasn't sure he could handle looking her in the eye and seeing the projection of her suffering and torment. He recognised her instinctively despite how changed she was in stature & demeanour. She was so thin now that even with the pale lose fitting peasant rags she was dressed in her fragile malnourished frame was obvious. It was a depressing image of her to behold. Aeryn seemed unsteady on her feet like she was helplessly caught between the soft tides of life and death. Julian wanted to save her, to dive into her ocean of despair and pull her out, but he dared not move an inch. This was Father Bachinger's stage and Julian was just a spectator blind to the true story he was telling. He had underestimated him up until now, and would not make the same mistake twice. He had questions that needed answers and he knew where to start. His resolve was brittle from the emotional onslaught he was under, but he couldn't allow that to stop him. There was still time to do something significant. With a heavy heart he looked away from Aeryn and back to Sina. She too had undergone a metamorphosis, one beneath the surface and unseen in nature… Julian needed to understand what it was and **why** it was. She stood there proudly, her beauty still ever present but now laced with something different… something darker. While looking at her properly for the first time in weeks, Julian realised how much he had missed her, her densely black skin always radiant with the glow of high priced moisturiser, her figure slim yet epic in feminine ratios and her hair always changing in style but never in beauty. Despite these familiarities he could sense that she was irrevocably different and that it was her who was emitting one of the two powerful life forces he sensed from outside the room, meaning that the other and most frighteningly powerful one belonged to Father Bachinger. Even worse was that he was indeed steadily rising, its ferocity palpable to those around of the superhuman persuasion.

One minute left

"I can see by the pain on your pretty caramel face Julian, that you have figured out the truth that I orchestrated everything since you arrived on the grounds... everything that has led you here to me." Father Bachinger's gleeful comment was ignored by Julian and instead he spoke directly to Sina, all he cared about in this moment was understanding **why**.

"Sina... pour quoi?" There was quiet for a second, The Priest was not letting Julian's shunning of his presence bother him into an egotistical rant, as he too was eager to *see* this exchange.

The following is translated from French

"I know that's your first question...I t always is for humans, but it's not relevant. Once I remembered the truth about who I really am it was only a question of how?"

"I don't understand, what you mean? How did you become this?"

"You see my poor little hero, it's the how that is important. I never became this, I always was this? The person you met in Gien, the person you fell for and got to know intimately was never real." That statement hurt Julian deeply. This whole time that he was fighting to save Aeryn worried that he was potentially losing one of the few people he cared for, the love he had for Sina was resting in a safe corner of his heart and mind protected from this fate. And now he was finding out that he had already lost it… lost her… lost another significant person to him. It was crushing… especially when revealed in the presence of his dying father and friend. Father Bachinger couldn't understand what they were saying but as he already knew what Sina was going to explain to him he could just do as he loved to… To lurk in the shadows watching the pain and suffering of people being illustrated by their bodies; the micro expression of hurt from the sharp stabs of painful words, the gesticulations of bewilderment and rage from a fragile mind trying to understand the horrors that have befallen it and the tears and violence that erupt from the acceptance of hopelessness or the hunger for retribution for a loved one's suffering. It was glorious to him and he watched intently… with an almost sexual lust in his eyes.

"I can feel your amazing life force… My senses tell me that you are not human anymore… sorry never were… but… it's just… Please Sina just make me understand how I lost you too?"

"After what I've done to the people you love since returning to fight beside my master, it's the least I can do." Julian didn't pick up on the insinuation Sina was making and just waited for her explanation in sad silence. "The earliest clear memory I have is of waking up in a group home for orphans aged around nine, I think. My memories before that, memories of my birth parents are very blurry…it's only now that I know that the reason for that, is those memories are fake and my entire history is a fabrication of *his* Controllers. Unlike all the Other Ones I and my master do not know how long we've been here trapped in *his* program. Our memories and histories were erased and re-written countless times to fit our situations and placement on this earth. You probably see us as the 'bad guys' but I wonder how many human lives had to be tampered with to keep this program running since the beginning of the human race? Can you justify that?" Julian slowly broke open his lips to ask

"But why are you different from all the rest?"

"Good boy, I see you're already learning to avoid the distractions and focus on the important questions, well that's because unlike the rest of masters Other Ones I was one of the two he created first, we were both was created with a higher concentration of his immortal soul. My design was to overlook and rule the rest like an earth General. I am more powerful and obviously far more dangerous than those you battled with up until now. I guess that's why my memories of who I really was were sealed like masters."

"But…when?"

"Remember my ex, Jonathan?"

"Yes..."

"When me and him broke up and we started our pointless little earth fling." Julian felt the sting of those words deeply and Father Bachinger saw this pain and it tasted sweet…succulent like the honey of fresh pollen-fed bees…Father Bachinger was licking and biting his lips in the periphery… watching… stalking…

"Since then??"

"No, first Jonathan went back home to England after we broke up… but then I got a strange text from him saying that he was back in Gien and wanting to speak to me urgently. That was the morning you got that weird phone call and left in a hurry, remember? That was in fact the last time I saw you." Julian's tired mind flashed back to that day, then to that moment… He tried to block out the memories of the passion they shared, as it would only make accepting this new reality harder. Then there it was the memory of her phone flashing and him seeing the name Jonathan appear on it! But he still couldn't piece it all together, what was the relevance of this?

"Still struggling to understand? You poor thing... Don't you realise that you have already meet Jonathan?" Julian searched his mind again, and couldn't find any evidence of anyone by that name... then suddenly the penny dropped.

"Do you mean Jo... the guard Jo?! The one left to die by your master??"

"Yes him... sorry for any confusion he did always prefer being called Jo... and correction he's dead not dying and master had nothing to do with it. I was the one who ordered those men to kill him, I will never tolerate the existence of anyone who questions my master's will. He actually expired only a few seconds ago, was always a weak man to be honest...not suitable for me then and definitely not now." Julian remembered the guard's explanation of coming back from France before he met the Priest, how hard it was getting over a break up and it all started making sense. He was in disbelief, Sina was always a strong women but he never thought she could be capable of this... it was all proving to him that this really wasn't the girl he knew anymore, but now a new and fearsome adversary. "You see, before his end, Jonathan had come back for me on master's orders because master could sense my residue life forces on him during his awakening. And so Jonathan was temporarily given the power to awaken me from my ignorance. It was incredible to suddenly remember who you really are... but soon those feelings changed to anger, anger that I had been sentence to such a demeaning existence! I wasn't going to let this slide so I came back here, to my rightful place. I vow Julian that *he* will pay for that insult! If you and everything being eradicated is what it takes then I only regret that it wasn't done yesterday." Pure coldness of intent exuded from her, Julian sensed it and instantly felt on the edge of worlds end.

Thirty seconds left.

With a demon's grin, Father Bachinger stepped forward to the front of his stage and proclaimed, "Julian! Welcome to the end! In these last few moments let me tell you a story... in my renaissance I learned that with time, the time you so nicely provided me, I could regain more and more of my true self, but not enough to return home sadly. Even now as you tremble at the sense of what I've become, its only twenty percent of my true self..." The pleasure he felt in saying those words caused his jaw to elongate like that of a Jurassic predator savouring the moment before his first bite of blood warm flesh. "But something *is* missing...a portion of my memory that has yet to return to me. I know that's the key to becoming myself again, the almighty Other One and true ruler of RATH. Being close to you Julian, for reasons I don't yet understand brings my forgotten past back to me, so to that end here you are... ripe, and bursting with everything I need." with a tone of pitiful acceptance Julian asked,

"How...? How will it end..?" His words filled the room like a black hole absorbing the last lights of hope from everyone and everything that was depending on him. Julian's dad collapsed face first into the patch of blood soaked carpet of which there was more on the floor than in his body at that point. Aeryn's sway amidst the tides of life and death ceased and she collapses towards the ground graceless like a malnourished calf. But before she hit the ground her fall was abruptly halted. Sina caught her by the hair then forcefully wrenched her head back so Julian could see her face. Aeryn was cut and contused almost beyond recognition, Julian saturated with misery was numb to the sight. Her eyes were swollen shut and in Julian's mind that was a minor blessing. It saved her from having to see him reduced back to a helpless boy too wounded to do anything about his own fate and that of his cherished.

"How, you ask? Simple. Once I remembered that my Other Ones were actually placed on earth at different points in time and not just here with me, the end was clear. I knew that once I had the power to recall them all back to me the consequences of that action would be devastating to your universe... It would cause a time space event that would end all life as you know it... But hey, why should that stop me..?" he said, brimming with happiness. "Me and my creations are immortal and would be back in our domain able to enjoy the screams of terror as everything here in this miserable place came to a much overdue end." Julian just hung his head quietly, his shame almost too heavy to bear. "No last words I see, well let me give you mine..." He stared deeply into Julian's eyes with a gratified expression of sexual perversion and said gently, *"The expert in getting the enemy to make his move shows himself, and the enemy is certain to follow. He baits the enemy, and the enemy is certain to take it. In so doing, he moves the enemy, and lies in wait for him with his full force."* Julian's head jerked up in shock, pupils dilated and mouth open he stared at Father Bachinger, who whilst excitingly trying to absorb the radiating melancholy said, "Sina didn't just tell me about the loss of your virginity, she told me about your training and the books you studied! I knew it all! You were never going to win! You are and always will be just a boy who's sad about losing his mummy."

3...2...1

"Times up, Julian." And with that declaration The Priest leapt forward and grabbed Julian firmly by the forearms! This physical contact between the two, just like last time caused an ethereal event within Father Bachinger's consciousness. But with the Priest's new exponentially increased life force it was immeasurably stronger. They both began to shake viciously, the force of which created a sound so terrifying it was as if thunder and lightning were being scolded by God. All those within that room were struggling to remain intact as they witnessed the beginning of the end. The force of this event was shaking the very earth beneath them, but among this chaos a small sign of life presented itself... François was conscious! The disturbance had violently awoken him from a perilous siesta on the steps of deaths door. He strained his head off the ground and looked up to see that the son he loved more than any world in existence was in mortal danger. Long ago he once swore to his wife..."Kalina, as long as I have air in my lungs I will never allow anyone to harm our son... sa ma chéri je te promais." And so he was going to live and die by these words. He summoned every ounce of strength he had in his body and began to crawl towards his son...He fought off the paralysing pain of each movement forward for that promise... the gale force winds, tremble of the earth and walls around him could not deter him from reaching Julian. He would not break his vow. The closer he got the more he could feel his body being filled with something familiar, something from long ago... he was only inches away now and he stretched out an arm. The force of the event occurring in front of him was beginning to tear at the fibres of his borrowed flesh. Just before he could make contact with the Priest's robe everything suddenly fell silent and still...

The Priest looked up and said "I remember... the key... I remember. You tried to steal away my immortal soul forever... but I remember now... its colour, its taste, its feel and IT'S NAME!" This was the final truth hidden from him and all Other Ones... Their true name... the key to their immortality, the knowledge of which was the only way to be reunited with that essence of spirit separated from them on the day of judgement. It was left in an empty place between worlds, sealed away from everything else in the universe. But today it would return… "I'm sorry I've forgotten you…and in that forgotten myself…but now come back and join me…let us be seamless! No longer distinguishable as two halves! No longer at his mercy! Destroy these shackles and ascend! I summon me back together! MY NAME IS KOROSU!!"

With those fierce exclamations a space and time bending explosion occurred… all things were eradicated from sight and nothing remained but two among a white silent nothingness.

No time was left.

Chapter 22

A being of inconceivable strength stands within the silent nothingness and reaffirms his truth.

His vocal oscillations and language indiscernible to a mind still caged by current evolutionary human constraints, require translation. The following words are the closest interpretations and understanding of them.

"***Agnoscere***...I am Korosu one part of the original whole, The Other One and chooser of the opposite path... the one who colligates his creations and their true names... their immortal souls. I bequeath onto them this forgotten knowledge so they too can recognise themselves. But... where am I? This place, ashen with no walls or floors, I do not recognise it. Maybe it is what's left of their assemblage...? Strange... I see that the fallible one has survived too, surprising... his misfortune... ***Kiranai.***"

"Where am I?" Julian said, puzzled and amazed in equal measure... for he too was here in this all white place of bewildering scope that only seemed to have solid mass beneath where he and the being in front of him stood. He dared not move an inch in fear of falling into the white emptiness surrounding him. "Who are you? What are you??" he asked, staring up at what was certainly not human or recognisable as anything he had seen before. It was twice as tall as him, unclothed, skin grey and mildly see through, human in shape but without the facial features or sex. From its stomach, a dark mass of deathly colours most of which Julian had never seen before were moving fluidly in 360 degrees while maintaining spherical integrity. The darkness of it seemed to spread throughout the beings entire body as if it was its engine and source of life. Mysteriously he couldn't even sense this obviously powerful life force, it appeared that the abilities he had before were now gone. His human instincts told him that he should be scared of it, but fear didn't seem to have found a settlement within him… He rationalised that the acceptance of his loss and the end of everything he knew had made him immune to it. So he continued to look, waiting for an answer. The being seemingly lost in his own thoughts didn't acknowledge Julian's question. Julian could hear vibrations and melodies flowing from the being, it seemed as though it was trying to communicate with him, but he could not understand it. He tried again with different questions. "Am I dead? Where is the Priest??" It responded with new vibrations and melodies,

"*Inferiore*…I am formally the one known to you as Priest, now Korosu is my only name. A creature of your standing cannot understand the tongue of gods. Intellection is for those with time, explanations for those with minds…neither belong to you. You are unexpected, yes, and your category is not yet found but needed it is not. Simply life that skipped its end through the actualisation of chance. I will perfect the equation, divide the fraction, disunite the cipher and reduce to zero…*Kesu*" It began walking towards Julian slowly, each step landing on an invisible surface. Julian was still unable to understand its way of speaking. He thought about retreating for a second, but realised that there would be nowhere to retreat to.

*

I don't understand... Julian lost... He had faith but lost! Like a mirror, I too shared his faith but I too like him lost! I could not do anything to help him save them, the everything that he helped me become was not enough and I am still here as nothing! All I could do is do as I always have done and observe... I do not want to see loss anymore, I do not want to hear or feel loss anymore! But like a cosmic punishment, here it is! I don't understand, how did you both get here Julian?? You and the one who now calls himself Korosu are in my place. Is my lonely existence of all white emptiness now all that remains?? What does that mean?! Is this death? Is this what humans say is the beyond? If Julian has passed, unfortunately I can see that, but the other one most certainly has not. So his presence here too must mean something else than the end. But now on the other side of my looking glass why can't he finally see me? He has come to me but is still beyond my reach. I am here for you Julian, can't you hear my pleas for your attention?! Listen to me, this cannot be the end you must do something, fight! Do not stand there waiting for the Priest to reach you, you have to find a way! Can't you hear him?? He is telling you that he *will* kill you, erase you from here. We can't allow it Julian! You have lost so much, but you haven't lost me! I am still here. LOOK AT ME! I must reach you before he does, otherwise all those years with you and yours were for nothing!! You did not see me then but please see me now!! I DON'T WANT TO OBSERVE ANYMORE! SEE ME AND LET ME BE MORE!!

*

Although Julian was being spoken to by two... He could not hear any one. The Priest now returned to his true form as The

Other One had finished his menacing approach and was stood inches from him, towering above like a parent before a child. It raised its arm up. Julian didn't move a muscle, and he recognised this moment as his true end and did not fight it. The final blow would be devastating and swift, all that he was would finish. A final vibration of communication flowed through Julian... He saw it as his requiem and so closed his eyes and listened. The Other One's fist was static above Julian's head, as the last failed communication between the two was completed the first began to syphon darkness from the beings core. *JULIAN!! PLEASE!! I'M HERE!!* The black, dark blues and purple colours began to grow dense as they collected in its fist, *FIGHT WITH ME JULIAN!!!* Quickly they reached opacity and at that moment that huge fist moved faster than eyes could see and instantly connected with its target! *JULIAN!!!!* An eardrum-rupturing explosion of immense scope and achromatic colour consumed the white emptiness...

Before the dust settles on his worn out path and the journey of our Atheist comes to it's conclusion, another story must be told... Its importance and connection to Julian is not bound by distance or time, for the power at work here is beyond limitations.

Year 2460AD

Japan

New Orléan (formerly Osaka)

The story is of the unfortunate life of an orphaned boy, son of an African American soldier and an Oriental women of noble blood. Only days after his birth he was wrapped in the finest materials of the era and left on the *engawa* of a wealthy family's home. They were the only family for miles that could afford to keep and maintain a traditional eighteenth century Japanese home. It stood out among the other more contemporary westernised structures. His mother left him there without shedding a tear and departed whispering her final words to him, "*Haji,* this is your new beginning".

It had been one hundred years earlier that the American and Northern European Alliance (A.N.E.A) had won the war against China for the resources of the United Lands of Japan (U.L.J) and occupied the territory. This combined nation of Korea & Japan was a neutral territory and for centuries had not got involved in the devastating nuclear war between China and the A.N.E.A. That war had left both sides decimated, populations dwindled and soils barren. The victorious A.N.E.A had claimed what remained of China although it represented little economic value. And so it was inevitable that admiring glances would be sent to the fertile, rich lands and ninety-nine percent pure-blooded population of their next-door neighbours. It was only two months after occupying China that they proceeded into the U.J.L. In the following one hundred years, the A.N.E.A were unrelenting and glutinous in using what they needed and moulding the nation in its own image. English and French gradually become the spoken tongues with only traces of their original culture remaining.

Year 2470AD

Now ten years old, the boy is kneeling down on the *tatom* flooring, enjoying an early morning with his adopted father. He was nose down in mathematics homework, completing equations designed for sixteen year olds, while his father smiled proudly and had his breakfast. He was left with the duty of raising a mixed race boy lost in between cultures and a living breathing crime against state law. The untainted people of the U.L.J were now a rare and precious commodity in this war-ravaged, toxic world of prolific inter-race breeding. This meant that all manner of criminal organisations would purchase such human specimens on the 'Red market' for a vast spectrum of uses. So profitable was this growing underground industry that the now corrupt governments passed a law whereby no one was allowed to mix western blood with east. This child was only saved from termination by the kind heart of the man who found him and the government bribes his deep pockets allowed.

This day was significant because it was the day that marked the birth of a new world power, and with it the series of events that would lead to a universe altering moment. As they enjoyed the last few minutes before the day's tasks would take their attention, a breaking news projection popped up. His father, better able to understand the enormity of the report, was ghost faced as he watched the holographic projection coming from his work tablet. The news story was explaining that the United Nation of Africa (U.N.A) who, ever since they closed their borders using stolen southern European technologies to seal off the entire continent from the outside world, had not been heard from for 150 years. It was the U.N.A's leader, Yannick Mufunga that was centre of the story, he was announcing live to the world that their scientists had discovered a new particle that was one hundred times smaller than the Higgs Boson. It was a particle that was present in every organism, but in humans these particles had slightly different properties; they were present at a far higher concentration, they were the binding agent for the atoms that made up the human body and in every strain of genetic information they were present like a protective membrane. The most incredible finding was that these particles were no longer present in the body after death. Billions watched in awe, listening intently to these revelations. He continued his speech, proclaiming it to be the 'Soul Particle', the first definitive proof of a divine creator. He went on further to explain that with specific manipulation, involving a meditative prayer and another unnamed stimulus, a person could promote its growth, causing them to undergo changes the likes of which had never been seen before. He stated that this was the next step in human evolution… that the creator had seen fit to halt the human body's development thousands of years ago but had left within it the seeds for the evolution of the soul.

The broadcast ended and looped back to the start. The boy's father turned it off looked at him and said, "*Musukosan*, today I think the world has changed forever."

Year 2481AD

Eleven years on the boy's fortunes had turned significantly; he had overcome extreme prejudice and envy to excel academically and athletically. So great were his achievements that he was now ranked among the top three best in the annual U.J.L Championships, a tournament created by the A.N.E.A. Participation was compulsory for all citizens, and though publicly it was said to be to encourage the ongoing health and entertainment of the nation, the truth was darker. It was in fact designed to secretly rank the entire untainted male and female populous on a plethora of criteria. Criteria then used to aid in classifying them into their appropriate merchandising categories, this would ensure maximum profit could be made from each sell on the Red market.

His achievements in the championships served to gain the attention of the military. They soon contacted him with a proposal that would alter the course of his life and again send him onto an unfortunate path. Using the previously unknown truth that his birth father was a former soldier of the A.N.E.A as emotional blackmail, they conscripted him into a covert task force. They needed his specific racial qualities, for their mission was to infiltrate the sealed nation of Africa and investigate the truth behind the rumours coming out of the country. In the past eleven years there had been numerous unsubstantiated reports from spies and journalists that President Yannick Mufunga had been creating a new breed of soul evolved humans that were mentally and physically superior. Some of these reports claimed that they were able to grow wings, others that they had telepathic powers and even some claiming these new beings were immortal. None of the spies or journalists made it back or lived long enough for any of it to be proven. This was the mission entrusted onto him.

To accomplish this the A.N.E.A had allied with the Southern European Territories (S.E.T) led by Pope Celestine V, a man whose rise to presidential level power was thanks to his family's achievements of uniting all of Christianity into one faith and transforming the previously crippled economies of the southern European countries into a combined wealth equal to that of the A.N.E.A's. His family's most controversial legacy was changing the language spoken in all of the S.E.T to Latin, though slightly modernised it was still at its heart the ancient language of Rome. Ironically The S.E.T was also the most technologically advanced power in the world and their technologies would be invaluable to the mission. Pope Celestine V was not the honourable man he portrayed to the rest of the world. His smile, charm and sophisticated good looks allowed him to conceal many troubling truths. One of those being that he had reasons for allying with the A.N.E.A that were beyond his claimed interest in Christianity's intellectual and spiritual growth. He intended to, if verified as genuine, steal the knowledge of Soul Evolution using it to conquer Africa (now completely Muslim) and convert it to Christianity. A feat that he believed would set him apart from anyone that came before him, making him the greatest Pope in history and the most powerful man in the world. To achieve this he would need a double agent within the task force…and he set his sights on our story's young man. His confused sense of self and conflicted national identity would make him easy for manipulation for one such as the Pope.

Year 2483AD

South America

A.N.E.A HQ

After two years of intense military training our young man had acquired the vast array of skills and experiences that would allow him to invisibly infiltrate and gather information in a Muslim nation. But this was not his only mission… and to that end he was also made to study Christianity's teachings and learn Latin., Pope Celestine had decided that this was a prerequisite of anyone working for him. Though a model soldier and pupil to the Pope, he could never completely shake off his inner Atheist and was usually just playing the role often feeling hollow and devoid of real faith.

United Nations of Africa

Cairo

The young man leads his team forward and with the skill and leadership befitting his training, covertly infiltrates the very top tier of the U.N.A. They discover that the reports, though exaggerated were in fact true. The scientists here were using volunteers, and subjecting them to a process they called 'Focused Salat'. It involved the subjects praying in a state of sensory deprivation for as long as ten minutes while their bodies are bombarded with a newly discovered form of radiation that reacts specifically with the 'Soul Particles'. This causes their genetic building blocks to alter and transforms them into something different. The extent of the transformation would depend on the subject and their level of focus or, as they preferred to say it, their faith. But one thing remained constant… every subject developed a peculiar glow from deep within their stomachs, and claimed they could perceive the world around them differently as if they were out of sync with time. This was the evolution of the soul and what the nation believed would bring them closer to God. The boy, though knowing the teachings of the two most prominent religions in the world and witnessing first-hand what a marriage of religion and science could produce, could not buy this explanation… His experiences growing up had left him lacking in the ability to believe in anything his own intellect had not proven to be true. He was bound by logic and had never felt the tingle of intuition.

The nation's leader had decided that he would subject entire cities to this process, and one by one transform the nation into physically and spiritually evolved beings that would live sin free, the way God had intended in the beginning. Some even harboured the hope that in seeing this God would be pleased and see fit to take them up to be with him far above, in a realm above the heavens. But as with most men of great power, the leader had been so consumed by his life's quest that he disregarded the dangers presented to him by his scientist. They had warned that expanding this process to such a degree would be dangerous and a single error in calculation could cause a catastrophic event on a global scale. Little did they know that this was at the very least a possible consequence and worst an end to all things.

The night of the citywide experiment...

On this night all that could go wrong had done, it were as though the God the people of Africa were trying to get closer to was pushing them further away. Millions willingly volunteered to undergo the evolution of the soul, but before the ten minutes could expire, a catastrophic chain of events began at the source. The scientist had in their pursuit of a new frontier, retreaded the age-old path of human error. The cities were in mass distress, united in their cries for a saviour, countless bodies reacting to the radiation, some contorting unrecognisably others imploding into nothing, but all praying not for transcendence but forgiveness and acceptance. The sky shook with fierce foreboding, lighting storms whipped the earth mercilessly and all the man-made structures began to crumble around the crouched people of this new Africa. Amidst this, our young man was still pursuing a mission he had not yet accomplished, ignoring the pain he felt inside for these people's suffering. He pitied them for their faith in the unseen. 'How could there be a God if such destruction could befall them?' he thought, as he raced through the bodies and wreckage that remained of the president's private Cairo research facility. He knew that there was still a chance to stop this world's annihilation. He had learned the source of the 'Focused Salat's' power and was only meters from it. This minor distance undersold the greatness of the task at its end. He knew that this valour would be his final act. He had already lost the team he was meant to protect in the violence and chaos of the citiy's destruction. But there was one he had already lost long ago, the pain of that in this time so close to the end caused him great sorrow. This person was his adopted father. Confounding this anguish was knowing that whether he failed and allowed the world to suffer the wrath of misusing God's science, or succeeded and learned the truth of death in humble sacrifice he would never see him again. The bond he had with his father was the only truth he ever really felt and throughout his life's relationships, hardships and successes nothing had ever felt more real… Nothing had ever felt more like faith than his love for his father, and no religion could ever match it. They were all man-made institutions and he had lost his belief in mankind many years ago.

The young man's destination was imposing in stature, making him more fearful with each closing step. It was an expertly constructed fully transparent room of near indestructible material, within which appeared to be an ocean of violently disagreeing natural phenomena. Not able to reconcile they fought each other seeking supremacy shredding the fabrics of space and time in the process. He gathered his composure trying to ignore the rumbling of the ground and fluctuating heat of the dense air around him. His heart, unlike his mind, couldn't. His impending death rattled the fractured pieces of his heart causing him to feel the sadness vibrate out from inside his chest. As he took the final march towards the sealed structure he remembered the morning his dad said to him that the world had changed forever. His father's face then was still full of hope and not as it was the last time… distorted by the pain he had brought him when he joined the army that had subjugated his native lands. Our young man filled with guilt and anger screams out to the heaven's "LOOK WHAT FOLLOWING YOU HAS BROUGHT???!!! NOTHING BUT DESTRUCTION! MY FATHER BELIEVED, AND YET HIS SON IS DRAWN

AWAY TO HIS DEATH! YOUR SO-CALLED CHILDREN FIGHT, SUFFER AND PUSH THEMSELVES TO THE LIMIT JUST FOR YOUR ACCEPTANCE AND YOU ABANDON THEM?! I DON'T BELIEVE IN A GOD LIKE YOU!! YOU ARE NOWHERE WHEN IT COUNTS AND CLAIM TO BE EVERYWHERE WHEN IT DOESN'T!!" Tears stream down his face as the overdose of adrenaline makes his body shake as he places one hand on the structures access door. "WHERE WERE YOU WHEN MILLIONS DIED IN THE CONSTANT WARS FOUGHT IN YOUR NAME?! OR WHEN TYRANTS KILLED WOMEN, CHILDREN AND FATHERS FOR COIN AND SOIL?!! WHHERE WERE YOU WHEN MY MOTHER AND FATHER ABANDONED ME?!! WHEN I WAS BEATEN AND ABUSED FOR BEING DIFFERENT?! WELL I DON'T CARE ANYWAY! I never needed you… I made something of myself without your help… I NEVER needed you…I've read all the Bibles created in your name and their pages read hollow… IT'S OUTDATED FICTION FOR THE WEAK! I will save my father and everyone else without your help!" He pauses for a second, realising he has to regain his composure and enter the pass code that unlocks the door… The time has come for his sacrifice and the world's rescue. He braces himself and keys in the numbers, the electronic interface reads **access denied**… He stares into the red glow of those words, his gaze so deep they blur and lose focus. His shock is accompanied by helplessness. "So after all that I've failed… I couldn't even save him, what kind of son am I?" Resigned to his and the world's fate, he utters his final words and offers them up to the God he said didn't exist, unsure even himself to their seriousness "I wonder… after all I've said… if I prayed to you now, would you save us?" With that a silent universe wiping explosion eliminating everything.

No time was left.

Chapter 23

Year 0 BC

In a time before the beginning there existed a whole being...

It existed here due to a rupture in the walls of space and time, a rupture caused by the events in 2483. The being once a young man of that time survived due to his incalculable amount of exposure to soul particle radiation. Instead of being dissolved into nothing like the rest of his universe, his soul evolved beyond the constraints of dimensional barriers. Despite the destruction the being remained whole, connected to all those there that night... a sum of all their individual parts. Our young man had evolved beyond flesh...existing without form as unchained consciousness. His memories still intact, he feared that this was in fact the truth of death, but his now astronomical intellect quickly understood the truth. He was not dead but placed before the beginning, able to witness the birth of the universe... and it was beautiful, a privilege he was saddened to be the only one able to enjoy. The only answer that eluded him was **why**, the *how* he could see was a matter of grand mathematics... In witnessing the birth of everything he could see an endless mesh of formulae on a scale beyond even his comprehension. The impossible physics of creation were materialising into twelve dimensional algebraic equations. Equations that even when at their most unbalanced, were gracefully met with a subsequent cascade of arithmetic perfection that intuitively brought balance back to the sequential flow of multi-dimensional fractions. The potential **why** of this was frightening even to the being he had become? In awe, he faithfully observed up to and beyond the big bang that announced its completion... hoping that the one who had created this world would reveal itself. Surely it was aware of his presence here, a presence that he was sure was not meant for this time and space, and it would certainly come to him...as he lived outside the equation of life and would have to be rectified.

For reasons unknown it separated into two singular parts...

He waiting and observed...but there was nothing...the creator never came to see him. Over time he grew lonely... the whole being by definition was alone, and though far removed from most of the confinements of the human condition, his soul was still the soul of a man. And with that came the innate need for others...no matter what form, the soul is designed to seek out connections, the kind that nourish it and drive it forward towards filling the space left onto us by the creator. Disillusioned with the creator's absence and suffering the inescapable sorrow of singularity, he made the decision to use what his consciousness was able to grasp of creation, leave this plane and reside in one of his own construction. He would spitefully name it The Realm above the Heavens and begin a process that he believed would eliminate his pain. The process, a separation of his wholeness into two singular parts that could exist in this new realm... free to express any desires they had and live in the eternal peace of each other's company. Although that was the plan, this being didn't truly understand the exactness of its wholeness. His human soul that had evolved him into a god-like state was for all its ascendancy still chained down by the parameters of its design. And in his arrogance, he had failed to realise that the human soul was designed with the capacity for good and evil, two parts of the same whole... providing balance... Therefore to separate it into two if not done with masterful precision would be removing the natural constraints built into their design. He further failed to understand that this process would be a regression into a less spiritually evolved, more human state... meaning becoming more fallible to the sway of emotions, thoughts and desires within him both positive and or negative. These driving forces are born of the denseness of life experience residing within the soul. The peace he hoped for in his new realm could not be born by such a thing.

The whole being separated… he was still new to the mathematics of creation and because of that his calculations failed to balance the equation of consciousness, and thus his soul was separated into three. His consciousness one part of the whole was a numeric remainder that splintered away into the substructure of existence. But before it was lost forever, it was found by the one who is unseen and always watching… the father that is forever attentive to the child, seeking to fulfil its needs even when the child's demands are immature and ignorant to the truth of the world. The child many times will always ask his father **why,** but a mind so young could never understand the answer. The father can only hope the child has faith in his love, for that is the most important of all truths.

A father's voice rings out across the dawn of time, echoing off his creations it's heard by all except one.

'You will not be lost… you will be protected so that you can save them all. I can forgive your transgressions as you are still a young soul and in your growth you must push, strain and tear before you can heal. No matter the sins never will you be beyond the reach of my grace.

I have created a miracle for you - but will hold you in my house until it proves itself ready. Though the process will make you forget everything that you are, the life of this miracle will remind you… observe him and remember the truth… This is your redemption and with it you shall redeem all those lost to you.

You once asked if I would save them all if you prayed..?

A father doesn't save their child because they asked for saving.

You once said that you didn't believe in me…

It never mattered if you believed in me, the crops do not know the farmer but bloom all the same.'

Our story now returns to the place of its conclusion, back to the present and the blank space where Julian's greatest adversary stands in waiting.

The explosion that consumed the all-white space has settled and only one stands, The Other One… Korosu.

"Get up Julian! it's time to fight, we have a lot of people to protect." Groggy and in a great deal of pain Julian hears the voice and opens his eyes, expecting to see someone standing over him. Through the blur he's surprised to see no one…

"Who is this?" he asks.

"Good you *can* hear me now, I can't tell you how happy this makes me, Julian… If only you knew how long I've been waiting to speak to you, how many years I've been nothing but a helpless observer to your life." Still gathering his senses, Julian tentatively responds,

"Umm okay, well I'm very happy for you but you haven't answered my question."

"The short answer is, I'm just another unfortunate young man like yourself who's been given a second chance. The complicated answer is that I created the being that almost killed you."

"You mean the Priest? As in that inhuman thing over there that used to be Father Bachinger?"

"I told you it was complicated… and I think he prefers to be called Korosu now."

"So that's how you pronounce it. Well I'm still confused to be honest,"

"Well before this is over prepare for a lot more of the same." Still strewn on his back, Julian temporarily forgot the pain he was in and smiled. Strangely he could also feel the other presence within him smiling too.

"I assume that's you I can feel?"

"Yes it is... You okay with that?"

"Without telling me your name or even buying me dinner? I don't know..."

"That's fair. Well mother named me Hajimaru but everyone used to just call me Haji."

"Cool name, but at some point you're going to have to explain this Japanese thing to me."

"I will, over dinner."

The two of them were enjoying the intuitive connection they felt with each other and to Julian it seemed as though he knew this voice, the peculiar familiarity of it made him scan his memories. And slowly small moments of déjà vu started to filter through. The pieces were there, but he was still not yet fully able to complete the puzzle.

"So... do you know how we're going to deal with that creature over there?"

"Of course... we're going to kick his ass."

"You sure about that? Did you not *see* him?? He almost killed me with one punch!"

"Julian that blow *should* have killed you. You don't find it strange that you received a hit from an almost god-like creature and are still alive?" Julian was silent, he realised that the voice was right. Why was he alive..? "Stand up Julian and look at yourself... you're not what you used to be." Julian, now more alert, can feel the pain that kept him prone on the floor subsiding, and stands himself up. As his balance centres, he becomes aware of the new power inside him, it's alive, an energy flowing through him and refreshing his spirit like a cool mint elixir. He looks at the opponent before him and as he focuses, his sight becomes different... To his amazement, now he can see everything that was previously hidden. This space in fact was not a blank canvas at all, but alive with countless colours and textures. The experience of witnessing it was like waking up inside an exquisite painting of a new born soul, the brush strokes exuding the grace of careful design and colours expressing the ethereal manifestations of love's immortality. It touched him deeply, giving him renewed hope for the task ahead. The only blight in this picturesque environment was the grey being of dark glowing centre. A glow from which Julian could sense a palpable malice, strong enough to traverse the gap between them and place a sword at his throat.

"**Adhuc vivens**...unexpected but not without solution. Your existence more resilient than the rest, but once more I will come to bring you your end. Without restraint I will strike your mortal flesh as though it were a reflection of my own...*Jihi nai.*"

Julian was now also able to decipher the grumbling melodies coming from the being and understand the threats they contained, but he was unfazed. This was because as he looked down at his new body and felt the strength within it grow exponentially. He realised that as of now the only one in a position to issue threats was him. Julian's clothes were torn up badly from the superficial damage of recent events and barely hanging onto his body. The exposed skin of his arms and portions of torso were glowing like white hot metal, the heat represented the power that came from the presence of the observer. The lost portion of the whole being had found its vessel, and together he and Julian had become an instrument of God. Angelic in stature and tempered in composition, they now guarded the fate of mankind. Only the one who thought itself a deity could not see the truth, the truth of the white room or the truth of what Julian was now and in its blindness it advanced.

"He's coming… okay, it's time for us to spread our wings Julian."

"Yeah, let's get to work."

The two opponents headed towards each other, the fate of creation resting on the outcome.

These two parts although from the same original whole grew to have different driving purposes and effects on the space and time around them…

The ensuing battle was fierce beyond measure. Blows with the force to tear the tops of mountains where being exchanged by the destined enemies. Their environment was being dented and deformed by the dimension bending nature of their power. Whether looking through the eyes capable of perceiving the Technicolor or those blinded by white, the view was the same. The landscape of victory only contained one.

These effects were not always complementary and from this a great tension arose…

Julian now an agent of God was expert-like in his delivery of consequence, his blows condensed by the vast pain those he loved suffered at the hands of the Priest. No matter how Father Bachinger had changed he would never forget his face, this ever-present memory of his evil would guide the grace and precision of his attacks. His opponent's way of war was wild and unforgiving to the surroundings. The more Julian pressed forward his advantage the greater risks his opponent took to secure victory. "Julian we have to be careful, our enemy does not understand what this place is and his wildness could lead to its demise."

"What do you mean?"

"This room is a creation of *his*. I know because our union has gifted me knowledge I didn't have before… probably it was seeded inside you waiting for this moment. This place is where I've been observing you from since the day you were born. It's separate from your world and the only connection between the two is you. So he took you both away from that church and brought you here to protect your world from this battle. If you let him destroy it then there will be no more protection for it and those still there."

"I would ask who you're talking about when you say it's his room but, I can already feel the answer inside me… Well, I'm just happy he's decided to lend us a hand. But the best news is that this means I didn't fail!… It means that my father and Aeryn are still alive!"

"Yes it does Julian, but not for long if this fight keeps up."

"Don't worry, I'm bringing it to an end now!"

Julian centres all his anger, resentment and hatred into one moment of tension-splitting focus. He gathers all the power afforded to him from the observer within and readies himself to bet everything on a final charge. He has let this man torment his spirit for long enough and has decided that it's time he returned peace to his heart.

"*Familiarise*… your energy reminds me of history, my history… it doesn't make cognitive sense for such things to be possible. I see with these eyes that you are less and insignificant to the causalities I can produce. How then do you posses energies akin to one of my transcendence? Antithetical in nature to the rest, but to reside on my plateaux? Insufferable insolence… you will be erased like the rest…*Fukanō.*"

Following this came a period of ever-growing friction between the two entities, now irrevocably opposing one another…

Like a vision from movies portraying a hero's valour, Julian ran towards his enemy with a speed capable of breaking every barrier, his fist ready to deliver the justice of two and the redemption of millions. Korosu, free from the burden of knowledge, carried within his grasp the destructive power of ignorance. His every pounding step forward was like the deafening beat of a war drum. Its rhythm grew exponentially in pace with each stride, until it was ferociously eating up the ground between them like an unfed wild animal. At the moment of their collision everything outside the sphere of this duel was instantly brought to its knees, struggling and pleading to maintain its integrity. Creation looked on as spectators at the culmination of a plan devised in light and etched into the black canvas of space. The opponents were locked in a struggle of wills, the observer within Julian reminded him again of the dangers of a prolonged clash and Julian could feel his feet deep within his belly. They were the sainted sword and shield, and together their power could not be rivalled. Though it would take many years to be able to use the full spectrum of its prowess, Julian and his observer within were always gifted students and had learnt enough during this fight to make their advantage definitive. With one final strained push, the chosen servants overcame the terrifying chasm of failure that stood before them, their hands clenched in judgement landed a strike that Julian designed to end his enemy's existence. But the observer within him held back and instead the final devastating blow only shattered their enemy's spirit, subduing him into a timeless sleep.

Julian stands over his vanquished foe, his body is damaged severely. He hopes that even in this form the consciousness that was once Father Bachinger, was still present enough to understand that each wound was retribution for the suffering of his father and Aeryn. Disappointed that he still lived he asks, "Why didn't you let me kill him? It's the least he deserves"

"I could feel that that's what you wanted... but as I'm basically your soul now, I have to help you make the right decisions, don't I?"

"My soul? You think a lot of yourself, don't you?"

"Well I thought guardian spirit was a bit much." Julian laughed... it relaxed him like medication for the stressed.

"So what now?"

"I'm not sure but I can feel the presence of another nearby."

"Another like him? Or another like you?" Julian was still basking in the glow of victory, with no desire or patience to face a new enemy.

"A bit of both actually." Julian, intuitively understanding the meaning of those words, prepared himself.

"I hope he's coming to get us out of here... or at least say thank you for a job well done."

The colour filled space was once again calm and swirling gently with its usual vividness and beauty. From within these colours a shape appeared, it was a large silhouette that shone bright like the sun. As it came closer the brightness dimmed and its true form was revealed.

Julian stared at it in fear, quickly changing his casual stance to one that was prepared for a worst-case scenario. "Why does it look like him?!"

"Calm down Julian, it's not him."

"Yeah it might be brighter but that large featureless grey-skinned body is just like his."

"I know, but it's not." Julian searched the waves of emotions within and found the reassurance he needed. His observer instinctively knew that the being now stood before him was the opposite of Korosu, it in fact was the other part of his lost being, The One... originally of his whole and here in 'person' for an audience with the chosen instruments. Although neither of these beings shared the form he had before, he could feel from within their glow portions of him being reflected back... like looking at the best and worst parts of his reflection in a shattered mirror. It reminded him of his moral fallibility and his life before the tragedy. Both of them were eager to hear what it had to say and listen intently for the slightest utterance. They didn't have to wait long, the being took a few more steps closer and began emitting the same vibrating melodies used to communicate by Korosu.

For reasons unknown they then created other beings from their own selves who, although only a diluted power, would share their driving purposes.

"***Agnoscere***...I am Iyasu one part of the original whole, The One and chooser of the opposite path. Hajimaru I come to declare truths. In subduing Korosu, irreconcilable equations have met resolution. Sooner interventions were postulated but I was told to exercise restraint by a nameless one... the nameless one, the true architect of this conclusion...***Matte Iru***."

"Is it calling me your name? Or does it know you're here?"

"No... not exactly, I think it recognises your identity by the nature of your spirit..."

"Meaning you?"

"Yes..."

Julian felt that this was as good a time as any to ask the dimly glowing figure a question, it had been on his mind ever since the night his father first told him about this world beyond theirs. He clears his throat, looks straight on and says,

"I understand that you and the other were once one and the same, but I don't understand how despite that, you became so different… so much so that you both created an army of followers to fight in a war between you."

"***Erratum***…reasons for the ones and others was not conflict. That was consequence, not cause. Cause was resistance to singularity. Even as two and no longer one, the singularity of consciousness plagued this existence. Becoming opposite from each in purpose prohibited a resolution to the resistance. The opposing purposes were destruction and healing, in creation the opportunities for both existed. Within our two parts there could become many. Energy possessed within could be seeded in new form separate from the singularity, this was the resolution…***Kodoku.***"

Julian found it hard to comprehend the exact meaning in the way these beings would speak, but his observer understood it completely and filled in the gaps for him. The truth was clear to the observer within because they were both a part of him, and it made him deeply sad to see just how similar they still remained to his previous self. This because his decision to divide himself into parts was with the hope of ending the inescapable ache of loneliness… but its citing of a 'resistance to singularity' being the reason for them using pieces of their soul to create new followers was proof of his plans failure. It seemed that the inability to escape this emotion was due to the nature of the human spirit that still existed with them, his spirit. What truly makes a person human is their soul, the shell around it by design or manipulation can change its form, transcend or regress, but the soul will always define it. The soul cannot flourish in solitude and will always seek company. Only a god can exist as a singularity... and unfortunately they were still only human. The observer had been taught this through his unique experience of Julian, whereas they were not as privileged. But it did seem that the separated part of him named Iyasu was on the right path. The observer within now saw the truth of the Rehabilitation program. In feeling a soft resonance of humanity within his immortal soul, The One must have understood that this was the origin of their propensity for a healing view on creation. Although that must have meant that there too laid the origin of The Other Ones desire for destruction. The One understood that only through the unique human experience of mortality could a respect for creation be developed.

Their time in his space was drawing to a close... the sainted weapons now sheathed and mounted could be returned. But before this, Julian had just one more sentiment in his heart that needed expressing. His observer had always seen this attachment of endless affection between him and her, but feeling it within himself too now he has moved by this love; gentle as an infant's kiss with infinite strength of a mother's forgiveness.

"Can you please tell her that me and dad still miss her so much and will always try to live in the way she showed us?" Though these heartfelt words were said loud enough to be heard by it, only silence came afterwards. There was no response from the one named Iyasu. Instead the colour-filled space around them slowly disintegrated along with The One. The sainted ones slowly rematerialized into the room of wood and stone, their re-entrance into the lives of their loved ones was magnificent for all those able to witness. They descended gracefully towards the floor, their silhouette pearl-bright with a soft outline of a majestic wingspan that enveloped the surrounding space.

As they touched the floor, their heavenly glow rescinded, so much as to make those present feel to have witnessed a mirage. They were now presented with the image of a mere mortal man, body tired from grand exertions and eyes filled with tearful joy. They were back in Father Bachinger's office, the room was in a very bad state, and not a single structure or furnishing remained intact. The only things that were there, were the two people Julian most wanted to see... They had been waiting for his return for hours and now the dawn was here with them, and together they would give Julian the warm hope-filled embrace of a new morning. The first to speak was Julian's father, he was stood beside the seated body of Aeryn-Sun and with his face gleaming proudly he says,

"Fils, comment ça va?"

"I'm good dad, just happy to see that you're okay. How is Aeryn?"

"Why don't you ask her your self son." Julian takes a closer look at Aeryn to find that beneath all her hair she is looking up at him lucid and smiling. A wave of warmth passes over Julian, he can barely contain how good it feels to see her look at him again with strength in her eyes.

"How are you feeling, miss?"

"Why don't you come over here and see? Isn't that what a hero is supposed to do?" Though her voice was still not back to its normal strength of tone, her sassiness was still there and it reassured Julian of her improving health. He approaches her, she still wears the scars of her ordeal but the brightness of her smile seems to fade all of that into the background. Julian extends his arms down to her and she grabs on to them, Julian pulls her up from the crimson stained floor like a lifeguard pulling a weary swimmer from the ocean and back onto solid ground. Once on her feet, she looked up at Julian noticing his physical growth since the last time she stood this close to him. Her heart almost bursting with relief and jubilation, she relinquished her normal character and flung her arms around him, hugging him as passionately as her worn body would allow. She wept onto his chest and said,

"Thank you so much… my faith in you never wavered, not once, not when you left me alone, not when he took me, not when they tortured me telling me that you wouldn't return. I knew that God had a plan that was bigger than both of us, that it wasn't my job to try to understand but just to persevere as long as I could. Wherever you were, whatever you were doing, I just knew that it was for you family and friends. I never lost faith in that Julian… Thank you for saving us all."

Julian was almost brought to tears himself by her ardent exclamations, but knew that this was not a moment for that, he had to be strong enough to take in everything she was feeling. It was a small act of repentance for failing to be there for her from the beginning. With Aeryn's frail body still in his arms a thought passes through his head and he turns to his father and asks,

"Dad, where is Sina and the others? I don't sense them anywhere."

"They are gone. When you and the Priest disappeared, things here went crazy. That girl, Sina, she tried to finish of what she started with Aeryn but I protected her."

"How? How could you stand up to her, her spirit energy is much stronger than yours."

"I think when I touched the Priest's robe during that event I somehow temporarily got some of my old power back, c'est incroyable… It's as close to being back there as I've felt since I was put here in the program. With it my wounds healed and I was able to defend Aeryn against her and all the rest of his followers that came in soon afterwards."

"I see, like father like son, I guess."

"Oui, but there were a lot of them and as I said the power was temporary. But before they could overwhelm me, the Controllers suddenly came and helped subdue them all. To be honest son I was shocked that they actually intervened… It's not like them… but it was how I knew you were still alive, somewhere fighting for us too, proving to them every ounce of your worth."

"I wasn't alone… I had help."

"Really, from who?"

"It's hard to explain, but let's just say that I found my inner strength."

Really is that all the credit I get? Tell him the truth that you were a beaten mess and I picked you up and carried you to victory.

'Haha, I think you have delusions of grandeur Haji'

Typical… the sword always underestimates the importance of the shield.

Julian was enjoying the banter but pulled himself away to finish off what he had to do.

"Okay dad, I think it's time for us to leave and get Aeryn to a hospital. Plus we have to call the police… We can't leave the bodies of all those poor nuns in the rooms at the other building. They deserve better than that. Their families should be notified and get the chance to say a proper goodbye."

"T'enquête, the Controllers have already taken care of that… their deaths will be placed in the memories of the families as humane and having happened long enough ago that the scars on their hearts have scabbed over by now. The damage to this church will be fixed as soon as we leave too. Those I feel most pity for are all my fellow Other Ones that were tricked by Father Bachinger into forsaking their Rehabilitation, who now find themselves sent back into the dark prison between our worlds, joining all those who originally refused to enter the program in suffering an eternal loneliness that is hard for either of us to imagine." The observer within Julian understood all too well that suffering, and felt grave sympathy for those lost souls… This sympathy flowed from him into Julian making him unenvious of their fate, and truly lament how Sina's life on earth ended. Julian distracted himself from those emotions by thinking of Aeryn and his father being alive and safe, he knew they would forever be the source of his happiness here on earth.

"Bon, on part?"

"Yeah lets go. Not sure how much longer I can stand carrying this cry baby on my arm."

"Err watch your mouth, mister. Don't forget you're talking to a nun and right now you're in my Father's house."

"Hahaha." For the first time in a long time Julian could laugh completely carefree. Their ordeal was over and they could move forward in family, friendship and faith. "True, true. My bad. Well I think it's time we get you to a hospital." The three of them make their way downstairs and head for the main church hall exit. Seeing the church in morning light after everything that had happened was surreal for them, but they continued on out the huge wooden doors and walked along the pathway talking and reminiscing, Julian's dad embarrassing him by telling awkward stories to Aeryn about his potty training years that Aeryn found hilarious. It was the first time that his dad and she had got a chance to speak properly and it made Julian very happy to see them finally getting to know one another. Then François looks at Julian with a mischievous smile on his face and says,

"Oh son, I forgot to mention that the Controller told me that I've completed my Rehabilitation."

"What?? You wait til now to tell me this??"

"I thought it would be a fun surprise."

"Huh? Fun surprise? You're still just as strange as always dad... So when are you leaving me then?"

"Mmm... I was going to leave as soon as I knew you were safe... but then I thought, I'd much prefer to stay here with you and welcome your mum home."

This was a period that was coming to a universe-changing climax.

The End